The
PARISH
and the
HILL

The
PARISH
and the
HILL

Mary Doyle Curran

Afterword by Anne Halley

The Feminist Press
at The City University of New York
New York

Published by the Feminist Press
at the City University of New York
365 Fifth Avenue
New York, NY 10016
www.feministpress.org

Mary Doyle Curran was a member of the Department of English at the University of Massachusetts/Boston for the last fifteen years of her life. This edition of *The Parish and the Hill* is made possible, in part, through the generous contributions of her colleagues there, including Martha Collins, Chancellor Robert A. Corrigan, Linda Dittmar, Mary Anne Ferguson, Edwin Gittleman, Vice Chancellor for Academic Affairs and Provost Robert A. Greene, Seymour Katz, Duncan Nelson, Shaun O'Connell, Vincent Petronella, Irvin Stock, and Cornelia Veenendaal.

The Feminist Press gratefully acknowledges the contribution of the AT&T Foundation toward the publication of this book.

Library of Congress Cataloging-in-Publication Data
Curran, Mary Doyle, 1917-1981.
    The parish and the hill.

    I. Halley, Anne.   II. Title.
PS3505.U784P37   1986   813'.54   86-14247
ISBN 0-935312-58-7

Cover art: Self Portrait by Elizabeth Nourse, reproduced by permission of Deirdre Doolan Dunworth. Painting photographed by Bruce Cathcart, Jensen Beach, Florida.
07 06 05 04 03 02 01   5 4 3

*To Eleanor Blake Warren
and Mary Theresa Doyle*

For there is hope of a tree, if it be cut down,
that it will sprout again, and that the tender branch
thereof will not cease.

Job, XIV, 7

Irish Parish and Money Hole Hill

I REMEMBER Irish Parish. It was Ward Four in the old days before the Irish began coming in. After the first great famine in Ireland, they came as rapidly as they could make up the passage money — Kerry men and women — and the one spot of green they named Kerry Park. They built their shanties around the park overlooking the river. Soon Ward Four was crammed with Kerryites, all coming for the money, and, above all, for the food that could be picked from the trees simply by lifting one hand. No one had told them about the work that waited for them. It was not until some of the first ones, consumed by a longing for the green land, went home to Ireland, sick with the consumption laid on them by their jobs, that the others learned it was the same work that the Irish were doing in the dark mills of Liverpool and Manchester. It was in the mills that they would earn their living, or laying the rails for the railway that was to stretch from one side of the new country to the other. There were those Kerry men who would not follow the rails, for laying the rails took them with every step away from the At-

1

lantic Ocean and that much farther from the old country. It was those who settled down in Irish Parish, and the mill owners were made rich by their decision. Shrewd Yankees that they were, they harnessed the water power and created the great dam in full view of Kerry Park. The Irish had that always before them to remind them that the tales of travelers can sometimes be apocryphal.

These Irishmen soon found they had exchanged the English landlord for the Yankee mill owner; and they took off their hats, these shanty Irish, as reluctantly to this one as they had to the other. As time went on, the shanties disappeared, but the shanty Irishmen remained, housed now in the long row of red-brick tenements put up by the Yankee mill owners. The tenements were dark and small; children filled the five rooms to overflowing. There were five to a feather bed and three beds in one bedroom — the other bedroom, dedicated to the mother and father, held only one, though the youngest slept in a crib near the marriage bed, where the next occupant of the crib was being created. The marriage room also held the great chest stored with the linen brought from home. There was always the mingled musty smell of babies, tobacco, and bread in the house.

The front room was the one facing the street, and that was sacred to the dead, for it was here, in the early days, that the dead were waked. This room was filled with heavy furniture, bought at the local furniture store, and a few relics of the past: a colored picture of

Ireland; perhaps a letter or two from home, placed prominently on the table; a pot containing some of the old sod that someone, in a last moment of desperation, had seized before he got onto the boat. Here, too, would be the most precious wedding presents carefully preserved, but the focal point of the room was the great family Bible sitting on a table in the center. In this all the names of the living and dead were carefully inscribed by the priest. Only for a death or a birth was the Bible ever opened. It was never read, for these Irishmen had no need to read the Bible stories — didn't they hear them often enough in church, and didn't they have, for entertainment, plenty of stories in their own heads, stories that had little to do with the Bible?

The dining room, with its great round table in the center, was not used much; often an extra cot was set up in there for the oldest of the children. Occasionally, when the old people wanted to escape the din of the children, they went in there to talk; but this was seldom, for an Irishman talks best when there is competition. The kitchen was the lived-in room. Here the family gathered to eat, talk, and play. Around the glowing wood stove the family, old friends, and even the cat, gathered on a dark winter night. The stove was the heart of the room, replacing the open hearth of the old country. The men were given the favored place, in front of the stove, where they could toast their wool-socked feet in the oven. The women gathered in another circle off to the side, sewing or knitting, hastily giving a full, round breast to a child

whose crying ·interrupted a story. The child, spasmod-
ically clucthing and unclutching its hands, would fall
asleep, its face still buried in the breast.

The teakettle stood always simmering, adding its
steam to the damp smell of the room made by the diapers drying to one side of the stove. There was never
a stove that did not have its teapot standing on the back
of it to keep the strong tea warm but not boiling. The
men and women both filled their bowls freely. On some
occasions there was whiskey, or "poteen," as it was still
called. The room was filled with the tobacco smoke
that issued from the T.D.'s that both the men and
the women smoked alternately. There was much talk
of the cancer of the mouth that they thought was
brought on by the rough stems of these clay pipes. It
was a miracle that any of these women could hold a
clay pipe, for most of them lost their teeth with the
first child. Some of the older ones took snuff, carefully
offering their paper packet to the one who sat next.
The snuff was always accepted with a prayer for the
dead — "The blessing of God be with the souls of your
dead." Occasionally a thanksgiving was offered for a
pipeful of tobacco, too. At seven-thirty the oldest children put the youngest to bed and came back to listen
to the talk, until, overwhelmed by the heat of the room,
they tumbled off the stools and were sent to bed. Determined to stay awake to hear the end of the story,
they were soon asleep with ghosts and goblins haunting
their dreams.

In telling the stories, there was always one man or

woman who was favored, depending on the number of supernatural visions he or she had had. The one with the longest memory was best, for he could tell visions that were none of his own, but belonged to those dead ones whose names were forgotten. Whenever an Irishman told a story, it became his own.

" 'Twas after the birth of Johnny there," he would start. "I was watching him, for he had little strength from the mother who died giving him birth. I was sitting by the crib when I heard a step in the kitchen. It was after twelve, a bad time to be up, but I felt no fear, for I knew who would be in the kitchen rattling pans after twelve. I went out to her, and she said quietly, 'It is I, come back to look after him, for it's a great longing I have to keep him alive.' I said nothing, but nodded. 'I will stay only until morning to keep those off that are after his soul, though he but a child.' I nodded again, and remembered my old mother who had sprinkled holy water on the doorstep the night my father almost died. My grief! but I found the bottle quick and went and sat by the child. She gave him the breast and wrapped him in the warm cloth she had prepared with steam. Soon I heard a great rattling at the doors. 'Are they locked?' she asks. I nodded, for I dared say nothing for fear she would go — it is not good to speak to the dead."

An old woman in the corner sucked on her pipe ominously.

"Soon they were at the window. I could hear them crying and banging away. I tell you the hair stood straight on my head, for I could see her struggling to hold the child from them. It was a fearful struggle and her sitting all the time with no strength to speak. They near broke the glass with their hurling. I knew then there was no help against them. What are windows to the host?" he asked.

The whole room in a body shook its head, sighing.

"With that, I jumped up. If the dead could not keep them out, the living would. I took the holy water and poured it over the window. Everything was very quiet. When I turned around, she was gone and the child was in its crib breathing easy." He stopped to mop his face. "I never want another like it," he ended.

No one spoke for a long time. Then a woman began speaking. "It's about the O'Sullivans I would talk, and this is my story," she said. "In the old days of Ireland when the O'Sullivans were among its kings and there was wealth and glory for them — conversing daily with the Fianna and even, some say, with Crom Dubh himself, for there has always been some of the Devil about them — they had seven golden castles and seven silver, and there was some said it was fairy gold. There has ever been a story that they had more to do with the Sidhe than they would say. There was even one O'Sullivan who was gone for fifteen years, and there was no age upon her when she came back."

All the older people looked knowingly at one another.

"Well, it's that one gave birth to a child two months after her return, and it was no natural birth, for the swans were circling the house the whole day. It was a boy, and they say he heard the Sidhe, and since that time there is no one of the O'Sullivans who has not had to shut his door tight on a windy night for the fear of them. Some say they took to the hills of Kerry with the coming of the English and lost their wealth doing it. I have seen the black-browed ones come into the town of a Saturday and there is something else comes with them. Some say that the old ones that went to the hills buried their treasure and the young ones have been seeking it ever since. One of the girls looked for it in dreams and was told to seek it in a fairy forth. She did, and lifted the rock which it was supposed to be under and found nothing but a heap of dung. Some say the Sidhe removed the crock of gold to America and there will be O'Sullivans looking for it yet. They say the Banshee cries for the O'Sullivans as well as the O'Briens — they both being of the old Ireland. There is a John O'Sullivan come over this week hunting for gold. Well, he'll find no pot of gold here unless it be the one buried at the foot of Money Hole Hill and he's more than welcome to Yankee gold, for I'd want none of it."

Usually these evenings ended at eleven o'clock, for there was no Irishman wanting to be up after twelve. One could never tell what one would meet then. Too, they all had to get up early in the morning to get to the mill by six. When the windows were still dark with the night, the women would be up taking the hot soda bread out of the oven for breakfast and the men would be shaving themselves before the kitchen mirror. Excepting for the thump, thump, of the razor strap and an occasional fretful cry from the bedroom, this was one of the rare times that the house was silent.

Gradually the whole tenement came to life, though the streets outside were still quiet. Just as the first lightness appeared, the men would come out of the blocks with their lunchboxes in their hands and there would be greetings along the still dark street. Sometimes the women, too, would appear, with their shawls wrapped tightly around them to keep the cold away, on their way to church. The men would walk along with one another, but there was no talk — it was still too dark and too early for that. The women and men both hurried along so as not to be late for the daily Mass which began at five-fifteen and ended at five-forty, so that the men could get to the mill by six and the women back to the children.

The church would be very quiet and cold, and the people huddled there, waiting impatiently for the altar boy to light the candles so that the priest might appear and get on with the Mass. Though they wanted to start the day right, they didn't want it to take too long. The people would kneel, quietly saying their beads, their rattling the only sound in the church. They rose as a body when the priest appeared and began: *"Introibo ad altare Dei. Ad Deum qui laetificat juventutem meam."* The women received daily communion; the men received it only on Sundays — they needed the warm breakfast to get them through the twelve hours in the mill. After Mass, they all came out, ready for talk and banter now, for it was lighter and the day had started right. Some of the old women stopped to light a candle, but the younger ones hurried home to their children.

While the men worked their shift in the cotton and paper mills, the women worked theirs in the home. They baked their own bread, and indeed cooked everything their families ate. Flour was bought by the barrel and potatoes by the bushel. On Saturday and Wednesday mornings, the whole house was filled with the smell of fresh-made bread. On Monday, it was filled with the smell of damp laundry. There would be a great kettle of starch on the stove and soapsuds foaming over the edge of the set-tubs used on Saturday night for bathing children and on Monday morning for beating clothes into cleanliness. The back yards of the tenements were filled in winter with freshly washed clothes, hanging stiff as boards, iced by the wind. The women hanging them, their hands red and stiff with the cold, kept up a constant barrage of talk. "There'll be no drying today with the weather the way it is, and me with another tubful to replace these."

During the afternoon, the women would stop in on each other for a cup of tea, and they would talk over the latest news of the Parish — a birth, a death, a new one from the old country, or — and this they talked of most frequently — a new female complaint. The cures suggested interested them more than the complaint itself. They were all self-healers. Doctors seldom appeared in Irish Parish even for births. There was always a midwife, worn from childbirth herself, who

would come to attend another's, her few instruments
gathered in her apron when she came up the stairs. All
the children were told it was the new child that made
the apron bulge so.

Some of the older women were "knowledged" in
herbs, and they knew a cure for everything under the
sun. "There is nothing to a bad heart that dandelion
will not sure." "Mullein is a fairy herb and it is dangerous to cut — do not pull it while the wind is changing
or it's your head you'll be losing and not the ache in
it. It's the one to bring children back when they are
away." Children and childbirth formed the core of
their conversation, and there was always a new story
for them to talk and sometimes laugh over. "John
Fitzgerald, who had so little sympathy for his wife and
she in great pain," Bridgie Meehan would say; "you
all know him, sour black man that he is. I put the pain
on himself, and he all doubled up and roaring with
it. He'll not be lacking in sympathy next time, I'm
thinking, now that he's had a taste of it himself."

Great warnings were issued to the women that were
carrying. "Don't be going to a house where there is
one in labor or your own will come on you too soon.
And be careful to keep out of the way of amimals, especially cats — there is a woman I know whose last was
born with a claw. She woke in the middle of the night
and saw the cat staring at her; and she knew the one
within her was doomed, for she could feel it scratching
from then on. And if it's born with a caul, keep the
child away from the fire, for it's in danger of death
by burning."

Some of these shanty Irishmen were better off than others, but there was little social distinction in those days. All worked in the cotton and paper mills twelve hours a day, six days a week; all had large families and all were behind with the rent. In summer, they all sat out on their front stoops in their shirtsleeves, calling warnings to the children who played in the park and talking with one another. The old women smoked their T.D.'s, able with no discomfort to hold the hot bowls in their hands, hands calloused with whaling the bottoms of many children. The men talked and told stories — the mill and the work of the day were forgotten as their minds, freed from the present, recalled the past and explored the future.

There was no social ostracism if one of the children went down to John the Harp's to fetch home a pail of beer. Since God had provided these children, there should be use for them. On Saturday nights the men would gather in the back room at John the Harp's, drinking straight whiskey and talking. Some nights there would be music — one man would bring his accordion, another his fiddle. As the evening went on, the music grew faster and louder and there would be great singing and dancing. A man would take the center of the floor dancing and leaping to the music. The higher he could leap, the greater a dancer he was. Old Dineen, aged fifty-five, was the greatest "lepper" in Irish Parish. "Sure and it's up to the roof he can go, and it's wings on his feet he has surely." At twelve o'clock the men would come home gay and warm with

the drinking and dancing. There was always a bottle
of something for the old woman in one pocket.

Everyone belonged to Saint Jerome's Parish, for Saint
Jerome's was the church these Irishmen had built out
of their own pockets, even sending to Ireland for a
Kerry man as their priest, "a fine strong man he was
with a great flow of words from his tongue." They
wanted none of these strange American priests who
would be on bad terms with the Sidhe. A priest who
had no charms against the powers of the "gentle folk"
was of no consequence to them, no matter what titles
he might have after his name. Above all, they wanted
none of the skinflint sort, always dunning his parishon-
ers for a new roof to the church when the old was as
good as ever. They would give, but not on demand.
And they could do without the theology if the man
could sing a fine Mass. They wanted none of him who
would give you a look if he saw a glass of whiskey in
your hand either. There was no good to a man if he
could not take a drink of whiskey at a gulp without
gasping, priest or no priest.

Until Saint Jerome's Church was built, these Irishmen
had no regular Mass on Sunday. Once every two months
a priest traveling from one small New England town
to another came through and said Mass for them. Along
with a few others, he was sent out from the Boston
Diocese to take care of every town in New England
that contained Irish immigrants. When the church was
finished, it was a fine building — red brick with five
stained-glass windows and an altar that was the pride

of the Parish. Inside, the church was a hodge-podge of color, every saint brightly painted. When my grandfather, John O'Sullivan, came to Irish Parish, the church had been added to, and a red-brick schoolhouse conducted by the nuns stood next to it.

John O'Sullivan was a Kerry man, born in the hills of Kerry. From the time he was born until he had set out to earn his living in a small Kerry town, he had heard nothing but pure Gaelic spoken, and he still spoke it himself as long as his wife lived. He was a strong, handsome man with the look of the black-browed O'Sullivans and there was many a girl who took more than one look at him. But John O'Sullivan had eyes for no one else from the time he first saw Johanna Sheehan walking down a country road in her bright red petticoat. She was the daughter of a fairly well-to-do farmer, well-to-do for those parts — didn't he own his own land and hadn't he more than one pig? John O'Sullivan was a hand on the farm next to the Sheehans', working for an old crochety man that had not the strength of a woman in either of his arms, and this from the great age upon him.

It was while he was sleeping in the loft that he heard the plotting going on down belowstairs between the old man and Mr. Sheehan. Though there was no strength left in the old man, he had eyes in his head.

"A girl like that would be a comfort to an old man in a cold bed, and a great one for the farm," the father said, "and she so straight and strong."

But the old man was crafty for all his great age; he

knew the farms joining each other had more to do with the offer than wily Mr. Sheehan would say. "I'll take the pasture of yours in the hollow as the price for taking the woman off your hands."

"There's plenty who'd take her with nothing to go with her," the father indignantly replied. "There's not many women as fine and strong as she. I'll make no bargains with you, you old crow — not many fathers would be willing to give up a daughter to one with so many years on him. Come, settle your mind on her and she's yours with no bargains to it, free and clear."

"I know well," the old man said, "that it's the land you're after and I'm a part of that bargain, but I'll take her, for all that you're winning over me. I have but a few years, and the land may go to her as well as another. Be careful, though, that it's not begetting a son I am, one who'll be making muddle of your plans."

Mr. Sheehan only chuckled: "The Devil has your tail and you know it — no man, not even a Kerry man, begot a child after eighty." The wedding date was set as early as possible.

John O'Sullivan slept little that night, and in the morning he put himself in the way of Johanna Sheehan as she went singing down the road. He repeated to her the conversation he had heard, and she, being a girl of great spirit, resolved that she would never marry the old man. Johanna said never a word, listening to the ravings of John O'Sullivan gravely and quietly. One morning she did not appear on the road, but there was a letter for John O'Sullivan left in the rocks where they used to sit. The letter said simply: "I have gone to America. I have saved all that I earned from my eggs and taken the bit Aunt Bridgie left me. If you want me, you will find me in a place where there are Kerry men. Signed Thomas Heffernan, Schoolmaster, written for Johanna Sheehan, in secrecy."

That was all John O'Sullivan knew when he left Ireland for America. He collected his wages at the end of the season; for he was not one to renege on an old man, no matter how much bitterness he felt in his heart toward him. He worked till after the harvest and then left. He had enough for passage and enough for some shoes. He sailed to America with other immigrants in the cold of the winter. When the boat docked at Boston, he was told then that it was there he would find most of the Irish immigrants. He took a job on the docks, and in the evening, tired and weary, he hunted for Johanna Sheehan, but no one had heard of her. Most of the Irish girls were working as house servants, but he could find no Johanna Sheehan registered at any of the agencies. In a saloon one night, he heard two men talking of Irish Parish and how it had become a settlement for Kerry people. He asked them where it was, and the next day he left for Irish Parish. He found Johanna there waiting for him to come. They were married, and Johnny O'Sullivan went to work in one of the paper mills.

Johanna Sheehan gave John O'Sullivan seventeen children. She was a good wife and mother, and, though she told no stories herself, she never tired of her husband's. She died of excessive childbearing, as most of the women of the Parish did, at the age of fifty. After her death my grandfather came to live with my mother, who was his favorite child.

All of the O'Sullivans went to church and sang in the choir, and the O'Sullivan girls were known far and away for their sweet, clear voices. The whole family was a singing one, and on the Feast of Corpus Christi they led the procession around the park. John O'Sullivan and his family occupied one of the tenements in the "Row," and, as he became better known, he was one of the men whom all Irish Parish turned to for advice. Even the priest would come to him if there was a Parish problem he could not cope with. And the priest, too, acknowledged that John O'Sullivan was the finest story-teller in the Parish. On summer evenings people would gather on the steps of the O'Sullivans' to listen to him, and there were plenty went home quaking with the fear he put into them.

For forty years the O'Sullivans lived in Irish Parish, and there were changes that took place, not within the old but within the young. No one thought of the Hill in the old days, nor much about education either. The seventeen children, with the exception of Agnes (God rest her soul, marked for death by the words of the blasphemous comparing her to an angel) had, as a matter of course, been sent to Sister School. The Order of Notre Dame, stern and severe in habit, taught them. They learned nothing much except to read, write, and spell. My mother's handwriting was medieval, each letter carefully and conscientiously drawn.

I was born in Irish Parish, but was lifted out of it, and with my family was one of the group to move to Money Hole Hill. The influx up there came gradually, and our move from Johnny O'Sullivan's block made us aliens for many years. The slow migration really began in my grandfather's day. It began with the marriage of Sidney Whitney to Bridie Flannagan. Irish Parish acquaintance with the Hill had only been a geographical one till then; but the Hill came to the Parish when it wanted a wife for its foremost son; for beauty and health, and a fine aristocracy, an aristocracy of the spirit, resided there.

Bridie was a paper cutter in the Whitney Mill. In six months, she was a lady in the Money Hole Hill sense of the term. My grandfather could see no difference and told her so — "a few more feathers in your hat," — he would say. But he was secretly pleased that she came to hear his stories, as she always had. But who wouldn't come to hear my grandfather tell stories! "He would have scared the Devil himself and kept him from his evil work," my grandmother used to say.

Bridie was one of the first wedges, but there was another. Nelly Finn moved up to Money Hole Hill, but her invitation was not so legitimate. Nelly was a great source of amusement to the ladies of Irish Parish whose husbands couldn't afford her. In their secret hearts, they were rather tickled to know that the men on Money Hole Hill were frail, even if their wives did wear so much whalebone. The ladies of Irish Parish were fond of Nelly Finn; the ladies on the Hill scorned her. They had their reasons. Many were the nudges and sly winks when, after Mass on Sunday mornings, she drove through Kerry Park, her parasol tilted rakishly, and as many birds in her hat as there were in a bush. My grandfather was fond of Nelly, too; he would wait for her to pass his corner on Sunday morning and inquire, "How's business, Nelly?" Nelly became a myth for Irish Parish. Long after her death, my mother would say, when I was pestering her, "Don't bother me now. I'm as busy as Nelly Finn."

We moved to the Hill because of my father, who was a foreigner and had little understanding of Irish Parish for all his having been born in Ireland. My grandfather blamed it on County Cork — "It's English he is, not Irish at all," — he would grumble. Others moved because the old ties were disappearing, and the Irish had little but the church and the mill in common any more. When we moved, Irish Parish was still at one with itself. Ours was looked on as the first great apostasy; for my grandfather, now old and childish, was still considered one of the archangels of Irish Parish. Everyone protested his departure, and none more than himself; for in Irish Parish, at least, he could still be shanty Irish with impunity.

And so we left Irish Parish for less green fields; and we became outcasts from our own race, and aliens among the race of Yankees into whose hallowed circle we moved. There were, it is true, a few Irish on Money Hole Hill; and they were the worst of all, imitators of imitators, neither Yankee nor Irish, but of that

species known as the lace-curtain Irish. They put the
curtains up in their parlors, and decked out their souls
in the same cheap lace. It was into this circle that a
lace-curtain father moved a set of the most shanty Irish
people that have ever been. My grandfather refused to
go back to Irish Parish because he would not leave my
mother, whom he considered the root and flower of our
whole family. My mother would not leave because she
could never abandon, defeated, a battle involving her
race. She would remain, though ostracized by both
sides; and before we left for the school of the Yankees
and our lace-curtain cousins, my mother enjoined us
to remember, in the battles which occurred every day,
that we were O'Sullivans, descendants of the kings of
Ireland, and we were not to come home crying. We
never did; and to the end of my days, I shall remember
my mother standing in the door, her black eyes flashing
out a fire that still serves to warm the worlds of the
Money Hole Hills that I have lived in since.

The Look of a Fixed Star

I REMEMBER when I was born. I walked down the long, dark hallway and emerged in an Irish parlor that was full of the sound of my brother Eddie playing his violin. I stood at the window. It was snowing; and while my brother Eddie practiced scales, I scratched away the frost on the window. On a sharp, piercing note of the violin, I was born, because, at that moment, I the unconscious became conscious that I was small, lost, unknown in a world cut off by the snow. I turned from the window and saw an old man sitting in a big leather rocker, an old man as small and lost as I.

His white hair was long and soft, and his eyes held the quiet, the sadness, and the loneliness of that moment. All that I saw, all that I felt, as I looked out on the snow, was in that old, gentle face. He nodded at me and smiled. I went to him and crawled into his arms. He carried me into that long dark hallway; and when my mother turned on the gaslight, she found us both sitting at the end of it. That was my grandfather, the refuge then, the symbol now, of my existence. We met in the yearning for life and the yearning for death. They were for him and for me the same thing.

From that moment on, my grandfather became my life. He was in his second childhood, I was in my first; and we understood each other in all the languages, spoken and unspoken. He opened up for me a world that has sustained me as no other ever could. I walked with him in that world of his as I have walked in no world since. It is a world no one else has ever been able to enter; for it was created by the imagination of an old man for the solace of a young child.

Everyone else in the family would shake his head and ask, "How is he today?" My mother would answer, "Failing, failing, fast." My grandfather and I would smile over that, for we knew better than they. In the morning we would go out for walks together. He was not allowed out alone because he could not find his way back again. I walked beside him, holding his hand, while he talked, talked in a language I have never heard since. His voice was beautiful, and as impossible of reproduction as pure music. The intonations were those of the purest Gaelic speech. The whole talk would be a long monologue, for he talked as though he were conversing with the disembodied, as indeed he was. Everything came to life as he spoke. In the world he created for me, the man in the moon was as real as the man in the street.

"And do you know, Mary O'Connor, what Saint Patrick was — do you know how he drove out the Druids disturbing the sleep of the dead with their hammering of stone? He drove them out, but they stayed in the green land and they still cause the dead to tumble in their sheets at night. Clever he was, and he grew into the greenest tree in all Ireland; shading the land and the people from the hot sun, keeping the harm of the storm from them. I saw him become a great tree; his arms spread out and became mighty branches; his feet sank into the earth and became mighty roots. All the rivers of Ireland water those roots to keep that tree green. When you go to that land, you will see him growing, for he covers the whole land with his greenness."

My grandfather spoke the language of his people, though he always spoke it in his own way. He was an Irishman, and twenty years in America or a million years in America, his roots were still planted as firmly in Ireland as Saint Patrick's. That was the land he was yearning for, that, and a land that has never been.

While my grandfather lived with us, we still paid many visits to Irish Parish. Though removed from the Parish, he was still an essential part of it; and every Saturday afternoon my mother, my grandfather, and I would go downtown. While my mother shopped, my grandfather and I would sit in Kerry Park. It was still largely Irish, but there were new people coming into the Parish — new people from another old country. Strange, old-fashioned-looking children with white hair played in the park, talking a strange gibberish. I used to sit on the bench next to my grandfather, smoothing my white starched dress, staring resentfully at these "foreigners." They had no right to be playing in my grandfather's park. My grandfather urged me to play with them, but I was too conscious of starchness and stiffness to be playing with these children with round, staring eyes and dirty faces.

Sometimes they would stand in a line before the bench, their round blue eyes fixed on my hand as it dipped in and out of the candy bag. Their eyes never left the hand. When I conveyed the chocolate to my mouth, their eyes would follow, watching me lick my fingers greedily before I went back for the next one. I was conscious of their flattering attention and licked my fingers all the more noisily while they stood there. When the bag was emptied, they would move away silently with a sighing movement.

My grandfather watched this performance quietly, saying never a word, but clenching and unclenching his hands with the effort of his restraint. One Saturday he bought me an extra large bag of chocolates, including some of the chocolate cherries he knew I was especially fond of. I settled myself on the bench, making a great show of smoothing out my dress and rattling the bag loudly to attract the attention of the children. The line formed and I began eating, licking the juice from the center of the chocolate as it rolled down my fingers. Their eyes went from bag to mouth, from mouth to bag. Their attention was as devout as communicants at the altar rail, following the priest's hand as it moves from chalice to communicant, eagerly awaiting their turn. My grandfather leaned over and took the bag from me, offering it to the children. They turned shyly away like animals whose joy is to observe unnoticed. He sighed and shut the bag, putting it into his pocket. I stared at my hands and dress, ashamed to speak or look up. I knew what the gesture meant, though I couldn't formulate the meaning. All week my grandfather shunned me.

The next week the children pretended not to notice us. I knew what had to be done. I stood shyly outside their circle, candy bag in hand, watching them, my grandfather watching me. I humbled myself further and sat in the grass near them, watching them as they built their stone houses. One of them looked up and spoke. They all laughed. I colored, but determined that I would stay until they had accepted my expiation. I held out the chocolate bag, smiling, but they paid no attention. One of them jumped up and headed for the wall above the dam. I watched him leaping like a bird from stone to stone. Some of the others began to run wildly about the park doing somersaults and cartwheels as they ran. They behaved like a cage full of monkeys, agile and graceful. I was amazed by their dexterity and daring, I who had always been so awkward.

I knew that this was a challenge I could not ignore; so I arose with great dignity, pulled up my dress and did the splits in the grass. It was the only thing I could do, something my cousin, who took acrobatic dancing, had taught me. The Polish children were impressed, but my victory led to my defeat, for I could not get up. I struggled while the children rolled in the grass laughing. My grandfather came and lifted me to my feet, and took my hand. The tears were rolling down my face, but I made no sound. "The salt is not so sweet to the taste as the chocolate," he said, putting his arm around me.

The Polish children came and stood, sobered and silent as ever. I kept my head down so that they could not see my shame. I still clutched the candy bag. My grandfather pointed to it and patted my shoulder. "Offer them some. They'll take it now." I held the bag out to them. Gravely each one took a chocolate and sat down in the grass to eat it, each one dreamily absorbed in this new experience. By the end of the hour we all were playing together. My grandfather drew no moral for me, but I heard him speaking to my mother that night: "It's the sense of ownership that divides people. It's happening in the Parish the same way as on the Hill. It's an evil that spreads, you will see. There will soon be no oneness there either."

In the winter, these visits to Irish Parish were spent in a warm kitchen with all my grandfather's old cronies gathered round him. They would talk about everything — the mill, the Parish, local politics. My grandfather wanted to hear all the details of the mill where he had worked, for since he had been retired his connection with the mill had been broken.

My father did not approve of his going back to the mill for visits, though my grandfather longed to. He missed the work he had done for forty years and, though he never showed it, he resented the position of the old man relegated to the idle seat by the fire. He had

stood in hipboots in the basement of the mill when
the canal overflowed to supervise the salvaging of pulp.
He had been a great hero, and people in Irish Parish
still spoke of the mill as "the place where Johnny
O'Sullivan worked," as they called the tenement where
he had lived, "Johnny O'Sullivan's block." On the
Hill my grandfather had no place, but in the Parish
he was still a legislator.

More and more on these Saturday afternoons the talk
turned to the disintergration of the Parish and the new
immigrants coming in, replacing the Irish who had
removed to the Hill. "The Dineens moved to Taylor
Street last week — it was the girl with big ideas in her
head always after the old man. Jimmy told me himself:
'She'll never be quiet until we've put up the lace
curtains like the rest. She says the Parish is no longer
respectable with all these foreigners taking it over.'"

My grandfather shook his head sadly: "Well, they
have surely the same right as the rest of us, and it's foreigners we all are in this strange country. It's little
enough any of us understand about it except that it's
swelling like a great balloon, and who is to prevent its
bursting into a thousand pieces, one piece dividing
against another if we do not make peace with one another."

"My son John, the one that's a foreman," old Mr.
Kelly announced with some pride, "he says that it's
our jobs the Poles are after and they're willing to work
for far less. He says there's a line of 'em as he goes by
the employment office on a Saturday morning. He's

after saying that it's the threat of cheap labor they are."

"Well, it's true that they may be that," answered my grandfather, "but it will do no good to be fighting with them. It's what the Yankees may be looking for. They're great dividers of the opposition, as you well know, setting one half of a country against another. You've all seen the waste in that."

"But they don't even speak English, John says, jabbering away in a foreign tongue with no one to understand them but themselves. He says they're no better than dumb beasts."

My grandfather flashed out at him: "And since when is it that an Irishman takes a pride in the English tongue? I tell you you're staring out of the back of your head, full of the pride of one who never looks before him. You're no better than any of these, though you've been here longer. You're an earner of bread by the work of your hands same as these, and you may hold your head no higher for that than they do. This country has plenty of room for all, but not enough if there's to be bitterness between those who have nothing but their hands to sustain them. There's enough bitterness between the Hill and the Parish as it is, with the Yankees looking down on the lace-curtains and the lace-curtains looking down on the shanties, and here now we have the shanties thinking themselves better than someone else so that they can have someone to look down on. It's a disease, I tell you, and if you catch it you're done for, that I know, for I see it on the Hill. You'll end up hating the person who eats and sleeps next to you. Let it be, for there's temptations enough without that, and it's enough to be hating the right things."

I had never heard my grandfather preach before, and though I did not understand what he said, I listened with attention and with a great feeling of seriousness, for he had the look of gravity and he used his cane to punctuate his sentences.

"Haven't you had enough of hate and bitterness with all that you've seen in the old country? Let us live in peace here. Let them who want persecution, persecute, and them who want peace, make it. I have no respect for the man who fights for the love of fighting. He's the worst man of all. He's the dumb beast. I have that kind of man close enough as it is to me."

The old men nodded. They knew he referred to his own sons.

One man said: "It was the war, Johnny, nothing else. They were good boys before that."

"That's easy enough to say," my grandfather answered, "but who can say the easy thing? It can't be left to that. There is something else that I cannot say, though I feel and know it. It has something to do with all of us and not the boys only. It's a wind from the north and who knows when it will stop blowing? Perhaps, Mary O'Connor will be the only one who will not feel it chilling her in her sleeping and waking — or it may be even colder than — who knows? Well, let us pray that none of us here will be welcoming it."

The old men sat silently with their hands folded. There was no sound in the room except for the wood crackling as it gave off the fire that filled the cold corners of the room.

On one Saturday afternoon, one of the local Irish politicians approached my grandfather, appealing to him for votes. He knew that my grandfather was a key man in Irish Parish; there was an old saying that whatever way he went, the Parish turned with him. Mr. Gaughan was a young man just starting his political career. My grandfather listened to him. "It's time we had an Irish mayor, Mr. O'Sullivan; there's enough Irish votes to put one in if we can get them all out. All you would have to do is speak to the old men and women of the Parish and ask them to do a little campaigning for Jerry Foley. He's a good man."

My grandfather sat with his head to one side studying the red glow of the stove. "What's his program?" he asked.

"Well," the young man said, "first we want to see the Irish have a chance in this city."

"Are you from the Hill, young man?" my grandfather asked.

"Yes," he answered, "but not exactly, for we're just on the fringe of School Street."

"Well, go on with the rest," my grandfather murmured.

"Well, we'd also like to see something done about this large influx of Polish."

"What exactly?"

The young man did not answer, but went on talking of other things: of how strong the Irish were becoming and the opportunities they were missing, and how, if the Parish and Irish on the Hill would get together, they could carry the city and there'd be plenty of reward for both. He talked to my grandfather as though he were catechizing a child. My grandfather never looked at him, just continued his contemplation of the stove.

When he had talked himself out in a style that he would have used at a political rally in the Parish, my grandfather spoke.

"Young man, did you ever hear the story of the Irishman who had a fire in his head and discovered that whoever or whatever he looked at caught fire? It spread just the way the heat of that stove spreads. Oh, he was better than pleased with himself with all that power he had to scare people. No one daring to look at him for fear of the fire. He had more than he wanted just for the asking. He could say to a man, 'You'll be giving me your pigs and your cows or I'll burn down your house,' and he would drive them home. When he was fatted with riches and had more than he could do with, he then decided that he would look for someone to share it, but neither by threats nor violence could he get a soul who would follow him except in fear. The more he offered to a woman, the more she would shun him. If he went in to have a drink, the place would empty and leave none to serve him. When he became head of a town, he soon found it empty.

"Soon he was left completely alone, and it was no comfort to sit in a big house with even the dogs shivering at your approach. The walls echoed with his own voice talking to itself and not even a cat would purr within that house. He took to the road, but there was no one who would walk with him or give him shelter. He walked up and down Ireland with the fire in his head, burning his way with the fury that was in him. When there was no more to burn in this way, he found a great ocean and thought to himself — 'There will be other countries. I'll set fire to this ocean and send it to the other side to burn the countries beyond.' He looked at the ocean, but it would not take fire — then he put his head in it, thinking that would do it surely, but all he got for his trouble was drowning. Now, Mr. Gaughan," said my grandfather, "you wouldn't want to be like that spalpeen and start a fire you couldn't put out, would you?"

Mr. Gaughan left, puzzled and annoyed. He contributed to the notion already established on the Hill that my grandfather was a crazy old Harp.

At the end of these Saturday afternoons, we would go to Saint Jerome's Church, where my grandfather made his weekly confession. I would wait in the pew while my grandfather was in the box. There was something very ominous about these occasions. The church was not quiet and peaceful at it was on other afternoons. It rustled with sin. I would watch the people going in and coming out of the boxes and judge their sinfulness by the amount of time they spent in the confessional. When my grandfather came out, he always had his hands folded, the beads draped over them. He never looked at me, but went straight to the central altar to say his penance.

This was another way of judging sinfulness, for the longer a person's penance, the longer he knelt, and therefore the more sins he had to expiate. It used to trouble me that my grandfather always spent such a long time at the altar and in the box, for I felt certain he was no sinner.

While he was saying his penance, I would examine the people coming and going, young women carrying their Saturday shopping, dressed for downtown with hat and gloves, some children giggling and pushing each other. Four o'clock was the children's confession time, and they used to try to beat each other to the confession box, some of the bolder ones standing beside it to be sure and get in first. One time the racket was so great that the door of the box opened, and this was the first time I knew that confession was made to a priest, for the awesome thing to me had been the belief that inside that box God was present, come down of a Saturday to hear the confession of his people. The priest was no God, but Father Feeney, familiar and forbidding enough. He spoke sharply to the children, making them kneel and examine their consciences before they dared set foot in the confessional. He motioned the older people in.

The fact that there was a man in there listening to a frank recital of your sins made the confession even more ominous. I was so sure that God was easier to talk to. The old women in their shawls stayed longest, and like my grandfather they always said the stations as well as their beads. I wondered what mortal sin they could have committed that caused them to crawl on their knees to every station. I used to stand by my grandfather while he knelt saying his prayers before each station. In the dark, dim church I could make out only the prominent figures on the plaques — a man who carried a cross, his position shifting from station to station, other men lifting whips, a few women with faces covered. Before each station my grandfather would name the text: "Jesus takes his first fall." The whole allegory made a tremendous impression on me as I followed my grandfather from the beginning to the end. Somehow at the end I felt a dim sense of triumph, but I did not know why.

When we came out of the church one day, I asked my grandfather what kept him so long in the box. Did he have many sins? He told me there were so many that he could not account for them all. "Lest any of them have slipped my mind in a former confession, I recount them all. These last years I make a general, beginning with my first and ending with, please God, my last."

"But why do you do it?" I asked.

"I cannot know nowadays," he said, "how long there will be. And though I'm not one to approve of fasting and fainting, I want to be ready to go back."

"Go back where?" I asked.

He did not answer. As we walked home, the snow began to fall, covering both of us. It fell with a great quiet and all sound was muffled by it. I hoped, as I walked beside my grandfather, that we were going back wherever it was he was going back to.

Whenever the front door was left unlocked, my grandfather would slip out and wander away. If he were asked where he was going, he always answered, "Nowhere." I remember one day my brother Tabby had gone out to do some early morning fishing. After my grandfather heard him leave, he got up, dressed quickly, came into my room, and asked me for my red hat. He would never make an excursion without that hat. It was a crocheted cap that came down around the ears. It was bright red and had a large red tassel on top.

My grandfather loved that hat because he had worn it the day he had had a polite run-in with my first-grade lace-curtain Irish schoolteacher, who had treated me badly because I was shanty Irish. My grandfather had gone to see her and, in his politest eighteenth-century speech, asked her if she had ever seen a falling star.

Puzzled and disturbed by what she considered a crazy old man in his granddaughter's red cap, she answered "Yes."

He then looked her straight in the eye and asked: "Have you ever, Miss Hogan, seen the look of a fixed star?" She shook her head. He pulled the red hat more firmly on his head, pointed his finger at her. "Well," he said, "Mary O'Connor has seen both — remember that."

With that he left her, came home, told the story with many chuckles, to my father's horror. Ever after that, wherever he went, he wore the red hat. It was for him like carrying the Sinn Fein banner at the Siege of Drogheda.

This morning, after I had found the red hat, which was always hidden from him, I asked him where he was going. He smiled and said, "One of the Sheehans died last night, and I'm going to see him off. Would you like to come with me?"

That was all I needed. I dressed quickly; we both slipped into the kitchen, filled our pockets with doughnuts and brownies, and set off.

It was a gala day. Since we had no money to ride in the trolley car, we had to walk. My grandfather said, "We'll follow the river to Kerry Park." Halfway down, we sat by the river and ate our food.

I asked, "Grandfather, how did you know one of the Sheehans was dead?"

His answer was quick, "I heard him going."

As this seemed quite possible to me, I went on eating my brownie. "Well, if he's gone, how can we expect to see him off?"

"He'll be there, you'll see," was his answer.

When we arrived, we were met at the door by Mrs. Sheehan. "And how did you know, John O'Sullivan, that himself was gone?"

My grandfather looked at her and smiled. "Your husband was always a polite man, Nora Sheehan. He would not go without taking leave of his friends."

I was fed, and my grandfather was given a drink of the strong whiskey provided for the occasion. There was no smell of death in that house, as there has been in the houses of the dead I have been to since. We went into the parlor, and what I saw there made me grasp my grandfather's hand and never leave his side. For the man was there! His whole soul shone nakedly from his face. There was in death no pretense, there could be in death no mask.

"Are you frightened, Mary O'Connor?" I did not answer. "Remember that whatever you do of good or evil, it will shine like this in your face when you die. There will be nothing hidden. Whoever says that the soul leaves the body at death lies. The soul is free and shines in the face of the dead. There is no will to stop it."

We knelt. My grandfather prayed always aloud. "My God, may my soul shine through in the beauty of goodness, as this soul does. I envy this man his going forth. The struggle is over, and he is at peace. If he walked with heavy shoes, have mercy on him, O my God, for his soul is light and beautiful. Oh, pray for me, Jerry Sheehan, as I pray for you that there will be love and mercy for both of us."

Some nights my grandfather and I sat on the back porch; even from there, we could make up a world larger than the real one. One night, as we were sitting in the porch swing, a great storm came up. We sat there and watched it. The house shook under us with the reverberations of the thunder. The lightning lit up the whole sky. I clung to my grandfather. He began to talk.

"There is a great war in heaven tonight, Mary O'Connor, and before morning there will be another fallen angel. The voice of God is raised in anger at him, and he, in defiance, has raised his sword. God will smite it from him; and on the last, fearful crack, he will fall, fall a thousand feet; and the lightning will describe his course. His beauty will diminish as he falls; and wherever he strikes the earth, a new beast will be born to prowl the world. Pray, Mary O'Connor, that he does not land in your yard. Those are the only beasts you have to fear, those generated by anger and hurled to earth as evil. Have no part of them, for their creator has repudiated them."

After supper, especially in the winter, we would all gather round the stove. I would sit in my grandfather's lap while he told stories. I can still hear the polyphonic voices of my grandfather and the teakettle. There was the warmth of the fire and the warmth of human intercourse; for neighbors would come in, as they had in Irish Parish. They were not Irish, though. Mrs. Carter was a Yankee woman and a "black Protestant." She was horrified and fascinated by John O'Sullivan, and came to hear him talk, consoling herself that she was thereby learning the ways of the Devil. My grandfather always dwelt on the horrors of Drogheda and the Antichrist Cromwell, the evenings Mrs. Carter came. He described the crucifixions of the Parish priests against their church doors. It amused him to shock her. The account became more than amusement, however, as he proceeded; for he passionately hated persecution of any kind.

His stories were always a curious mixture of religious, political, and social thought. My grandfather had the zeal of an antiquarian, ·but no respect for his sources. His stories would be mixed and collated and the text that emerged was his own. I have never seen in any of the texts of Irish legends and fairy tales the stories printed as he told them. The traditional Irish fairies and little people became hobgoblins, fantastic creatures of his own imagination. There were no Pucks tipping over milk bottles, for my grandfather had too great a sense of sin to be whimsical in his stories. The creatures of his imagination were horrible and dire agencies of Nemesis meting out to sinners punishments that fitted their sins. The man who had refused to give a pair of shoes was condemned to walk barefoot over the hot coals in Purgatory. The man who refused to pray for the souls in Purgatory was condemned to live in this world with the cries of those same souls ringing in his ears. The woman who refused love was condemned to wander the world howling at the windows of men to let her in. Her cries were more unearthly than those of the Banshee.

When the stories were told, the chairs were pushed back, Mrs. Carter left hurriedly, and my grandfather knelt at a wooden chair in the center of the room to say the Rosary, mysteries and all. I am sure he prayed, as I know I did, for all the fantasies of his imagination: the woman who could not love, the man who could not give. I prayed especially for the souls in Purgatory, not out of Christian charity, but for fear that I would hear their cries. I said my prayers for them very loud.

As time went on, my grandfather grew more and

more feeble, and my mother, though unwillingly, held the same notion as the rest of the family that old John was getting childish. She would say quietly to my aunts that his memory was going. No one in Irish Parish would agree with her, for he was as sharp and witty there as he had ever been. It was the Hill that stifled him.

"What's the use of talking there when no one has the mind to comprehend you?" he would ask. "If you meet a man on the street and stop him to tell him that through the window last night you saw a great procession pass and that he was among them, he would think you crazy, but if you tell that to Bridgie Flynn in the Parish, she would wash herself, put on her best, make a visit to the priest, say good-bye to her friends and go home to die. A dog howling on the Hill is only the howl of a dog — in the Parish it is an omen."

How could he tell his stories to his own sons and daughters, who would only hush him for his superstitions? Hadn't he been eating a sandwich in the corner next to the water tank last night and put out his hand and felt it quake, and during the night didn't he see the woman walking the coals with no shoes to her feet? He'd set a pair on the porch the next night and weren't they gone in the morning? At times he grew querulous over the disbelief in his children — "only yourself, Mary O'Connor, and your mother to listen to me and she but half believing."

One moonlit night I heard my mother get out of bed and go out of the room. There was something eerie about the house, and I crept down the long dark hall-way after her. I watched my mother go up to my grand-father, who was standing at the window clad only in his nightgown. The moonlight flooded the room, glanc-ing off the white hair of my grandfather, who had the look of a straight statue. My mother touched him, but he didn't move.

"Are you in your sleep, father?" she asked.

He stood motionless. "I heard the voice again, and it has come now for the second time — a great whispering cry out of the night with even lonesomeness lost in it. It is not of this world — it is not like the cry of the dog and he sitting with his back to the world crying to the moon. It is not even like the keening — no human voice could make it. It is the dead and they no dead at all. It whispers and swells till your ears are full of the sound of it — a great whispering wail and the whole sadness of the world whistling through it. It is the second time. I shall hear it once more," he said, "and that will be all the weeping and wailing I'll want. It cries for the O'Sullivans. My father heard it too."

My mother said nothing. She put him to bed and returned to the room. I heard her take her beads from under her pillow. Shivering with fright, I wondered how she had known he was up unless — and of this I was convinced — she, too, had heard the cry.

After this, my grandfather was not allowed to go out by himself, nor was he allowed to go to Irish Parish. My Aunt Josie maintained that the "fairy tales" he heard and told there excited him too much, and so he sat in the living room of our house rocking back and forth in the big leather rocker, listening to my brother Eddie playing the violin, talking to his sons of their misbehavior — sometimes leaning out the window to converse with some of the people passing by. "A fine morning, Mrs. Carter," he would say, "almost good enough to let the cat out of the bag you're carrying." Mrs. Carter would clutch the bag to her, assuring herself that that was a loaf of bread in it. Sometimes in his perversity he would call to a stranger, "Be careful not to look around quick, for there's more than you bargained for behind you." My grandfather would chuckle when the man looked cautiously behind.

My mother finally put a stop to this practical joking. "Now, father, it's not like you to be doing this to people. It is very unkind."

"Well, 'tis only a little fun I was having — an old man put off in a corner has to have something to entertain him."

"Well," my mother would say, "talk to your granddaughter. She'll listen to you day in and day out." That I did, too.

When I was seven years old, there was a great fight in the family over my grandfather. He was almost completely paralyzed now from the shock he had had, and my mother had to lift and carry him like a baby. He used to say to her as he sat at the table, gruel dripping down his chin: "You'll be having to feed me next, and then it is back to the cradle for me — no teeth, no hair, not able to lift my head and it wobbling like the day I was born. That will be the end then, I'm hoping, and an end like the beginning."

My mother used to say to him, "Don't talk foolishness, father. Thank God you have your mind."

He'd look at her slyly. "You're none too sure that that's left me either," he'd say, "the way I hear you and Josie going on."

He was a great care, but my mother made no complaint. One day Aunt Josie came to the house and talked with my mother and father. They went into the living room so that my grandfather could not hear them.

I stood unnoticed behind the portière of the bedroom. I heard my Aunt Josie beginning quietly: "Now, Mame, we've taken a look at father's bankbook and there's over a thousand dollars in it, and I've talked it over with James here, and some of the boys, and we all feel that father should get some good of his money before he dies. He worked for forty years every day of his life to earn a little comfort in the end. We all agreed that he should have proper attention and care — and so we've decided that —— "

Before she ended, my mother interrupted: "Hasn't he been getting the best care and attention here, Josie?" Her voice was quiet, but her eyes were not.

"Of course he has, Mame, but it's too much for you, and he's taking up your whole dining room. James here agrees that you're wearing yourself out from him."

My mother turned to my father: "Have you ever heard a word of complaint from me about him?"

My father shook his head and said: "Now, Mame, be reasonable. Maybe you don't complain, but anyone with eyes in his head can see that you're tired out from him, trying to lift him and dress him and feed him."

My mother's hands were trembling as she held to the arms of the chair, but she said nothing.

"Well, if you'll just listen, we'll tell you what we've planned" Josie went on, "all the arrangements are made. He can go to the Reilly Home for the Aged. It's a good Catholic Home and the nuns there are as nice as can be. He'll have plenty of company with some of the other old men there, men the same age as himself. He won't be as lonesome as he is here with no one but a child to talk with him. It won't cost any of us a cent. There's more than enough of his earnings to take care of him, for there's not much time left for him. There may even be a little left over, and of course," she said piously, "whatever there is should go to you for your grand care of him all these years. Not that the rest of us would not have done the same if he had chosen to come with us." She added the last a little acidly.

My mother's hands still held on to the chair tightly after my aunt had finished. Then she began to speak, at first slowly and quietly, but with the anger flooding her so that the words at the end tumbled over her tongue and could not get out fast enough. First she spoke to my father: "And how would it be with you, old man, if two of your children sat in the living room with you lying helplessly on a couch and talked of how to dispose of your carcass as though you were no better

than a dead dog in the gutter? How would it feel to
have the ice creeping up slowly from your toes till your
very heart knew the cold of it? Not much comfort in
that to an old man who has lived and loved and begot-
ten serpents for children."

Then she turned to my aunt. "You're like the worms
that feed on the dead, already making ready for the
feast before the corpse is cold. So it's worrying you are
about how to spend the old man's money. Well, I'll
tell you — take it and spend it while he's living. He'd
rather see that than to use it all up on himself in a
morgue. Oh, it's fine to have a daughter like you picking the pockets of the dead before they are dead — no
better than a scavenger, though you're so fine and respectable. I've seen the Home all right and the old
men sitting in front of it, their hands folded on their
sticks, waiting and waiting to die because there's none
in this world will have them. Cast out they are the way
one would cast out old rags and bones. A fine way to
spend your last days in the certain cold of a Home for
those who are not wanted! They crying in their beds
at night for the love that no one gives and a nun coming
down the long halls to speak pityingly to them. I remember John O'Sullivan and the light step of him
coming home and picking up his children to swing
them and hug them for the joy they brought, and the
home he made warmed by the very presence of himself
in it. Have you left off remembering the past, Josie,
that you can so easily dismiss the joy of it? Let you both
put your heads together and make certain of misery
for an old man, I'll have no part of it."

She rose, there were tears on her face, but her anger still filled her. At the door she stopped: "As for the dining room, we'll get along without that, for it's no part of this house anyway, and I'd rather have love in my house than a fine dining table set with stone-cold dishes."

I followed my mother down the hall. When she reached the dining room, she turned into the bathroom to calm herself before meeting my grandfather. I went in to him. He had heard all. The voices had been loud enough. There was a great deep hurt in his eyes and he had pulled the shawl of his loneliness tightly about him.

The following week, despite all my mother could do, he was taken away. The afternoon he left, I rattled around the cold, empty house. My mother was baking in the kitchen, though it was not Saturday, trying to keep herself busy. The dining room was not changed. I sat in a corner of it for the whole day nursing my loss.

The first week went by, but my mother remained adamant. She would not go to visit him. Aunt Josie went twice, twittering over how gay and comfortable he was. When my mother could not bear my pestering any more and her own loneliness, she broke down. I had a fine new white coat and hat which my grandfather had not seen. My mother dressed me in these. We packed a basket full of her bread and cakes and started off. The Home was on the road to Springtown; we had a long trolley ride. When we arrived, we jumped from

the streetcar and crossed the road, climbing the long
hill to the red-brick institution. "It looks like a jail"
was my mother's comment.

In front of the building old men were sitting, just
as my mother had described them. They were staring
at the ground and did not look up as we passed them.
They expected nothing. Inside, the place had the clean,
clinical smell of a hospital. I did not think it resembled
a home. One of the nuns directed us to my grandfather's room. He was sitting propped by many pillows,
staring out the one window. He was alone in the room.

When we came in, he said, "It's Mame and Mary
then, and it's a long time I've been expecting you." I
climbed up on the bed and kissed him.

My mother stood at the foot looking at him. She said
quickly, "Are you content here, father, as Josie says
you are?"

My grandfather did not look at her. He stared out
the window as though he were looking many miles beyond. "Well enough, Mame. They are good to me and
all, but I miss you and the boys and Mary. If you would
not mind, perhaps you would ask some of the old
people in the Parish to come and have a look in occasionally, for it gets dark and lonesome here." He
pulled his shawl around him again as he had the day
he knew he was leaving.

"Would you rather be with us again, father?"

He answered: "I do not wish to come between children. I would rather stay here than be the cause of
bitterness. It is only, Mame, that I am silly like a

child — old man that I am — fearing that I will hear the voice the last time and there'll be none by me. That I would not like. It's not good to die alone. I would have you by me, Mame."

My mother rose and went down the hall. Soon she came back with a nun. "Well, Mr. O'Sullivan, you haven't been with us long and here is your daughter taking you away with her."

My grandfather's eyes followed my mother as she dressed him and packed his things. We all rode home in the ambulance. It was a gay ride, my grandfather talking all the time, my mother and I both content that we would not have to face an empty house again. When my father came home, he took his defeat philosophically and told my grandfather that he was glad to have him back.

We all settled in the kitchen that evening. My father had carried my grandfather into the kitchen and placed him in the big leather rocker, and while my brothers Michael and Tabby played checkers and Eddie read quietly in the corner, I watched my grandfather. My mother was reading the paper to him. As I watched him he seemed to grow small, the big chair engulfing him. His hands were folded in his lap and they had a look of death. Every now and then he would lift one to his face as though he were verifying his existence. He was not listening to my mother but for another voice — a voice he no longer feared.

During these last months my grandfather told me many stories about the early days of Irish Parish and of my mother as a young girl. He was remembering all the past as a man does when the present is no more.

"A long way off, I can remember hearing great bells as I walked through green meadows expecting every moment that behind the stones I would meet with the future. I would run through the fields leaping as high as a great deer, filled with the joy of May and thinking myself as wise as the salmon. And when my mother would tell the story of the old woman of Beare and her living until none could count the years, I used to think, And what is that to me, for I have eighty ahead of me, and no fear on me with plenty of strength in my arm? I would come home from the running and put my arm under my head lying before the peat-fire, dozing off with the light of it still dancing in my eyes and my brother carrying me like a lump to the loft. There was little thought then of what was to come — I would be running and leaping the rest of my life the same as now with never a care on me.

"It was with great sadness that I left a country which could give a lad the joy of all its own liveness. I remember getting on the boat and thinking, now I'll maybe never come back and perhaps it's here I'm leaving the best of me." He would sigh deeply — then: "It was good in the Parish when I first came, more like the old country than Boston just a hundred and fifty miles away. I did not like the darkness of that place. The Parish itself had nothing of the look of Kerry, but the people were the same, except that I missed at first the red skirts to brighten up the look of a woman. But there was the same gay look in the eyes of these people and there was love among them. None of us who were used to the fresh shining air of the sea and the green grass of Kerry liked the dark mill, but there it was and a man could earn a living for himself and his family in it. It was better than the old country for all that, where a man could watch his children starve and he not able to bring them a bite.

"There was no dissension then. We were all the same, and if a woman made a cup of tea there would always be a friend by to drink. No one ever had to shake a teakettle in an Irishman's house. There was always plenty. You will never see those days again, for they are gone, all of them, and it's the Hill did it, the Hill with its pot of gold and Irishman fighting Irishman to get at it. Irish Parish was full of peace till the time came when the serpent got into the garden and none content after — all of them making the gold rush to the Hill and trying to outdo the Yankees at their own game. A few at first, then the whole Parish tumbling over one another to get there. I saw it first in Boston where some of the young ones had gone and come back to disease the old. Trying to prove they were as good as the next when no proof was needed. It's a sad story, and there is no end to it yet."

I did not like this kind of talk. "Tell me about my mother," I would say to turn him away from the sadness.

"Well I remember the day she was born. The first O'Sullivan of our branch to be born in America and

she more Irish than any O'Sullivan in the old country
— her eyes with the big black look out of them, and a
brogue as thick as a knife when she was five. She was
like me, dancing and leaping, though she had two or
three younger than herself hanging on to her skirts.
And a temper that went up like kerosene. I mind the
time she took care of the bully of the street and she
only up to his shoulder. She had him on the ground
before he knew and she did not scratch or kick like a
girl. She fought him like a boy and then came home
crying because she could not bear the hurt she had
given him. No, she was not beautiful like her sister
Hannah, but she had a greater thing than Hannah — she
had a joy in herself that would swirl out like shooting
stars. She was the best dancer in the Parish and had
many a beau, but she took your father above them all."
He shook his head over this. "They had nothing alike
in them. She had the spirit in her, too, but it did not
ruin her as it does so many of the O'Sullivans."

"What spirit, grandfather?" I asked.

"The one that can hear and see when there's nothing
visible," he answered. "I mind the time when she went
to the table-rapping at Bridgie Flynn's. Bridgie was
a great one for raising the spirits. We all sat around
the table, your mother next to me — only fifteen then
she was. Bridgie had a queer blue flame going and
she was rapping away at the table as hard as she could.
Then the table began to rock and Bridgie says in a hollow voice, as though coming out of a well, 'I have a
message for Mamie O'Sullivan — Nora wants a word

with her.' Nora was your mother's old friend, just
waked a week before. I could feel your mother trembling beside me. 'Rap twice,' says Bridgie, 'if you wish
to communicate.' Hardly were the words out of her
mouth when your mother jumped up, tipped over the
table, and was out of the house in a flash.

"I went home after her and found her sitting next
to the stove, talking to your grandmother, telling her
the whole story. 'And I saw her, mother, as plain as
day standing right behind Bridgie crying because she
had not confessed her last sins and begging me to do
it for her.' Your grandmother was a quiet woman, but
that evening she was angry. 'John O'Sullivan, will you
never give up this foolishness, putting ideas into a
child's head, scaring her half to death with these foolish
notions? Had I known where you were taking her, I'd
been after you with the broom. Now, Mamie, never
mind Nora's sins, but mind your own and go to confession tomorrow and tell the priest the whole story
and tell him it was your silly old father that led you into
this sin, for it's against the Church to be raising the
dead. And if I was the priest, it's to your father I'd
be giving a good penance.' But for all that your grandmother said, I noticed that she was uneasy herself the
rest of the night."

"Did she really see a ghost, grandfather?" I asked.

"Well, who knows? There's some swear to them, but
you'll have to ask your mother yourself," he answered.
"There's no way of telling, but perhaps the door between these two worlds is not shut as tightly as some

would like to have it." And that was all he would say.

I remember the day my grandfather died; for on that day a world died for me, and I was left walled into my own small spirit, and into an isolation I knew would never pass. The only other member of my community had gone, and the world was as empty as the day I was born. I did not know then what it meant to die, I only knew that there was absence, an absence as real and fully savored as any I have known since.

The long hall was dark, and I sat at one end of it. It was six o'clock in the morning, and everyone was out of bed. This had been for me the first sign of disturbance, for we were a sleeping family, Saturday mornings especially.

I was in my night clothes. The hallway was dark and cold, and I was afraid, afraid as I have never been since. The doorbell rang; and my mother, clad in a wrapper, her hair down, opened the door that led to my grandfather's room, and came rapidly down the hall. She carried a lighted candle in her hand, and I could hear her weeping as she came. My soul turned into a small, heavy lump, for I had never seen her before guarding the small light of a candle as though it were the most precious light in the world. She was for me at that moment the symbol of all my grandfather's weird tales, and she was, I felt, as lonely and sad as those tales. I could not move for the heaviness that came over me. She opened the front door, knelt; and a man, garbed in black, carrying the sacrament as carefully as my mother had carried the candle, came in. They moved slowly down the long dark hallway, the door closed, and all the lonely, sad creatures of my grandfather's imagination reached out their hands, bent back in pleas. There was nothing but terror and darkness, and the unknown.

I ran to my grandfather's door and called him. There was no answer, only the quiet voices of people praying. Something awed and quieted me. For ten minutes I stood there; and as I stood I was comforted, for there was a presence near me. Then someone moved inside the room, and I heard weeping again — the warmth of the presence was gone, and I was alone. I knew then my grandfather was dead; I knew it as inevitable as if the newspapers were before me with their dishonest words: "Death takes John O'Sullivan."

In that moment I knew, as only a child can know; and I did not call upon the dead, but the living. I screamed for my mother and beat the door that separated her from me. The door opened. At a glance, I understood. My grandfather was gone, my mother remained.

Daughter of the Kings of Ireland

I REMEMBER first the singing voice of my mother. Every evening she rocked me to sleep. The parlor was filled with a dark quiet, and I, lulled in and out of sleep by her rocking, felt no distinction between sleeping and waking. That time, that place, her voice, her presence, were a sleeping-waking dream. Whatever she sang became a mournful keen for those asleep or awake. There was no body to her voice. It sang, as a ghost would, thin, shrill, sharp, poignant. She sang the songs my grandfather had taught her: "Eileen Aroon," "The Bard of Armagh," songs with or without names, songs I no longer remember, but hear every now and then as if from a long, long way. In that singing my mother performed a ritual. My sleep all night. was pierced with her long lamentations of woe.

During my childhood, up until the time my grandfather died, I did not have any clear conception of what my mother looked like. The voice of her, the smell of her, were the two clearest notions. She was for me mainly a pair of gentle hands. One day I came upon a picture. It was of a young girl gotten up, I thought, something like Nelly Finn. Through the feathers and fur, I saw a face, a good face, dark eyes — smiling, a face I had seen somewhere. I took the picture in hand, went to the kitchen, looked at my mother. They were the same, though the eyes were more intense, blacker — they filled her whole face. Not one of her children resembled her. I was so taken by the look of her that, for days after, I mourned when I looked in the mirror.

Our home on the Hill was a tenement, but it was a more respectable tenement than the one in the Parish. It was one of the few blocks on the Hill and housed only six families, whereas Johnny O'Sullivan's in Irish Parish had housed twelve. The street we lived on was known as a run-down street, although several Yankee families were still living in old wooden frame houses along the street. The Parkers were two houses from us — we used to be fascinated by their old carriage house in back which we didn't quite dare investigate. Across the street from us, the Rowes lived in a small ginger-bread-yellow house. The chief thing I remember about these families is that we had little to do with them. There was a complete air of mystery about these houses because, in all the years we lived on the street, we never went inside them. We used to see the families on Sunday morning when they would come out of their houses garbed in black and go in the opposite direction from us toward the Congregational Church. Their houses were frightening because there was never a sign of life about them. About seven in the evening, one could see a dim light deep in the house. At nine there would be no lights. When we played run-sheep-run and some of the pursued hid behind these houses, I would never hunt for them, but go and sit on the stone steps of the block cracking between my fingers the green leaves from the shrubs that surrounded the building.

The reason that the street was not quite respectable was obvious. It was behind the only business district on the Hill. Hampden Street with its row of small stores ran perpendicular to it and the backs of these stores formed the main view we had from the block. Our back porch faced on the alley behind Rowe's grocery store, and the back of that store was always littered with old orange crates and the boxes in which the fancy foods that the store dealt in had been packed. Rowe's was, when I first remember it, the most popular store on Hampden Street — that store and Foster's drugstore catered chiefly to the moneyed people on the Hill. After school I used to cut through Rowe's store out the back way into the alley and home. This route was very popular with the children of our neighborhood, but it was discouraged by the owner of the store. I can still remember the smell of the place. It was dominated by cheese, for the old-fashioned cheese cases with roll-back windows filled one side of the store. The enormous cheeses crowded the cases. I used to watch the Yankee ladies of the Hill, some carrying their own baskets, some with liveried chauffeurs behind them carrying the baskets for them, carefully slicing a small piece of the cheese to taste before buying. Occasionally my brother Michael and I would steal a piece of the cheese.

Toward the back of the store, the smell of fish predominated, for in the back room, separated from the rest of the store by a swinging door, was the fish room. Despite the smell, I loved going in there with my mother. I would scrape the sawdust on the floor into little mounds as she selected her fish. The fish lay in tubs separated according to type. After she had selected the haddock she wanted, Mr. Bowen, the fish man, would chop off its head, slice it open, and clean it. Sometimes we stopped at the meat counter, but very rarely, for my mother still bought all her meat from Mike Flaherty in the Parish where she had traded for thirty years.

Behind Rowe's there was a long hill leading into the alley which formed the rear view of the block. In the winter, as soon as school was out, the children from all over the Hill would come there for sliding. At five o'clock, I would drag my sled behind me down Hampden Street, cold and wet, so sleepy that the store lights blurred into a haze before me. I would gratefully enter the warm kitchen. My mother would pull off my wet clothes, putting them to steam by the side of the stove. I would sit in the corner as close to the stove as I could get, letting the warmth soak into me until, half asleep, I was aware only of my mother's hazy figure moving from stove to pantry, from pantry to stove.

Beyond Hampden Street the exclusive section of the Hill began. As I walked down Pearl Street toward the grammar school, large Victorian houses with enormous stained-glass windows gave an air of sanctity to the section — *cave canem*, no trespassing, private property. I never dared walk the cement walls in front of those houses. It was this section of the Hill that had once been exclusively Yankee, and it was this section that was becoming, when I first knew the Hill, the promised land for the lace-curtain Irish.

When we first came, the block we lived in was mostly occupied by poor Yankee families, with whom we had some association. Though at first there was coldness, by the time I was old enough to feel it the chill had diminished. My mother and Mrs. Carter silently respected each other; my father and Mr. Carter exchanged cigars. The children broke down all barriers, but the parents remained acquaintances only.

In the early days our house overflowed with the O'Sullivans. My mother was the oldest of the seventeen. She had saved all her brothers from the truant officer; she was now saving them from what my father considered a fate worse than death — jail. The O'Sullivan boys ran true to form. Every Saturday night, after the dishes were washed, my mother went out and rounded up the seven of them. She would herd them home in one or another state of drunkenness. Beds would be made up, scoldings administered, my father would sulk — but every Saturday she went out and led them home, respectability or no respectability. That was her way. Whatever she did was done in this grand style.

One day, when I was starting to school, she suddenly announced, "There'll be no school for you today, Mary O'Connor. I want you with me." She dressed, took my hand, and we started. I was exultant. We boarded the trolley, and got off in Churchill, one of the worst slum districts of the city. I had, of course, pestered her with questions, but received no reply. We climbed and climbed stairs in one of the tenement houses, dingy, dirty hallways filled with the smell of offal. Squeamish, I held my nose. My mother had her grand-style look — with that she could rise above anything. At last we arrived at the top and stopped before a door to one of the tenements. I could hear children's voices, quarreling, laughing. In my smug contentment, I wondered if they had an excuse from school.

My mother knocked; there was silence, then a great rush for the door, which was opened by a girl of about twelve, ragged and dirty, surrounded by children equally ragged and dirty. My mother announced, "I am your Auntie Mame." I remembered vaguely an O'Sullivan uncle with a large family. They all smiled as if they knew her, and we went in. She sat down and talked with them. She had a way with her. I was the only one in the group who remained awkward and stiff. I couldn't bear their smell. Finally my mother sent one of them for ice cream. While that was being eaten, she talked some more, asking direct questions, carefully learning names: "Where is your mother"— "Working." — "Your father?" The older children looked abashed. "Dunno" was the answer.

Then my mother settled down to her business. "Rose," she said to the eldest, "you heat some water. I'm going to wash all of you, and then I have a surprise for you." She scrubbed for an hour — there were nine of them. When they were red and shining of face, she lined them all up in a row and directed Rose to hold the baby in her arms. She took a bottle from her purse. I knew the bottle; it was kept in the pantry. It held holy water. She used it every time there was thunder and lightning. Often I would be awakened from a sound sleep drenched with it. My mother sprinkled it everywhere during those storms — on the walls, the furniture, everything and everybody susceptible to lightning. Once in her excitement she had mistaken bluing for holy water. She scrubbed the house as well as my brothers and me for weeks after.

When I saw the bottle, I knew what she was going to do. I remembered then who the uncle was — Jim, who had married a Lutheran. I recalled whispers from the dark of my parents' bedroom — my mother's indignant "None of those poor children baptized!"

She baptized them all, going straight down the line. Her seriousness impressed them — they were, even to the baby, grave and quiet. In the stench of that place, her voice rose sweet and clean: "I baptize thee Sarah, in the name of the Father and of the Son and of the Holy Ghost." "I baptize thee Sean" — she made the little German boy, in one breath, both Irish and Catholic. Over each head she poured the holy water and made the sign of the cross. Never in her life had she had a better time. This done, she gave each of them pennies, for, like Saint Thomas, she believed in talking the language of converts.

That night I heard the satisfaction in her voice, as she turned over to go to sleep: "Poor but Catholics." None of the children were brought up Catholics, but my mother's satisfaction never ceased. Babies in Limbo were her greatest terror.

My mother loved children. She often visited the local orphanage and was always besieged by children who wanted her to take them home with her. I remember Brightwood chiefly as a great source of terror, and when my mother decided to take me with her to see a show the orphans were putting on, I hesitated a long time, but the ride in my cousin's car tempted me and I succumbed.

Brightwood had become a nightmare chiefly because of the tales my brother Michael told. Whenever we rode by it, I would stare at its Gothic horror, expecting at any moment to have a great hand reach out and incarcerate me behind its great brick walls. Michael would pull me down to the floor of the car, telling me that we were safe there. It was a Catholic orphanage run by nuns, set back far from the road, with a long wooden staircase leading up to it — the grounds were wooded and dark, and there were never any children to be seen. Michael had a secret theory that the children were never allowed out to play. He told me that the nuns probably killed them, anyway — something I didn't quite dare believe, though in their black sinister costumes they seemed capable of it. The evening my mother suggested taking me to Brightwood, I had an immediate vision of myself climbing that long wooden staircase with a shabby suitcase in my hand, homeless and motherless. Solitary and bereft, I saw myself becoming smaller and smaller until only a dot representing me appeared from the Springtown Road, and soon I disappeared as mysteriously as all the small children disappeared who went up that staircase.

The ride to Brightwood in Billy Dempsey's car lasted only too short a time. As we went up the long road to the orphanage, I clutched my mother's hand. I was surprised to find the place so brightly lighted up, and was equally surprised to find a great many children very much alive in the hall where the show was to be given. They were ranged in rows according to age, very quiet and well-behaved, and were all dressed in blue serge. The show was the usual children's show, singing and reciting, piano-playing; the costumes were inexpensive and crudely made. I was enchanted by it and was annoyed by the long pause before the last act. Suddenly we heard a little girl's voice crying behind stage. When the curtains parted, she stood in the middle of the stage, tears still running down her face. She was dressed in a prisoner's striped suit. In a trembling voice, interrupted every now and then by a sob, she sang

> If I had the wings of an angel
> Over these prison walls I would fly.
> I would fly to the arms of my darling,
> And there I'd be willing to die.

She continued through several stanzas, the song becoming even more of a lament.

As the children were filing out after the show, I carefully held my mother's hand. My mother, tremendously affected, went up to one of the nuns and asked for the little girl who had sung the "Prisoner's Song." The nun directed her to the dormitory room. It was a dark room with thirty cribs. All the children were from five to six years old. Some of them were already undressed and in their cribs. A nun, Sister Mary Joseph, was helping others to undress. She led my mother to the little girl's crib. She was still crying. "She wet her pants before she went on," Sister Mary Joseph said. "There was no time to change. It nearly broke her heart." She leaned over and patted the little girl. My mother took her up and wiped her face, saying soothing words to her. The little girl cried harder. Awkward and shy, I stood to one side while my mother was comforting the child. I stared around the room. Its mud-colored paint contributed to the gloominess. I was frightened and tugged at my mother to come home. Then I noticed the children. They were standing in their cribs, eyes full of hostility, staring resentfully at this intruder who had a home and wore her father's name.

After the Brightwood experience, nuns terrified me. I associated them with darkness and loss. I used to watch the black-robed figures walking down Main Street. Always there were two of them, looking unapproachable and out of place on a busy Saturday street. I remember my astonishment when I saw one of them buying bloomer elastic in the five-and-ten. I asked my mother what they used it for, because it seemed incredible that

they could ever wear bloomers. My mother's answer
was shocking. "To keep up their drawers, same as anybody else." She did not have my sense of the great
gulf between herself and a religious. There had been
too many cousins whom she had played with as a child
who had later entered the convent. As a matter of fact,
the Sisters of Notre Dame had urged her to enter the
convent, but she escaped, saying she had no call.

My grandfather was relieved. He had no desire to lose
his favorite daughter behind the veil of silence, as one
of his cousins had. That was old Feeney, a distant
cousin of my grandfather's whom my mother referred
to as Uncle Seamus. Five handsome sons he had in the
priesthood and four daughters took the veil — "the veil
of sorrow" Uncle Seamus said. That was a record even
for Irish Parish, but when people congratulated Uncle
Seamus, he would turn his head to one side and spit.
"They're after the last one now, Lizzie, the youngest,
but if they come with the old Pope himself, they'll not
be getting her. A fine thing for an old man," he'd say,
"five sons to bless him and five daughters fasting for
the good of his soul, but nobody in the house to peel his
praties for him nor keep him company in the dark
winter. What good is the Masses? I can have plenty of
those when I'm dead." Every time we saw Uncle
Seamus, he shuffled up to my mother with the same
complaint. My mother wisely did not try to comfort
him. Secretly she agreed that it was a hard life for the
old man, no matter how many prayers were said for
him.

One night we got a call from a friend of Uncle Seamus's in the Parish. He wanted to see my mother. She
let me come with her, not suspecting the cause of the
call. Before we got to the second floor of the tenement,
we could hear the old man pounding the floor with his
cane. "She's gone!" he said to my mother — "gone in
the dark of the night with a word to no one but themselves over there." He pointed his cane in the direction
of the convent. "Oh, the black hearts of them! Sure
and hadn't they enough of mine?" His voice was trembling with anger. "The yahoos. The black-hearted
yahoos. If ever I meet one of them —— " his voice
trailed off in wordless anger.

My mother became the mediator, but nothing would
persuade Lizzie to come back, nor could Uncle Seamus
be persuaded to see her. "If I went there, I'd have no
control of myself," he said. "I'd snatch the bonnet off
her and drag her home by her cropped head." When
the time came for Lizzie to take the vows of the novice,
Uncle Seamus would not go, but my mother decided
after much teasing to take me. About ten o'clock in
the morning we arrived at the Mother House. It was a
very hot day and I was sweating from the long unshaded
walk up to the house, which stood on a hill. When the
door opened in answer to our soft knock, the coolness
crept out. I went into the dark hall lit only by a votive
lamp flickering before a statue of the Blessed Virgin.
We were directed into a reception room filled with solemn, quiet people.

After fifteen minutes of the reception room smell of

leather and wax, a nun came to lead us to the chapel. No one spoke. The deeper we got into the building, the cooler it grew and the more persistent the smell of wax became. The chapel, too, was dark except for the altar blazing with candles. I sat with my mother, straining my eyes in the dark to distinguish among the visitors people we knew. Just before the service began, the novices filed in walking as solemnly down the middle aisle as a bride would walk to the altar, clothed entirely in white covered with a white veil. Only the orange blossoms were missing. Chills ran up and down my spine. I had the same feeling that I had had the day of my First Communion, but I had known that day that I would emerge from the church into the June sunlight and the smell of tea roses. I suddenly felt sorry for these girls who would spend their whole life in coolness, smelling the clean smell of wax. The only thing I envied them was the gold wedding ring each wore on her hand and the great cross she wore dangling from her habit.

After the Mass, my mother and I went up to kiss Lizzie and to ask her to pray for us. As these girls had walked down the aisle, I had imagined their slim, gliding bodies matching ethereal and angelic faces. I was tremendously disappointed to find that Lizzie still had a wart on her upper lip and a red face. On my way home, I asked my mother what nuns did all day. She answered in an abstracted way, "Oh, they fast and pray and go to Mass," and she added with a smile, "I suppose they wax the floors. You know," she said, smiling wryly, "cleanliness is next to Godliness." "Oh," I said, looking out the trolley window and sniffing the sweet June air, then and there making up my mind that I would never be a nun nor ever very close to God. Nuns never frightened me after that.

Wakes or "crepes," as they were known in Irish Parish, were a great source of amusement in our family because of my mother's unfailing attendance at all of them. Every night she read "religiously" the death and birth announcements in the paper. Later in the evening, she would put on her hat and coat to go out. My father would ask, "who is it tonight?" "Johnny Finn, my father's cousin, is being waked tonight," she'd answer. "But I didn't know he was related," my father would say. "Oh yes, he was a sixth cousin. His mother, Brigid, was Dinny Meehan's third cousin, who was" — and so on, and on, like a page of Genesis, begetting cousins, until she ended triumphantly with "and that makes him John O'Sullivan's fifth cousin."

Of course kinship was not really necessary to attend a crepe in Irish Parish; but as the times changed, my mother grew more and more apologetic about her constant attendance. My aunts considered it a scandalous thing to do, atending every ragtail-bobtail crepe in town. My mother never said a word. She just went. In her eyes everyone was related to her; and literally there were nearly seven hundred of our relations in the city.

Attending wakes was part of my mother's social ritual. She was continuing a tradition. In the old days in Irish Parish, a wake was social. It was not the horrible deathwatch it is now. People went to wakes, not to mourn the dead, but to comfort the living. The function of attendance was to give tongue to the dead and say to the living the consoling things the dead could not say.

I attended my first wake when I was ten years old. When my mother and I entered John D. Shea's Funeral Parlor, the dead man's wife and children were standing in a receiving line at the door. My mother went up to them. The wife murmured, "Mamie O'Sullivan, it's that glad I am to see you." My mother put her arms around her, kissed her, and said, "The thanks of God be with you, Mary O'Donnell. You've lost a fine man to Him. He'll be grateful to you, for he's needing such company in that lonely place." My mother had a heart like a homing pigeon. Without a thought she could find her way to the heart of others.

We turned from the family and walked to the casket. Again, as at the sight of Jerry Sheehan, I fell to my knees. Here, if ever I met it anywhere, in the face of the dead was the peace that passes understanding. I could hear my mother praying, as my grandfather had done, aloud. I prayed with her. As I prayed, I could hear my grandfather's words: "No man ever dies, Mary O'Connor. He just leaves quietly to go home."

After our prayers at the casket, we went to the back of the room. There were many people seated around, mostly women, all talking intimately in low voices. I had been so awed by the sight of death that I wondered how they could talk so easily. I soon found out. All the talk was about the dead man. Everybody came with his most beautiful memory of Seamus Flaherty. The whole conversation was a memento to the dead man, the most beautiful that could have been offered. His whole life was preserved, as was my grandfather's, in this oral tradition. It was from the old Irish women at such wakes that I learned of the early days in Irish Parish and my grandfather's youth.

The memories were not all proper and expurgated — what these old women did was resurrect the living from the dead in their warm, rich rememberings: "Do ye remember, Annie, the time Seamus caught us scrubbing? I was like to die for shame, and the scolding of him. 'Woman usin' snuff on their gums,' he said. 'Go get yourself a husband, Katie Flynn, or you'll be having bad dreams next.' " There was a sighing laughter.

"Ah, couldn't he sing, though," my mother added — "a voice like a very bird. Do ye remember Father Feeney, the one who thought he'd a voice, though he'd croak no better than a frog? Seamus sang the response one Sunday, and we all near half-killed with laughing. Father Feeney with his cracked *Gloria!*" Here my mother raised her voice, imitating him. "And the sweet bitterness of Seamus's response. Sure, himself was like a rooster. He apologized to the Ladies of the Sodality, saying that he was not in good voice, and Seamus was so slow in the response it confused him."

The men, after they paid their respects to the dead, usually gathered in the kitchen. Soon the smell of their cigar smoke seeped into the other room, and the clank of the whiskey glasses turned the wake into the kind of social festival it was. Every now and then, I could hear laughter, and I know that they, too, were remembering not the dead man, but the live one.

At twelve o'clock, the whole tone changed. There was a great, silent, somber tone now, and I sat in my chair, feeling the doom of the hour. The dead man was departing and the keeners began to sing the farewell. I trembled. That *coainim* was the most elemental cry I have ever heard. Only the wail of a child coming from the womb resembles it. These women were not professional keeners, as those who now attend Irish wakes. They were friends of the dead man, and their cries were those of people bereft of one whom they loved. The cry rose and fell with the passion of their woe. It was the wordless wail of man issuing from the womb of earth, the cry of the wounded, woeful animal. It was the cry of the living clutching, clasping at the departing spirit of the dead, begging, beseeching his return. It was the cry of those who knew there would be no coming back. It rose and fell, to the words, *Olagon! Olagon! Olagon!*

At twelve-fifteen, almost exactly, the keening ceased. There was nothing again but the deep silence, and the quiet sobbing of those who were left. The casket was closed. The dead man had gone home. Suddenly, from the back of the room, a voice began: "In the name of the Father, and of the Son, and of the Holy Ghost. . . . I believe in God, the Father Almighty, Creator of heaven and earth; and in Jesus Christ, His only Son, our Lord: Who . . . was crucified; died, and was buried." It was the beginning of the Rosary. A deep peace came over the room. The words rose as a tide of comfort, filling the room with their warm familiarity. "Hail Mary" — the great round went on — "Glory be to the Father." The solid round beads of the rosary formed a warm comfort in the pocket of my hand as I walked home with my mother.

Because my mother was so much concerned with more important things, she never noticed what people wore. This lack of concern led her to ignore her own dress and her children's as well. People were constantly giving her clothes for all of us. There was one woman, a schoolteacher, living near us, Miss Clark, who like a great many Yankees never threw anything out. She had saved all her clothes from the time she was six. Each year that I added, her old trunks would be opened and I would be given the clothes she had worn at approximately the same age. I would go to school smelling of mothballs, and looked, as I said indignantly, like an old ragbag. The other children had great sport, and I began to hate school more and more.

It was the brown beaver hat that caused the revolution, though. It was one Miss Clark had worn when she was eight, a tam o'shanter, flat as a pancake with a great wire through it to give it a round shape. Since it was much too big for me, by the simple expedient of a pair of pliers my mother had pinched the back together, making a great lump, and so I went to school feeling like the sacrificed Isaac. The hat slipped down on my forehead and I was constantly pushing it up. I had the unfortunate habit, anyway, of wriggling my nose to keep my glasses adjusted. That action upset the balance of the hat and caused it to come down even farther until my head was squeezed by the wire vise. Then I took to looking over my glasses, letting them stay where they were so that I could keep the hat in place. I felt my own ludicrousness painfully as I walked to school, peering over the glasses, the great awkward hat sitting squarely on top of my head.

I bore with my discomfort until the day I was nicknamed because of the hat. We had been studying history, and the teacher had told us exciting stories of the American West. When I went to the cloak room at recess time and put on the fur cap, someone called out, "Look at Daniel Boone!" All recess I was plagued unmercifully. That afternoon I went for a long walk after school. When I came home I was not wearing the hat. I had gone down to Kerry Park and flung it over the railing into the river. Somehow that seemed the only place to rid myself of the pain it had caused. I was gone until eight o'clock, and my mother was so frightened by my long absence that I was not scolded for what I had done. After that I wore no more hand-me-downs.

My mother's kindness to people was of a sort I have never met with since. I never heard her pass an absolute judgment on anyone. Only persecutors she could not tolerate. If a man did not pay his bills, she would say, "How can he? He has no money." If a man got drunk too often, she would call it "nerves." There was never any gossip in our house; that, she would not tolerate.

If Mrs. Parsons's husband was stingy, she gave an excuse or the matter was not talked about.

She had surely a great gift. When the little Polish lady came to our house selling apples, my mother would answer her "Appuls today?" with "No appuls today." I, homely and eye-glassed child, never realized my ugliness because my mother had a photograph of a seraphic, blonde-haired, blue-eyed child, representing an angel, on the bedroom wall. With complete aplomb, she answered all my doubting questions with "That is you, Mary O'Connor." I was spared much anguish because of this kind untruthfulness, and I made no connection between the face in the mirror and the actual Mary O'Connor. I was always that angel, hanging on the wall.

I have seen my mother feed not only her own large family, but the ones upstairs and downstairs as well. Wherever we lived, there was always some poor girl with several children and a drunken husband. My mother never ate with us, but served us, then carried the rest of the food upstairs or downstairs, and came back to eat left-overs. This was not martyrdom on her part. She had no concern for her own belly. In feeding others, she fed herself.

My mother was unaware of her generosity, and she was saved from a soup-kitchen consciousness by a fine Irish trait, that of satire. No one was spared it, for she, like my grandfather, made no distinction either of rank or of occupation. She lampooned the priest as well as the grocer.

We had a very young priest come to visit us, Father

Colum, who had just been ordained. My mother was very proud of him because he was one of the innumerable children whose diapers she had changed. For weeks my mother had prepared for his coming; and all the uncles, disreputable or not, were invited.

We formed a great circle at the table. Father Colum spoke. Every word came out of the adolescent sermons he had written as class assignments for his preceptors. All of us grew more and more uncomfortable. I suffered acutely for the innocent young man, for I could see in my mother's eyes the fires of hell burning for him. In his rôle of priest, he felt quite comfortably conscious of the necessity for moral regeneration on the part of my drunken uncles. My uncles slumped as one abject body over the table. My mother grew more and more fiery over what she looked on as a breach of good taste.

At last, she rose from the table, went to the sideboard and with deliberate banging and rattling uncorked a bottle of wine, with which she immediately filled all glasses, Father Colum's first, and then each uncle's. After that was done, she sat down with a great clatter. Father Colum, unabashed, went on, pushing his wineglass aside with a gesture of distaste.

My mother fixed him, as one does an insect with a pin: "Colum Foley, my brothers hold their liquor better than you ever held your water. I changed your diapers fifteen times a day when you were a child, but I'll not put up with your childishness now. In this house, we enjoy our food and our drink; and if God provides, we drink and are merry, and we always remember that forgiveness comes from Christ, not from a smug seminary student."

Father Colum never came back to our house; my uncles got riproaring drunk that night. My mother summed up the whole episode in one phrase — "collar conscious."

We all laughed at my mother's sharp tongue, but we all avoided it as far as we were able. Her great epithet, "Boob," which she hurled indiscriminately at pastor or child, was feared by all. She could often put more meaning in to that one word than she could into a whole sentence. Her "clouts" were much less to be feared than her tongue.

My father's toadying to his boss she could not bear, as she, in her Irish independence, could bear no cringing self-effacement. My father was known as a good, dependable worker, one whom the Yankee boss could depend on. It burned my mother to the soul to hear my father's boastful remark that he was the only Irishman the shop had ever hired. They were a high-class organization that hired only Yankees.

My mother was not chip-on-the-shoulder Irish, but how she hated any racial derogation! She showed her contempt for what she considered my father's betrayal through a satiric portrayal of his behavior. Some mornings, before he left for work, she would take his hat and stand by the door. As he came down the hall, she would put the hat on, and bend over, crouched and cringing: "Good morning, Mr. Hayden — Fine morning, Mr.

Hayden — So happy to see you, Mr. Hayden." The hat would be going on and off all the time. "I want you to know, Mr. Hayden, how happy I and all my family are to be earning twenty-seven dollars a week in your light, airy mill. It's very good of you to keep on a poor, unworthy man like myself, Mr. Hayden. I want to live and die in your mill." This act was described by my mother as "taking your hat off to the boss."

My mother was a great politician, and politics was a live and burning issue in our house. My father was a Republican, my mother a Democrat; consequently our dinner table was never dull. My father always lost. The reasonable answers he gave were always treated as the babble of a child. My mother's tongue would flash out, "Listen to the boob! Vote for Goodman, the only honest man, Goodman put in there to split the ticket!" My poor father could never win because his tongue was neither sharp nor quick enough. Logic always disintergrated before wit in our house.

For years my mother was chairman of the Democratic Party in one or another ward. She won the position because she had innumerable relatives whose votes she could swing. But she herself never voted for a man because he was Irish. She voted for him only if he stood for what she considered the most essential needs, social tolerance and the rights of the workingman. To her a Boston Irishman was as low as an Orangeman. She hated the Boston Irish because they represented the stronghold of the lace-curtain Irish; the whole of Boston was for her an even stronger Money Hole Hill. It was to Boston that the lace-curtain Irish on Money Hole Hill moved when they rose in the hierarchy; that is, when they acquired more money and more intolerance.

While she was chairman of the Democratic Party, a great Boston Irish politician came to our city. All the lace-curtain Irish turned out for the great dinners tendered him. My mother stubbornly refused to go. One evening he spoke at the final Democratic rally. My mother, as chairman, was obliged to introduce him. She did so, gracefully. He rose, winning, charming, suave, his talk full of the promised land if only we'd "get rid of Jews, Protestants, Polacks — make America really American — make it a land of pure, honest-to-God, one-hundred-per-cent Americans — make it Irish!" The orchestra struck up "When Irish Eyes Are Smiling," there was a great cheering and shouting. That night my mother left the Democratic Party. She has never returned. Her only comment was, "Boobs, boobs, boobs!"

More and more, my mother grew ashamed of her race. She was puzzled and painfully distressed because, deep down in her soul, she did not understand what was happening to her people; and though she lashed out at them, her alienation from them made her sorrowful. She repeated over and over again what my grandfather had said so often: "The Irish cannot be transplanted. In their own country they suffered persecution; over here they will turn it on others." My grandfather had the eye of a prophet.

When Father Coughlin, star of the lace-curtain Irish,

rose, we listened, but we listened only once. My mother said, "He's no priest, he's a politician hiding behind the skirts of the Church." That night she wrote a letter to the Bishop. She received no answer.

Mr. Adelson, an itinerant peddler, was a great friend of my mother's. He came about once a month to our house. It was always an exciting time because he always brought presents for both my mother and me. He was a European Jew, and he and my mother saw eye to eye on almost everything. They had a great joke together. He would always say to her, "I'll join the Catholic Church, Mrs. O'Connor, if you'll join the Synagogue." We finally did attend the Synagogue as his guests. Neither my mother nor I felt out of place there, as we did in Protestant churches.

After Mr. Adelson died, my mother received a package. It contained a set of beautiful silver candlesticks. A letter from his wife came with the package, saying that these were the candlesticks that Mr. Adelson had used on the eve of the Jewish Sabbath. He had willed them to my mother with the one request that she continue to use them in the same way, and that she pray for him. For years those candlesticks stood before the Blessed Virgin and were lighted every Friday night for "the repose of Mr. Adelson's soul," as my mother would say.

My mother's religion was made up mainly of candles and holy water. Those were the things that most expressed her loving kindness. Every Holy Saturday I was sent to the sacristy, to fetch back her holy water supply for the new year. Her year dated from Easter to Easter. I partly loved the errand and partly hated it, because I was ashamed of the great jug I had to carry to the church. All the respectable people would come carrying small bottles made for holy water. I would slip in the door, ashamed of the great water jug I had to fill. And I had to fill it very carefully so that I would not spill a drop. I learned from sad experience to carry a tin dipper along with me to fill the jug. In my scrupulosity not to spill a drop, I gradually accumulated a large and specialized equipment, a funnel, a dipper, and a wagon to fetch the jug home in. At length, because of my mother's enthusiasm, I would carry home in my wagon enough for the whole neighborhood. Stopping from door to door to drop my supply, I became a hawker of holy water.

Candles were the same. In every corner and cranny of our house was a candle burning for some intention or soul. My mother not only burned them at home, but went every day of her life to the church to light a candle there. She was greatly annoyed when the candles were blown out at night for fear of fire. She issued a strong protest — Wasn't it at night a man most needed a candle burning for his soul!

I often accompanied her on these afternoon visits to the church. She took seriously anyone's request that she pray for him. We would drop into church and kneel first before the Blessed Virgin's altar. The church would be filled with the deep silence of a sanctuary — only an old woman or two quietly whispering her beads, the votive lamps burning and beating like red hearts in that dark place. We always knelt longest before the Blessed Virgin because she was woman's chief intercessor, and she was, of all, most accessible. My mother would light two or three candles before her for women in childbirth. There were always plenty of those.

We would then go to Saint Joseph's altar. Before him, my mother would light one candle for the seven uncles. She would have preferred one for each, but candles were expensive. Our ritual concluded with the stations of the cross, said for all the people that candles were not lit for. I don't believe she ever prayed for herself.

My mother burned candles instead of using patent medicines. It was a pleasanter remedy. Whenever anyone was ill, she cured him with candles, though she was never so self-assured that she wouldn't bring in the doctor or give a broth. Those remedies were ignored later. "Sure, wasn't it the candle that saved himself, and he dying of pneumonia?" This was always the way the story of my father's illness began, a favorite, told over and over by my mother. "Dying he was, crying and screaming out at the Banshee that had come to fetch himself, 'Take that woman away, she's coming at me!' " Here my mother's voice would rise to a wail. "Arrah, I rushed for the Virgin's altar, lit a candle that she'd whisk the ugly devil away — and whisk her away she did. Not a whimper out of himself after that, and he as whole and well as a live chicken in the morning."

My father never had the heart to tell her that the "ugly divil" who threatened him was no Banshee, but Saint Teresa, whose picture hung at the foot of his bed.

I attended Mass with my mother every Sunday, and after this great drama would come home and put on one of my own. My brother Michael and I celebrated Mass in the kitchen. We would usually have as a congregation the Carter children, the Beatons, but no Irish or Catholics. The Protestant children were fascinated. I would put on my mother's apron that fitted like a chasuble, fling a dishtowel over my arm as the maniple, enter from the pantry, with Michael as altar boy, and Mass would begin. The Mass proceeded very rapidly until the consecration, and then the whole procedure became a slow, solemn mimicry of the real Mass. I would turn from the kitchen table, lift my hands high in the air, make the sign of the cross, mumble words full of *is* and *us*, modeled after the *In nomine Patris et Filii, et Spiritus Sancti.* Then I would turn back again, bow low, and mumble. My brother Michael would come up to me with a pie-plate filled with grimy bread pellets, which he had rolled during the early part of the ceremony. Sometimes these were sugared because the faithful balked at the innumerable doughy pellets they were forced to swallow without chewing.

I would empty the pellets into a water goblet, and turn to the solemn part of the Mass, the consecration. A great deal more bowing and scraping went on, while my brother knelt behind me, holding up the apron, and banging away on a push-bell. I would lift the water goblet high in the air, always saying the same words, a small poem my mother sometimes said at night. She would come creeping down the long hall, saying in a sepulchral tone:

> I am the ghost of thy father
> Doomed to walk in the night.
> If I could be released
> From these prison walls,
> I would tell you a story
> That would make your hair stand on end!

The last words would be said with a shriek and a leap at us. It was the most fearsome experience I knew, and these were the words I repeated at the consecration of the Host.

I would lift the goblet slowly, imitating the sepulchral tone of my mother: "I am the ghost of thy father — " then, slowly lowering the goblet — "Doomed to walk in the night" — bowing — "If I could be released from these prison walls" — slowly turning to the kneeling faithful — "I would tell you a story that would make your hair stand on end!" I would spring at my terrified audience, shrieking the last words at them. Then, before they recovered, I would start serving the Communion. My brother would hold up the back flap of the apron, while I administered the Host with the solemn injunction, "Don't chew it. Remember, don't chew it." With that, the Mass would be ended. There was no sermon, no gospel.

This play continued with no interference from my mother. It never occurred to her that it was blasphemous. We were stopped finally by an aunt, who considered it a disgrace to allow this mockery of Catholicism before "black Protestant" children.

Such play-acting was stopped even more thoroughly by the priest who was giving us instructions for Holy Communion. Every Wednesday afternoon we went for instruction, and a thorough instruction it was, aimed at putting the fear of God into us. The thought of that first confession terrified me; the Communion I did not fear half so much. I would come home after instruction drooping with my sense of sin. All the joy of my earlier religion was beaten out of me. I no longer would go to church with my mother. Before me always was Sin written large on a white, disembodied, fluttering thing called my soul. I would wake up at night, try to catch that white, round-winged object and count all the black spots on it so that I could make a "good confession." I became overwhelmed with guilt at the number of times that I had picked my nose, gone to the toilet outside, taken down my pants.

I could neither sleep nor eat. My mother became much troubled. She went to Forbes and Wallace and brought back a beautiful white dress, and my first pair of white shoes. I was a little lessened of my fears in my joy over the white shoes. I fondled them, and carried them with me wherever I went. On the way home from showing them to Mrs. Parsons, I dropped them into a mud puddle. It was all too symbolic. They were as mired and muddied as my soul. I wept by the side of the puddle until my mother found me.

She rescued the dripping slippers, took me in her arms, and carried me into the house. She rocked me in the great leather chair. Inarticulately, I cried out my gasping grief. She rocked back and forth. I could hear the tormented working of her mind. "Never you mind, Mary O'Connor, what the priest says. You come home to me when he troubles you with his stories. There is no truth in it. God does not want you sad. He wants to comfort you. He'd be kissing and cleaning you all over, as Rainbow does her kittens. That's what He does when you go to confession. He takes your soul and scrubs it clean, putting it back into you as fresh and white as the day you were born. Before you leave confession, He bends over and kisses your soul three times; so that when you are outside you are leaping and laughing with the joy of all that cleanness inside you. Never you mind the priest. He is only the ear through which God hears you. When you go to confession, you talk to God. He's hanging on the cross, above the wicket. You talk to Him, and forget the priest. Now, I'll clean your white shoes as clean as God will make your soul, Mary O'Connor; and don't you be after catching that soul. It must be free to fly. That is why it has wings. It must be free to go between you and Himself. It pays Him a visit every night while you are sleeping. If your soul were caught in your hands, you'd be having no chats with God, and it would be then that you'd be having a real cause to fear."

That night, when I went to sleep, the shoes, as fresh and clean as when they were new, were before me on the dresser. They shone white in the darkness. I slept long and well. After that I talked to the crucifix when I went to confession: "Bless me, God, I mean Father, for I have sinned."

The Sunday I made my First Communion, my mother's only admonition was, "Don't chew, remember, don't chew!" When I received my Host, my mouth was so dry that I could not swallow. I was supposed to lead the children back to their seats after Communion, but I could not move. The Host, stuck to the roof of my mouth, would not budge. I did not dare touch it with my tongue. Wasn't it Christ? Who would dare to touch it? In desperation I called on my soul to release it, so that I could get it inside my clean self, where in my childishness I thought it would rest as hallowed as in the tabernacle.

Finally, the priest tapped me on my shoulder. I had knelt for ten minutes, holding up the procession. I stumbled back to my pew, remembering, however, to fold and point my hands high before me, as I had seen the saints fold theirs. I knelt in the pew, my mother's words crowding my ears: "Don't chew — remember it is the body and blood of Christ." Gradually the thin wafer began to melt, and I swallowed it in little pieces, apologizing to God all the time for this desecration of His unity.

After the horror of that experience wore off, I went visiting with my mother. I received many gifts, mostly money. These gifts were placed in the holy candle fund, and every day I lighted a candle with the solemn intention that the Host would not stick so badly next time.

That prayer was never answered. As I grew older and bolder, I decided my own way of serving Communion was much better — adding a little water. My mother agreed with me.

After my grandfather died, family prayers were given over. The stories no longer told, there was no reason left to fend off the fantasies of his imagination. We said our prayers to my mother every evening, ending always with a prayer that she had taught us:

> Mary, attend me,
> Christ, defend me,
> All angels, sleep with me
> In this clean, fresh bed.

Some nights in the winter, when the parlor was closed off, we would congregate in the kitchen. The big leather rocking chair would have been brought into the kitchen for the winter. My brothers would have on the headphones to the crystal set. My mother would be reading the births and deaths in the newspaper. My father would be sitting without talking, smoking his pipe or reading in the *Atlantic Monthly,* silently wording it with his lips. The leather rocking chair would be rocked back and forth by my brother Michael's foot; and I, curled in the corner, hazy with sleep, would see only a red glow of warmth, feel only the sweet peace of those who are wanted, hear only the humming song of the kettle with the warm, rich voice of my mother reciting aloud birth and death, death and birth. Oh, I remember rocking in and out of birth and death, not preferring either one or the other as long as it was my mother who rolled them richly from her tongue.

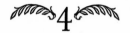

Aunt Maggie's Boy

I REMEMBER being perched uncomfortably and insecurely on a bony knee that jiggled me up and down, while a cold, tuneless voice sang over and over again the same words, "Lizzie on the pickle boat, Lizzie on the pickle boat." There was a coldness and a sense of distance from anybody — only the knee and the voice seemed present. I squirmed, as a dog does, and tried to wiggle up against the warmth of a body which I knew, instinctively, must be there; but I never got close to that body. It always receded. Finally, greatly puzzled, I turned around to see if anyone was there. I looked into a long, thin face, consisting mostly of cold blue eyes and a bony nose. I was fascinated by the icy quality of the face, all white and blue. I continued to stare. Abruptly, I was set down hard on the floor. An annoyed voice said to my mother, "She's wet my new trousers." My mother laughed heartily. "Well, I'm glad one of them caught you," she said. That was my father, a proud stern man, a man whom the past had frozen over.

That past he never spoke of until years later, when, softened and mellowed by the present, it no longer was freezing and frozen within him, and he told me his story: He was born in Youghal, County Cork. His mother was thirty, a blonde, big-boned woman; his father sixty, wizened and withered as farmers often are who live on barren land. The farm was small, and it yielded only a small crop of potatoes. There were nine sons, no money, and not enough food. My father often derided the potato legend: "The Irish ate potatoes because that was all they could get, and there's not much enjoyment or nourishment in them, I can tell you that."

My father was the youngest of the nine. Of his early childhood, he remembered most vividly the humiliation of going to school. The school was run by the English and taught by an Irishman educated in England. He was worse than the English. After my father had walked the seven miles to school in his bare feet, "the Irish toad," as my mother called him, would beat him for not bringing his weekly shilling, the price set for instruction. After three years of beatings, my father was taken from school. Even now, his handwriting is like the scrawl of a seven-year-old.

When he was ten years old, the whole family was taken with typhoid fever. They were removed, with most of the village, to the charity ward of an English hospital. The mother and father and six of the sons died. My father survived only by luck; he'd had a "light case." Afterward, the three remaining boys went back to Youghal. The two older brothers were desperate over the ten-year-old. They could not put him to the work that so many Irish children were doing in the dirty, dark mills of Liverpool, nor could they support him. They wrote to a rich, respectable aunt, who had gone to America thirty years before. They begged her to take the boy, and to send passage money for him. She did, though reluctantly. He would have to be "a good, clean boy," she stipulated.

He sailed from Queenstown early one Sunday morning. He took his last look at the green land and the white cottages against it. The cathedral, high on the hill, opened its doors, and the people coming out turned into tiny black specks, receding into the gulf the ship had set between. That gulf became wider, and the Irish people were pushed farther and farther into oblivion by that removal to America. There was no regret then, and none now, for the ocean wall that had been set between him and his people. The imagination of a child builds high walls for the mature mind. Those walls hold back the painful past.

The boat that he sailed on was, he told me bitterly, a cattle boat, and he was quartered with the cattle. The voyage took four weeks. He arrived in America hatless and shoeless, smelling of cattle dung.

Aunt Margaret was a respectable and accepted member of a Yankee community. With her began my father's lace-curtain training. The Yankees referred to her as "Irish but very obliging." She had come to America before the large Irish immigrations, and had married a man who owned a furniture store near Boston. They had changed the name from Cavanagh to Cavendish, and did a flourishing business. Aunt Maggie, as my father called her, was as wise and wily as the Yankees she moved among. She voted the Republican ticket and served popcorn and milk for Sunday night supper. Corned beef and cabbage was anathema to her, as was the vaudeville Irishman with the thick brogue. She repeatedly said that the young Irish boy was "a thorn in her side"; but she was "bound and determined to do her duty by her dead sister's boy." Her duty, as my mother said, consisted of removing every trace of Irish from his mind and manner. She did it by making him ashamed of his heritage.

She said to her husband, when her nephew walked into the room, "Well, Mr. Cavendish, we'll just have to make the best of it. He can work in the back of the store until he's adjusted." The boy, tired and dirty, was put to bed in the barn the first night, his quarters until he left Aunt Maggie's. The next day, Aunt Maggie, who always referred to him as "the boy," gave him his first lesson in lace-curtain manners. He was outfitted in an old pair of shoes and pants, hand-me-downs from Mr. Cavendish. He neglected to say thank you. Aunt Maggie tartly reminded him that he was forgetting his station. The boy never forgot again. All day long he was corrected and scolded. There was no question of education. "After all, Aunt Maggie fed his body," my mother used to say, "and that was all her duty demanded."

If he used an Irish phrase, it was changed into what Aunt Maggie called "good American English." "Boy, when in Rome do as the Romans do," she would com-

mand. Before he came into the house, he was required to remove his shoes. If he sat out on the front
steps to cool off on a hot summer evening, Aunt Maggie
would hiss at him through the lace curtains, "Boy, come
in here. What will the neighbors think?"

That was her great phrase, and she lived according to
what the neighbors thought. She remained loyal to
Catholicism, but that was, as my mother said, "watered
down by Protestantism." They had Protestant grace
before meals, recited sanctimoniously: "We thank thee,
Lord, for these Thy creatures Thou hast blessed to our
use." The boy used to search his soup uneasily for the
blessed creatures. They went to Mass on Sundays, but
secretly and slyly as though it were sinful. The boy was
enjoined not to mention these forays out of town.
There was no Catholic Church in Sherwood. Public
Opinion would not allow it. Aunt Maggie would say,
"Keep quiet about it, boy. What people don't know
won't hurt us."

But as time passed, and the Irish grew stronger, Aunt
Maggie became actively Irish and openly Catholic. She
had her picture on the front page, along with that of the
pastor, on the tenth annniversary of Saint Joseph's
Parish. Her activities were largely devoted to clubs, of
one of which she had been Past Grand Regent. She
also organized minstrel shows. At the end of every
minstrel show, when the people, sated with homemade
fudge and homemade entertainment, were eager to go
home, Aunt Maggie would rise with a flourish. "Let us
be thankful for the blessing the Lord has conferred on

us in making this program a success." She would then
read off a financial statement, telling how much more
had been taken in than had been spent. "Occasions like
this, with all this fine singing, remind all of us, I am
sure, of the old country, where we used to gather around
the hearths and listen to beautiful Irish voices," she
would say. The Cleary boy, who had sung "Danny Boy"
in a shaky tenor, would blush with pleasure, and the
Gogarty girls, who had rendered "I Dreamt I Dwelt,"
would shyly stare at their dresses. Aunt Maggie's speech
would always end with "Erin go bragh," the only Gaelic
she knew. One night she lifted her arm to emphasize
her last words — she got out the "Erin," and dropped
dead on the stage.

There were many Masses said for Aunt Maggie, and
she had the biggest funeral ever given an Irishman in
Sherwood: the Knights of Columbus marched behind
the coffin; the Daughters of Isabella in front of the
coffin; the pastor, who had fostered and feared her, rode
in the first mourner's car, telling my father what a fine
aunt he had lost, and Mr. Cavendish what a fine wife
she had been — "a good Catholic woman."

After Aunt Maggie's death, my father, now twenty-
seven, left Sherwood and never returned. He left with
no friends, no regrets, and no money. He came to Irish
Parish. Here he found what his aunt had indoctrinated
him against, the shanty Irish. Here the buckies and the
brogues were thick, and there were only the first glim-
merings of a lace-curtain consciousness. He had arrived
in Irish Parish to find no place for him. He walked up

to Money Hole Hill the first night, and saw little difference between that and Aunt Maggie's world, but he
found no place there either.

The next day he started looking for a job. In all the
mill offices he read the same signs, "No Irishmen need
apply." One morning, after a week of hunting with
no success, he was loitering outside the employment
office of the woolen mill. It was the lunch hour; a
worker came out and started talking with him. My
father learned from him that wool sorters were wanted
and that all training would be given in the mill. He
went into the employment office and gave his name.
The man asked, "Are you Irish?" My father said, "No,
English." He had no trace of brogue. Aunt Maggie had
seen to that. He was hired. He took a room in a boarding house with the other English workers. It was outside of Irish Parish on the fringe of the Hill, run by
a Yankee woman who was "in reduced circumstances."
It was a "genteel" boarding house; and whenever there
was a room available, Mrs. Jenks would put a genteel
vacancy sign in the window.

My father was apprenticed to an Englishman, Mr.
Hamelin, who spent all his time telling him coarse
stories about Irishmen. One night he took my father
to walk in Kerry Park. The dam was high, and all Irish
Parish had turned out for a look at it. Mr. Hamelin
turned to my father and said, "Dirty buggers, you can
smell 'em a mile away." My father remembered the
smell of the wool shop, but said nothing. Aunt Maggie
had trained him well.

That night my father saw my mother in Kerry Park. She was with a group of girls who sat on the railing staring straight at Mr. Hamelin and my father, giggling and laughing at their stiff collars and stiff airs. My mother remarked the Irish face and shouted, "Hey, Bucky, who was after taking you out of the bandbox?" Mr. Hamelin stared at my father. "Say, are you Irish?" he asked. My father shrugged his shoulders and grudgingly admitted, "Only half." He was shunned in the wool shop after that; and though Mrs. Jenks admitted no need for the room, he was requested to leave. Everyone said that he neither looked nor acted Irish, but added, "If there's a drop of it in you, it's bound to show sometime."

My father took a room in Irish Parish, but made no friends. He sat in solitude in his room, or in silence in Kerry Park, smoking his pipe. He saw my mother often and stared at her silently and bitterly. Finally, the loneliness he had known since he had come to America was too much for him, and he spoke one night to a white-haired old man. That man was my grandfather. Though my grandfather was suspicious of this cold stranger with the accent of an Englishman, he took him to his house for a drink of whiskey and a cup of tea. It would have been heartless, as he explained later, to do otherwise. When my mother came in, she found him sitting stiff and stolid in this shanty Irish house. She poked fun at him, but felt "the need in the man." He came every night for three years, whether she was there or not. She danced at the Hibernians', visited Boston, and laughed at him, cutting him with the name "Bucky," but surprised that he did not act like one. Persistence won her, as it had won him a place in the wool shop.

When they were married, they lived in Johnny O'Sullivan's block, overlooking Kerry Park. My mother was unhappy because all the gaiety had vanished from her life. There were no stories, no people dropping in at every hour of the day. The strange, saturnine man she had married did not encourage either people or stories. He had no sympathy for either the Irish people or their imagination. My mother was lonely until the children started coming. Then she built her life around them and tried to bring them into her world, discouraging entrance to my father's. But that was impossible. I remember standing in a doorway with my father pulling me one way and my mother the other. Full of pain and panic, I wondered why neither would cross the threshold. With the clear logic of a child, I realized that I could not go both ways.

The struggle between my mother and father was at first a silent one, but it gradually became bitterly voluble. It was then that my grandfather came to live with us. He was my refuge, for a child cannot live "torn between," as my grandfather put it. My father had won the first great battle. He came home one night and announced that we would soon be moving to the Hill. Even my grandfather sided with my mother, as did all of Irish Parish. But we moved, and I grew up on the Hill, with my grandfather and then my mother protecting me as well as they could against the misery and shame of being shanty Irish on Money Hole Hill. All of us, for the first time, were introduced to an insecurity and isolation that has not lessened during the years. The cleavage we met first within our family spread to school, church, everything that our life consisted of. There was no escape from it and no hope that it would not leave its mark. We all bore it, the children of a shanty-Irish mother and a lace-curtain Irish father.

My father's image was overshadowed in those early years by both my grandfather and my mother, but I grew increasingly aware of the stern, proud man as his influence grew stronger. After my grandfather's death, we were visited less and less by the people of Irish Parish and more and more by the people of the Hill. My father encouraged visits from the Yankees he worked with. They were all poor, but their names of Fuller and Parsons gave them social position. My mother, who did not like them, was nevertheless happy over the prospect of conversation.

I would slip shyly into the living room and sit quietly in a dark corner. The conversation, dull and dreary, was mostly shop talk. No one ever felt comfortable. My mother's wit flashed out occasionally into a shocked silence. At the end of the evening, my mother would go to the kitchen to prepare refreshments, homemade elderberry wine and cakes. After the "company" left, my mother would explode. "Not even good wine could loosen the knots in those tongues. Stiff as boards they are. Enough to make a person perish of boredom. I

won't have them again, I tell you, with their 'Yes, Mr.
Parsons,' and 'No, Mrs. Parsons,' and their wooden respectability pricing everything in the room." My father
never answered these tirades, but the following Sunday
we would have "company" again.

But my mother was too social a woman to remain
completely isolated, and after a while she began to
make friends among the Yankees, and even to maintain
(to their detractors in Irish Parish) that they were good
friends, but she seldom made friends with the members
of her race on the Hill. Her scorn for the lace-curtain
Irish was constant. She used to say, "Put an Irishman
on a spit and you'll find a lace-curtain Irishman to turn
him." My father paid no attention to her remarks; but
he did not invite the lace-curtain Irish to the house for
many years. Instead, every Saturday night he dressed in
his best blue suit, put on his stiff collar and high kid
shoes, and went downtown to meet his Irish friends and
have a drink with them. Many of the things the lace-
curtain Irish did he did not approve of, but out of a
desire for respectability he joined ranks with them.

That desire for respectability drove my father into
parental tyranny. We children were not allowed out of
our own yard for fear we would disturb the neighbors.
On the fourth of July the neighborhood exploded with
fireworks, but we had none. I was required to play with
children who disliked me and whom I disliked, to
placate my father's sense of respectability. But all this
play for a respectable position was in vain. Most of the
Irish Parish visitors had been discouraged, but my

father had not reckoned with the O'Sullivan brothers. Saturday nights the patrol wagon would deposit one or another of them on the back porch. When this first happened, my father, horrified, explained to the neighbors that it was all a mistake. But that explanation grew weak with the frequency of its repetition. "My God, what will the neighbors think?" grew to be a standard phrase in all our vocabularies.

My father did not dare to turn the brothers away. He knew where to draw the line, but he tried the impossible feat of getting them into the house as quickly and quietly as possible. This worked occasionally with all but my Uncle Smiley, who would come rolling up the street, singing at the top of his lungs the lewdest verses of "Mademoiselle from Armentières." The lights would go out in the living rooms all along the street and curtains would be slyly pulled aside while respectability gaped. "They're a disgrace to the Irish," the lace-curtain Irish yapped. The little Horrigan girl would say, sidling up to me the next day, "Does your uncle drink?" "Tell her it's a touch of sun," my mother would shout sarcastically from the kitchen window.

My father's tyranny never took the form of physical cruelty until one night when my brother Tabby came home in a state of drunkenness. My father, shaking with the indignity of it all, flew at him with a poker, shouting, screaming, "You're another one of the O'Sullivan bastards! It's all bad blood. Well, I won't put up with it, put up with it, put up with it!" As he repeated each phrase, he struck Tabby with the poker.

My mother and the rest of us stood by helplessly. In the face of an animal fighting for the thing he had struggled so hard to secure, there is no defense. My father saw in Tabby the defeat of the values he had struggled to win. He was not responsible in the eyes of his world for the drunken uncles, but for the son, yes.

I, brought up by a grandfather and a mother to whom violence was anathema, flung myself on the floor, roaring out my despair and grief, beating and pounding the inanimate floor in my sorrow for the cruelty of the animate world. I had been "torn between" too long. All the grief and pain stored up for so long was roared out long and loud. Tabby had disappeared out the front door, his belongings flung after him by my father. I would not rise from the floor nor cease from my weeping until he had been brought back. Sheepishly, my father allowed my brother Eddie to go after him. When he came back, I clung to him, patting him and sobbing out my grief. For days after I would steal past my father, not looking at him, blaming this cold, stern man, in my childishness, for the thing I did not understand.

My brother Eddie, a shy, lame boy, was my father's great pride because he played the violin so well. My father, with the same lack of understanding he betrayed in all things that touched upon the security of his values, would sacrifice Eddie ruthlessly for the entertainment of his friends. Eddie would be forced to stand in the middle of the room with people surrounding him, painfully conscious of the brace he wore on his leg, while my father would ask requests of his friends. Standing there, all eyes upon him, was painful enough, but to play was almost impossible. The music would come out thin and shaky because he had no heart for it. People would hum their favorite songs, songs he had never heard before, and he would be required by my father to attempt a reproduction of the songs. Always the last request would be for a song he detested, "Ave Maria," to which even the Yankees listened with moist eyes. I, sitting in a dark corner, would watch the white line around his lips growing thinner and thinner, his hands shaking, the bow quivering, and would remember the soaring joy of the violin when he played it for me. I would put my head in my lap to hide the white anger and terror of that face from my sight.

Against this aspect of my father, my mother was powerless. She knew that whatever she said would only make him more stubborn in his determination to indoctrinate his children; but in political argument, she could and did win. My father, in her opinion, was always on the wrong side politically. He had been well schooled in political conservatism by Aunt Maggie and he always voted against his own group, even against the lace-curtain Irish. If the name Cabot or Lodge appeared on the Republican ticket, my father would vote for it no matter what its qualification. It was sound, good business. It represented security of the first order.

In the early days, I would sit at the table and listen with surprise and dismay to the fiery fighting that went on between my mother and father. My earliest remembrance of political fighting was over something called the tariff and over another mysterious thing called immigration. Both of these were, in argument, always connected.

My father's voice, logical, cool, calm: "If you let all those foreigners in here, they'll be competing with us, and our wages will go down. It's the same with lowering the tariff. Those foreigners will send over a flood of cheap goods and prices on American goods will go down and wages with them. I tell you it's the old law of supply and demand, you can't beat it. You just don't know the first law of economics."

My mother's voice, passionate, angry, and often illogical: "To hell with economics and all your old laws! Whose demands are they, whoever *they* are, supplying? It's a hoax and you're too dumb to see it. Enough talk about foreigners and you one yourself, I'm thinking, until I rushed you down to the City Hall to take out papers just before Edmund was born. Me, marrying you, you old Bucky, and almost losing my citizenship, not knowing it!"

Later the political arguments became more immediate, what my mother referred to as a matter of "bread and butter." My father could never get over the white-collar complex. He was never a "mill worker." That appellation was too unrefined. He was a "skilled worker" with a "trade." The wool shop was superior to the mill, and the wool sorters superior to the unskilled mill worker. "After all," my father would say, "I am the only Irishman in the wool shop." My mother would snap back, "A fine lot of difference being a wool sorter and the only Irish one makes in your envelope. You're no better than the rest of them, though you don't get your hands as dirty." She had picked up the phrase "company man" from some conversation she had had, and she hurled it at my father constantly.

He was that, too. He would come home nights completely worn out from standing ten hours at the wool board and say: "Fine little man, that Joe Hayden. Why, he had his chauffeur stop and pick me up this morning on the way to work and, by golly, I rode right beside the boss himself in the back seat." My mother, disgusted with my father's simplicity, would say: "And why not? Sure and you're paying for the car as well as the driver of it. Next time you see him and he offers you a lift, tell him, 'Never mind the ride, you dear generous man. Just put it in my envelope.' "

We all enjoyed these battles because of the wit; but underneath that there was a grim note, a note that promised more than table talk. This grimness came out over the unionizing of the wool shop. My father refused absolutely to have anything to do with unions. "I read my paper every night and I know just what rackets unions are, and what racketeers unionizers are too," he said. "Joe Hayden has always treated me all right and I'll stick no knife in his back. If the men want a raise, all they have to do is go up to Joe Hayden's office and he'll treat them right." The whole mill organized, except the wool shop. "It's all right," my father would say, "but I tell you we know what we're doing."

One of my father's friends, a strong, fiery young Scotchman, used to come to the house and talk to him. He was one of the new kind of workers — aware, intelligent, and, as my father said, "radical." "Hugh's all right, but he's too damn radical," he would say. "He'll find himself in plenty of hot water." My mother knew nothing about the economics of labor, but instinctively she took the side against the powers that be and came out strong for unions. She learned all the phrases from Hugh and dinned them into my father's ears from morning till night. Finally, in desperation, he voted for joining the A.F. of L. My mother smiled; my father scowled. She could never keep quiet over a victory; her crowing could be heard all over the Hill.

When the mill was sold, my father, accustomed to the methods of old Joe Hayden, could not believe that his wool shop could change so. Managers and efficiency experts moved in. The quiet, slow pace of the old mill was revolutionized. The whole mill was put on a system of piece work to speed up production. The quality of the cloth my father had been so proud of degenerated. They began to put rayon linings in suits instead of the finer cloth previously used. "Rayon!" — my father's contempt was spit out — "Toilet paper!"

With the change of ownership came a complete change in policy. One night my father came home long-faced and grim. Not a word did he say all during supper. My mother kept demanding, "What's eating you?" No answer. He sat in the dark living room all night completely silent. In the morning, when my mother called him, he finally divulged his bitterness: "I am not going to work." My mother's face clouded. "A lay-off?" she asked — the most dreaded words in our house. It was the menacing threat that hung over all mill workers, even the superior wool shop.

But this time it was not a lay-off. In my father's opinion it was something far worse — a strike. My mother's face cleared like the sun on a cloudy day. She beamed. Then suddenly she demanded, "And what are you doing here, then, if there's a strike on, with a face like a stony squid?" My father turned his back to her, not answering. "I'm asking you. Is there no place for you? Is it that you're too full of sympathy for the other side to want to be hurting their feelings?"

My father, filled with anger, turned on her. "I tell you I'll join no strike. Strikes are radical."

At that moment the doorbell rang. My mother rushed to answer, eyes blazing. It was Hugh. My mother asked him into the living room.

He refused, saying, "Tell Jimmy to hurry. We're supposed to be at the mill at eight."

"What for?" my mother asked.

Hugh answered, "We're on the picket line today."

"Well," my mother said, 'he's sick; so I'll be going myself to take his place."

"Now, Mame, there's no need for that," Hugh told her, knowing full well what was wrong. "I'll just say Jimmy is feeling low."

My mother looked at him sternly. "I will go because there will be someone there to represent this family.

There will be none to say that the O'Connors do not stand with the people they belong to. I can fight as well as another."

When I came home from school at noon, I found a note on the table: "I'm out on a matter concerning bread and butter." I puzzled over it a long time. There was plenty of both in the house.

My mother walked up and down in the picket line all day carrying the sign that was to have been my father's. She reported, "I walked with my head in the air for a good reason, though there are some" — and she looked at my father — "who hold it high for none." She had responded to jeers and cheers with the same look. Her picture was in the paper, and she was the scandal of the Hill. My father could hardly bear to look at her. The word "picket" became poison to him.

Sometimes, infringement of my father's values precipitated more than amusement. There would be bitter quarrels, with my father's subsequent departure to Mrs. Jenks's. One of these occurred over my black bloomers. I wore them during the winter on school days because I used to slide down the ice on the hill in back of the house with only a thin piece of cardboard between my bottom and the ice. This pastime I refused to give up, though it dirtied and wore out rapidly the white bloomers I wore. My mother, who was for the most part unconcerned in general about appearance, solved the problem with sturdy black bloomers. Only on Sundays, out of respect for my father's refinement, did I wear white ones.

One Sunday after Mass, my mother had changed them to black because I wanted to slide. I appeared in the doorway of the living room, one black bloomer leg hanging down, the other slightly hiked up, my face as black as the bloomers and my mouth full of the licorice that decorated hands and face. My father was horrified; not only was it Sunday, not only was I wearing black bloomers, not only was I dirty, but also we had "company" — lace-curtain company. They tried to make the best of it, though distaste was written all over their faces. One red-faced man even made overtures to take me on his round belly.

With the quick sense of a child, I smelled the disapproval. I turned to the whole company, stared, and struggled out of the fat man's lap. At the door I turned and said, "I don't like you, fat man, nor you, fat lady, and my mother doesn't either." With that, I went into the next room.

Soon after, the company left with polite smiles and refined "thank you's," my father apologizing, "After all, you know children." Then the scene began, my father raging at my mother, "You not only can't make those kids behave properly, but you don't even keep them clean." My mother was too much amused to be angry. She came out and patted me on the head. That angered my father more. Out came the ancient Gladstone bag, bang went the drawers, out the door went my father, without a word. My mother smiled, "He'll be back when he's had enough of Mrs. Jenks's kidney pie."

My father's Catholicism suffered, as well as everything

else he believed in, for being touched with lace-curtain refinement. It was tinged, as is almost all lace-curtain Catholicism, with the Protestantism of the Yankees they imitated. Catholicism for my father held none of the joy it did for my mother. It was a grim, respectable business requiring monthly confession and Communion and a get-to-Mass-on-Sunday-or-die-in-a-state-of-mortal-sin attitude. Going to church was the respectable thing to do. We went in a body at a slow pace, gloved and gloomy at the prospect of a long, dreary sermon. My mother preferred the High Mass with the elaborate ceremony and singing; but the nine-o'clock Mass, stripped and bare of all but the most essential part of the ritual, with its homely sermons and its raspy boys' choir, was the family Mass and the one we attended. My father, with the pride of his station, deposited a dollar in the poor-box every Sunday, and we were all given pennies to deposit in the same place. With a complete lack of conscience, we contrived all kinds of ruses for missing the box so that we could pick the penny from the floor and buy gum with it. My father was inexorable, though. We would have to march up after church and give the penny to a collector. Little did he know that my brother Michael attended church after Mass every Sunday and collected the pennies that had fallen on the floor. We occupied a whole pew for which my father paid "pew rent." He was chagrined that, unlike the members of the Protestant Church, he could not have his name on the pew. We always occupied the same one, which was the next best thing.

My brother Michael and I, crowded behind a pillar, squirmed and suffered during the whole Mass. My father paid more attention to us than he did to his beads. My mother ignored us completely except during the sermon when she yawned with us. My father would come out after Mass and say: "A fine man, Father Finn, educated at Holy Cross. He knows what he's talking about. He's an educated man." My mother, remembering Irish Parish and the fine voice of the real Irish orator, would answer tartly: "Sure, there's no good sermons any more, nothing but a recital of the sins of the poor people not sending their children to parochial school to give them a good religious education. Not that I'm against a good religious education, but you have to have something besides that." She had removed all of us from parochial school because we learned, as she put it, "too much of the big R and not enough of the three r's."

The sermons were always the same, a young, thin voice rasping, putting r's on the end of everything, the same recital, every Sunday; "Saviet Russier is a gadless state." My mother shook her head. "I never heard politics preached in a church before." My father's answer was always the same. "It's blasphemy to criticize the Church."

When we filed out at the end of Mass, my father smiled and shook hands with everyone in range. It used to annoy him that Father Foley never was at the door of the church to give his parishioners a greeting. My mother soon put an end to that complaint. "You'll be

wanting to have him call you Brother O'Connor before
you're through."

We must have made a great impression, the six of
us lined up in one pew every Sunday morning, during
Communion especially, all heads devoutly bowed, hands
folded precisely. Those were the most comfortable
moments for me. I could daydream myself out of the
church into worlds that had no walls or parents caution-
ing children to look devout. During those moments,
when the silence of the consecration descended, I was
drawn into a solitude where I could forget self and
selves. It was certainly not religious, though it had the
peace and quiet of the genuine religious experience. I
always woke out of it with a start because my father or
one of my brothers would punch or pinch me, and I
would lift my head to find I was the only person left
kneeling in the church. Everyone else had settled back
comfortably in his seat awaiting the *Ite, missa est* that
would send him home to his Sunday dinner, Sunday
newspaper, and Sunday nap.

Despite his many shortcomings as a parent, my father
was always defended by my mother when any of us
criticized him. "Remember one thing, your father is a
good provider." He was that, too. He worked in the
dark, dreary wool shop all those hours to support his
family; and he was proud of his family, though he
showed little affection. Every Christmas he received a
"bonus," and that money went to dentists and doctors
for the care of us, his children. We all looked forward
to the bonus because it was paid in large silver dollars;

and though the money was spent before he ever got home, there was a tremendous excitement in seeing him empty that great bag of silver dollars on the kitchen table. They would go wheeling and whirling in all directions while we all gaped. Each of us received one of them in the toe of his stocking every Christmas morning. My father would caution us to put them in the bank, but invariably they went for college ices at Bill Zuchini's.

The thing that broke my father was his inability to maintain, in the eyes of the neighbors, this very position of "good provider." Even in the early days, lay-offs were frequent, but they were of short duration. Agonizing while they lasted, there was always some hope because they were temporary. I was schooled from the time I became conscious to a dread of those periods. The earliest one I remember was tragic. I watched my father come home that evening. I used to meet him. He climbed the Hill slowly, as usual, but I knew, by the way his long face had lengthened out still further, that something was wrong. I smiled at him and took his hand. With the tact of a child, I did not break his silence. He hung his hat on the tree in the hall and we walked down the hall, still silent.

My mother knew what was wrong the minute she saw his face. She said, "Lay-off?" He answered bitterly, "Yes, and there'll be lots more." Then he broke out in one of his infrequent self-revelations. "By God, I've struggled all my life and I'm no better off than the day I began." He took out his billfold and laid a hundred dollars on the table. "Here, I saved this to take you to Niagara Falls. You'll have to use it for expenses now." My mother picked up the money silently and put it in her apron pocket. She went to the kitchen door and stood, paring knife in hand, leaning against the open door. She did not cry, but I could hear the words she was saying to herself, "I pray God that none of my children will ever end in the mill." Neither of them had had a vacation since their honeymoon when they went to the Hippodrome.

That lay-off began what my father called his "bad-luck" days. He was "called in" less and less often. He stubbornly refused to believe, however, that the mill would fail him. Every night he would read the stock-market reports in the *Transcript,* especially reports on the wool market. "It says here, Mame, that wool is going up, and it will soon be steady again." That was 1929. The mill finally closed down altogether. My father proudly refused other jobs. He was a "skilled laborer," and other work was below his position. He finally accepted some painting for one of his friends, but he refused the money offered. One day, while he was painting, he fell two stories and broke his leg in three places. After the long hospitalization, doctor's bills, nurses, the family had nothing left. My mother retained her humor: "Sure, himself was imitating the financiers jumping in Wall Street," she said.

When my father recovered, he was filled with hope. Every day he went downtown to meet "the boys"; every day he came home with the same report. "Hugh says the shop will open next week. He was talking with someone who knows." Week after week, month after month, year after year went by, but the shop did not open. Instead, other shops closed down and the streets were lined with loafing men.

Finally, in desperation, he started hunting jobs outside the city. He had to hitch-hike because there was no money. He found occasional work and would write home in his childish scrawl that ran diagonally across the paper.

> Dear Mame:
> Here is the twenty dollars. Am saving enough for my room. I am fine.
>   JAMES

Usually, he would get home before the money. He suffered all kinds of indignities. He was awakened one night in the Springtown railway station, where he was sleeping on a bench, by a rough policeman who pounded the sole of his thin shoe. "Where's your ticket, bud? No bums allowed to sleep in here." Fortunately, this was one of the occasions when he had a ticket. He thrust it angrily in the policeman's face, saying: "I'll report you for this. What do you mean by disturbing respectable people? I'm waiting for my train." The policeman waved his club airily at him: "Oh, save it for the cops," and went on herding men out of the station.

When out-of-town work was no longer available, my father simply sat. My mother pulled every political string she had trying to get him a job. She prayed for anything, "not for the money, but to keep the poor man

from his grave." My brother Eddie, who was supporting
us on fifteen dollars a week, used to slip quarters in my
father's pocket for cigarettes. He would take money
from no one, but when no one was watching he would
pick up my brother's cigarette butts and smoke them
secretly. We all schemed to keep him from worrying.
When we could get no more coal, we would go up in
the attic and chop down some of the beams for wood.
I used to get the newspaper from one of the neighbors
without letting him know. That was the only thing he
cared to read now, this man who had schooled himself
to reading first out of public school textbooks until he
could read well enough to take the *Atlantic Monthly*.
He steadfastly refused to go on welfare. "I'll take no
charity from anyone." My mother by some mysterious
means would weekly acquire enough beans and flour so
that we could continue to eat our depression diet of
beans and biscuits.

The most painful thing was his constant listening to
stock-market reports. Regularly at noon, he would turn
on the radio. I can still remember the time signal
blaring out and then the cold, indifferent voice of the
announcer: "Anaconda Copper down 10 points, American Tel and Tel down 15 points," on and on, down,
down, my father's face descending with the descent of
each point. Somehow this mill worker, poor, one of
poor millions, considered himself involved actively in
the rise and fall of the vast American market. That, to
the end, represented security. And if he changed per-
sonally, none of his ideas about what constituted se-

curity changed. He voted for Hoover and damned
Roosevelt. The W.P.A. was a lazy man's out for which
he had only contempt. When my mother urged him to
work on W.P.A., he said: "I'll take no charity, and
that's what W.P.A. is. I'll not earn money by leaning on
a shovel." He considered everything Roosevelt did
"radical." And when my mother would defend him,
saying: "Well, if you weren't such a boob, you'd see
that he's trying to help you and every poor man in this
country. If it weren't for him, we'd be starving surely."
My father would answer: "I tell you, Mame, you'll
never see the end of this till you get him and all his
brain-trusters out of office. Another bunch of efficiency
experts, trying to control production. If they'd let the
market alone, the old law of supply and demand would
take care of everything." "Yes," my mother would add
contemptuously, "everything, except filling your belly
and putting clothes on your back."

My father grew more and more silent, more and more
bitter. "Damn fool efficiency experts, with their new
ways and new methods did it, that's what," he used to
say. Even that line stopped. He said nothing finally,
silently walking the long dark hallway from kitchen to
parlor, silently staring out into a blank nothingness. I
watched him, his head bending, his shoulders beginning
to stoop, the hands he had been so proud of beginning
to shake. I watched him at the same window day after
day, week after week, sighing and staring, staring and
sighing. All the values he had worked for, all gone. His
shoes were still shined, but they were stuffed with card-

board; his suit was still pressed, but it was shiny with wear. He would not go out, he would not see his friends. He just stood and stared at the past.

It was then he began to talk about that past, and Mary Walsh, his mother, who had nine sons and lost six of them through poverty. It was when he was hungry that he told us of the awful hunger he had known. He would talk mostly to me. I would sit silently in the dark living room listening to the woes of the past while I suffered the woes of the present. A stern, proud man was reduced to a small frightened child, a man who had had his beginning in a child born in Youghal, County Cork.

5

Spare a Drink for a Hero

I REMEMBER VIVIDLY the first time I saw my seven uncles. They had come for the Saturday-night supper of home-baked beans and fresh bread. I was concentrating on the heel of the bread which still had not been taken, hoping no one would take it before the plate reached me. It was a special delicacy that Michael and I usually quarreled for. I was completely absorbed by this hope when someone coughed. I looked up quickly to see a strange dark-eyed man lifting a coffee cup to his mouth. All thought of the bread was forgotten as I stared fascinated by the way his hand shook. He lifted his other hand to steady the cup, but it still shook violently, and the coffee slopped over onto the tablecloth and his suit. Swiftly I glanced around the table to see if this was happening to the others and discovered that the other six strange men were looking at me. I dropped my eyes — ashamed of something I did not understand.

When I looked again at the slim, dark man, he was smiling at me. He said, "I am your Uncle Patrick and my hands shake because I have been shell-shocked." He continued studying me carefully. "You want to know what shell-shock is, don't you?" I nodded. He fingered the handle of his coffee cup as he considered his answer. "Shell-shock is fear, the fear of everything that you know and do not know, and that fear" — he spoke quietly — "is occasioned by war." The whole table was silent — the six men sat dreading the next revelation. My Uncle Patrick was still looking at me, but his eyes shifted now to his brothers. "And what is war," he said, "but death by a slow, creeping fear that paralyzes the hand as it lifts the cup and raises an unuttered cry in the night and leaves the mind with the thought half-spoken and throttles the soul with its choking vision?" His trembling hand reached for the salt-shaker. No one spoke, and I, who had not understood, began to weep for those sad, silent men who understood too well.

The rest of my uncles I do not remember as vividly as my Uncle Patrick and Uncle Smiley. They were the most colorful. The other five disappeared before I was ten, and during the time when they had come to the house, they were too many for me to take in. I remember all of them collectively as ill-dressed, handsome, happy men, full of song and beer. At least every Saturday evening they would appear for supper and song. After supper was finished, my mother and the seven O'Sullivan brothers, with the O'Connors trailing, would go into the living room. Smiley would sit down at the enormous grape-legged piano and play. The rest would gather around and sing. They all had beautiful voices. The sweet, reedy voice of my mother would soar above the strong voices of her brothers. They sang a great many Irish ballads — "The Bildowns of Binnorie" was a great favorite, the one that my Uncle Smiley generally sang by himself with the rest joining in at the end. My Uncle Smiley's voice was strong and deep and he filled the song with the heart of him. The song began softly and tenderly with his voice taking the notes gently and lightly. I cursed the sister, blessed the harper, and wept as we all did for the young girl with the golden hair.

After the beer my uncles had brought with them was finished, the singing, too, ended and my uncles rather shamefacedly made their excuses. They never left, though, without solemn promises to my mother. "Now, Mame, we'll give you a kiss and a promise not to have the protection wagon out tonight." After eleven, though, the wagon was out hunting the O'Sullivans. It was not unusual for the Black Maria to draw up before our door, especially after the first of the month, for the first of the month was payday.

All of the seven were veterans of the first World War, and all of them received pensions. They had been in the infantry, and none of them had escaped the marks of it. My mother used to shake her head over the results. "They were all good boys until that horrible war." She had pictures of all of them in their khakis just before they went overseas — a group of young, handsome boys, bright and gay, slim legs wrapped in the khaki leggings, balloon pants, and, what seemed to me ridiculous, sombrero hats. None of them came back as he left.

My mother never tired of telling of their heroism. They were all wounded, decorated, wounded and deco-

rated again. "Glory be to God, Patrick there was reported for dead. I heard it from Mrs. Murphy and
rushed down to the City Hall to see the bulletin board
for myself. Sure enough, there it was black as black,
Patrick Aloysius O'Sullivan, private in the infantry,
missing. I near died with the sorrow of it. When I got
home, there was the telegram. We had Masses for him
and cards galore, when six months later he walked in on
me when I was doing the Monday wash. I kept staring
at him through the screen door, not even moving for
fear of scaring him off. I thought sure he had come
back to communicate the death of Smiley or one of the
others. 'Aren't you going to ask me in, Mame?' says he.
'If you're alive, I will,' I says. 'Well, I am, though God
knows how.' "

He had been in a hospital near the front when it was
bombed. All identification marks had been lost. He
was labeled "a shell-shock case," and he lay in a ward
for months unknown to himself, unnamed by others.
He finally remembered his name because it began with
the same letter as the surname at the foot of his bed.
Shell-Shock O'Sullivan. The army absolved itself with
a pension and sent him home with the rest of the newly
baptized.

My uncle Patrick never recovered. He moved restlessly from job to job, unable to keep any. The drinking
that he had started in the army continued, and he became, in the parlance of the days when heroism was
forgotten, "a drunken bum." I used to see him and
my Uncle Smiley lined up with the others on the stone

wall before the City Hall when I went downtown with my mother — a whole line of forgotten heroes; abject, lonely men with no hope and no help from any quarter.

My Uncle Patrick is one of my clearest memories, because he almost killed me once. He alternated between fits of unnatural gaiety and depression. When he was depressed, he either drank himself stupid or tried suicide. One afternoon, when my mother had gone to the store, and I was taking my nap, he turned on all the gas jets. Fortunately, my mother came back in time to save both of us. I remember still the choking sensation of the gas, but I remember even more painfully the sad, dark face of my uncle watery and dim through my tears, but full of unsaid contrition and woe.

Regularly, after that, when his pension came in, he would take me to the finest store in town and spend half of his check on me. I was allowed complete freedom of choice and would come home with elegant blue velvet dresses that were much too long and much too expensive. My mother would smuggle them back, returning with sensible middy blouses and blue serge skirts. The expensive toys were never returned.

My Uncle Patrick was a great lover of music, and spent most of his pension money on records. His "bats" — a term which always mystified me — occurred only when he was seized with fits of depression. He would disappear for a month, then reappear and stay sober for two. During those sober months he lived with us. He had a large victrola and a collection of nearly two hundred records. After everyone had gone to bed, he would sit in the dark living room and play music. My room was right off the living room, and through the red-tasseled portières that hung over my door I would hear the grinding as he cranked the machine. Softly, I would get out of bed and slip into a dark corner of the living room and listen. He always knew that I was there, but he never spoke. I could make out only the dark shadow of him sitting there directly in front of the victrola. During the quiet parts of the music, I would hear sometimes the rattling of the papers in a half-empty chocolate box, for he ate candy all the time, trying to stave off the great thirst that would come upon him.

He loved vocal music best, and in the dark of the living room, the rich warm voice of Caruso would rise and fall, flooding the room with beauty. Gradually, in the darkness, lulled by the sweet softness of the music, I would slide into sleep. In the morning I woke in my bed where my Uncle Patrick had placed me gently so as not to waken me.

My Uncle Patrick had wanted to be a priest. As a boy he had served at the altar. It was this image that my mother always remembered: "robed in red, carrying the book from one side to the other, with the goodness and grace shining clear in his face." The war had dissolved that ambition in him, but when sober he lived like a priest. He did not attend Mass nor fulfill any "Catholic duties," but he remained nevertheless a saintly and ascetic man who fought off devils in the night while others slept in their beds. The only time he went to church was on some occasion when there was to be special music. Only music brought him any peace. He took me once to a great cathedral to hear the most Solemn High Mass sung. I remember sitting stiffly beside him, not performing any of the usual ritual because he did not, trying to listen as intently as he did to the exalted, exultant swell of the music that poured from organ and choir. After the Mass, the two of us went and drank chocolate and ate sundaes. I was very sick going home on the trolley car. He held me out the door, talking all the while about the sanctity of good music.

He always looked on with general opprobrium, and he could not bear the general moral lectures delivered by respectable Father Feeney, whom he had served as an altar boy. He avoided him by crossing the street when he saw him coming. Father Feeney lumped all sinners together and gave them the same advice, "Make a good gineral, me boy, make a good gineral confession, and you'll find yourself feeling better," my uncle would parody him. If any confessions were made, they were made to my mother, who was the only one he could talk to. He would talk to her, as he said, "because she was so simple in her soul and so morally clean." This tortured man, diseased with doubt, found balm only in music and the people who were filled with faith. My mother gave him what he needed most, warmth and love. There was no one who could give him peace.

He suffered generally in silence the scorn of the lace-

curtain Irish who considered him and all the rest of
the O'Sullivan boys a "disgrace to their race." My
father reported all their remarks as a sign of what he
had to put up with. He only once mentioned the pos-
sibility of the Veterans' Hospital. My mother looked
at him before she spoke, waiting for her anguish to
turn into healthy anger. "I've seen them, I've seen them
up there on the Hill, caged and barred like animals,
sane and insane together until they are all the same:
No brother of mine will ever be locked there." That
was all she ever said. It was enough.

One night my Uncle Patrick came home when we
had lace-curtain Irish visitors, Mr. and Mrs. Sheehan
and their daughter Kate. Mr. Sheehan was in the con-
tracting business, "a good solid businessman," as my
father characterized him. Kate, a pretty girl, was singing when Uncle Patrick came in. He appeared in the
doorway; the singing stopped. Kate began nervously
plucking at her dress. Mrs. Sheehan thought perhaps
it was getting late. Mr. Sheehan looked his disapproval.
My mother rose, introduced Patrick, and then calmly
sat down waiting for the music to continue. The Sheehans were caught in their own web of refinement. Kate
started the song again, Uncle Patrick sat there scrutin-
izing his long fingers spread out on the arm of the chair.
The voice, carefully trained into a kind of mashed,
mushy, quality, began its sentimental dirge:

> I'll take you home again, Kathleen,
> To where your heart has ever been.

The "been" matched meticulously the "Kathleen." "A fine voice and a fine song," said Mr. Sheehan sententiously. Mrs. Sheehan blew her nose very gently. I shuddered for the girl; I knew how my Uncle Patrick hated what he called "sloppy, sentimental Irish-American ballads."

My Uncle Patrick smiled politely at Kate and moved to the victrola. "Now we'll hear some real Irish music," he said. "This girl's voice has not been trained at the Misses McCormack's School of Music. She is a tinker singing of her love for Ireland."

The gypsy girl's voice was pure and untrained. It was filled with an emotion that belonged to all men. The voice was sweet and honest, and the song was too full of grief to be pretentious. The Sheehans listened uncomfortably. When it was over, Mrs. Sheehan said, "It's pretty, yes indeed, very pretty. Come now, Kate, we must be going." Kate got up and said, "Well, I guess it's a good voice, but I don't care for the brogue. It's so — so — oh, you know," she simpered, "so shanty."

My Uncle put the cover down on the machine, looked at her and smiled. "Yes indeed, that's surely the difference between your voice and hers. A great singer sings from the heart. Good evening, Miss Sheehan." My Uncle Patrick left the room. That night he listened a long time to the music in the darkness. I could see only the red glow of his cigarette. There were no chocolates. The next day he was gone.

When he came back, he asked my mother if he could take me to the opera. It was to be in a near-by town, a performance of Mozart's *Magic Flute*. I shook with excitement for days before. My mother even allowed my Uncle Patrick to buy me a dress for the occasion. It was red velvet with lace trim on the collar and cuffs. I had for the occasion my first pair of silk stockings. All the way on the trolley car, I stroked the velvet, feeling the warmth of its color, and smoothed the stockings, feeling their sleekness. We sat in the Family Circle, sharing an enormous box of soft-centered chocolates between us. All the gaudy gilt seemed real gold, the excitement of people coming and going, rustling programs or looking through mother-of-pearl opera glasses; I felt the whole thing had been arranged entirely for my enjoyment. During the performance I was on the stage singing every note, making every gesture, playing every instrument. My Uncle Patrick was very gay going home on the jolting trolley car, singing and whistling all the tunes. I went to sleep with the song of a bird-catcher sounding sweetly in my ears.

When I woke the next morning, it was very late. I remembered almost instantly the joy of the night before, and the tune of the bird-catcher that I had fallen asleep hearing. I could not catch it, quite; so I jumped out of bed to ask my uncle to whistle it to me. I ran down the long hall, but found the kitchen and dining room empty. I called. There was no one in the house.

I went out on the back porch. Mrs. Carter was hanging up clothes. I spoke to her, feeling some panic over what was not comprehensible — a completely empty house at ten o'clock in the morning. "Do you know where my mother is, Mrs. Carter?"

She turned and saw me. "Oh, Mary, I thought you'd gone with her. The whole family has gone to the hospital. Patrick is sick."

"My Uncle Patrick?" I asked.

"Yes, he took sick in the night. Your mother didn't say what it was," she said evasively.

I stared hard at her. "He wasn't sick last night, Mrs. Carter. He took me to Court Square."

"Well, something took him sudden." She bundled the clothes into the basket and started to go in. "You get dressed now and come over. I'll give you some ginger cookies."

I didn't answer her, but went into the house. I knew what had happened.

I went into my bedroom and knelt by the side of my bed. I started to pray that he would not die. I prayed him into life as hard as I could. Constantly, the image of a dark figure sitting in an armchair kept coming between me and my prayers. I would put my head down, cover my face to keep out that image of him, sitting there quietly fighting off the devils of his despair. I saw his face as it had been the night before and as it was when he came home, after a long absence, bloated and defeated. When my mother returned, I was still kneeling by the side of my bed, not praying, just remembering him with love and with pity, not understanding at all why I pitied him. My mother, weeping, rocked me in the armchair, saying over and over, "It is better, it is better," and I knew that she was right.

There were not many Mass cards or condolences, as

there had been when he had died a hero. Father Finn made a great concession, and he was buried in consecrated ground. He left his music to me. My mother and I sat in the darkness that evening and listened to his favorite piece of music, *Pace, pace, mio Dio.*

After my Uncle Patrick's death, my Uncle Smiley came to live with us. Unlike my Uncle Patrick, he was a gay, talkative man. He was known all over Irish Parish as Smiley O'Sullivan, but even the people in Irish Parish shook their heads over him, for he was the worst of the O'Sullivans. My mother sadly remarked, over and over again, the difference between John O'Sullivan and his sons. No one understood how or why this difference had occurred. My mother blamed it on the war, my father on the O'Sullivan temperament; my grandfather had blamed it on the fact that his sons had no place. Smiley made himself a place, unwanted though he was, by sheer good nature when sober and by sheer bad nature when drunk.

Smiley had been my grandfather's favorite son, and it was to him that John O'Sullivan handed the tradition he had brought with him from Ireland. Smiley was Irish from sole to head, but not as my grandfather had been, secure in being that. He was Irish, right or wrong; and he bore a chip on his shoulder, as big as a log. He had the wit and charm of my grandfather, but not his desire for peace and justice. Persecuted himself, he looked for others to persecute, and regularly once a week he swaggered into some bar to find a victim, the victim being always of a people he considered beneath him, either Jewish or Polish. It was from him I learned the temptation of persecution. He had a magnificent voice both in song and in speech, and he used to sing me a terrifying song about the persecution of a Christian boy by an old Jew. I would sit in his lap, smelling the stale beer breath of him, while he sang with all the pathos and terror he could muster about the little boy who was playing ball in his back yard and had been enticed out of the yard and taken to the old Jew's house — kidnaped and tortured. There was a fascination of terror about this song that made me ask for it constantly.

After I heard that song, I used to run and hide when Mr. Adelson or the ragman came to the door. As I grew bolder, I would stand bravely in the front yard, my insides shivering, and shout "Christ-killer" at the old Jewish ragman. This went on until my mother heard me. Her indignation burned me. "Who taught you such a thing, Mary O'Connor, for you've never heard it in my presence?" My father, too, was upset. I told her Uncle Smiley. She sat thoughtfully silent. "You know Christ himself was a Jew, surely." I nodded. "Then we'll hear no more of that kind of talk. The wicked killed Him, and wickedness is not confined to a race, remember that."

That night, when Smiley came home drunk and truculent, my mother faced him. She had no fear of him, though there were plenty who had. I heard the sharpness in her voice as she called him and his reluctant "Now, Mame," for he respected her. He never sang the song to me again, nor did I hear any more remarks about the Jews or Poles from him.

I did not like the drunken Smiley. He moved me to fear in that state. Unlike my Uncle Patrick, who was quiet and grave, he flamed and flashed with physical violence, and he always came to us after a "bat," with terrible cuts and bruises covering his face.

When I had first known him, he was a young man, slim and alive, a man of wit and brilliance, but even as a child I had watched with fear the slow signs of degeneracy appearing, first in his eyes, which were slowly bloodshotted into a dull blear, then in his voice, which became thick and blurred, and most horrible of all in his spirit. He would lurch home the last days with the peaked cap he wore awry on his bald head, his pants sagging under his bloated stomach, his face red and blotched. In the morning we would find him on the back porch, curled like an animal, lying in his own vomit.

My grandfather had been proud of this man, proud of the voice of him, and had taught him all the poetry and stories he knew. My Uncle Smiley could not tell the stories as my grandfather did; but the poetry he remembered and recited in the beautiful speech that he had learned from my grandfather. He had been a brilliant boy and had gone farther than any of the O'Sullivans in schooling; but his only interest was in the literature and culture of Ireland. This he knew as well and better than many scholars. He used to send to Ireland for books. This I remember because he gave my brother Michael and me all the stamps for our collection. My mother would tell of seeing Smiley sitting on the front steps with some old Irish man or woman, when we still lived in Irish Parish, writing down the words of a story or poem exactly as it was being told. That way he collected and pasted into his books many poems and stories that never appeared in the text.

Sometimes, in the early days, when my grandfather was still alive, Smiley would come up from Irish Parish and spend the whole evening reciting for us. I can still remember my grandfather's prose story of some great Irish hero; the slow, soft voice of him telling the woes of Owen Roe O'Neill, then Smiley's translation of the prose into the fiery speech of the poetry. The political poetry of the Irish is full of demonic fury. I can still hear Smiley's voice, loud and full, roaring out the angry syllables, exciting the vowels into a live and real anger.

Did they dare, did they dare to slay Owen Roe O'Neill? I wondered how they dared to dare, listening to the challenge in Smiley's voice. The cry of injustice and contempt shuddered through the lines. All the woe of the Irish and their hatred against the English was the subject of the verse. The face of my grandfather wore the look of fixed sadness that is the look of those who lament the dead and mourn for a past which is irrevocable.

Wail, wail ye for the Mighty One! Wail, wail ye for the Dead!

Quench the hearth and hold the breath — with ashes
   strew the head!
How tenderly we loved him! How deeply we deplore!
Holy Saviour! but to think we shall never see him
   more!

When Smiley was through, my grandfather shook his
head sadly. "That is enough of the violent, Smiley.
Let us have a gentle poem, if there's one to be found
in Irish." Once Smiley had started on the violent,
though, there was no stopping him. Like an old bard
reciting war-songs to stir great heroes, he would roll
out the poem, his eyes flashing, his whole body leaning
to it. I wondered at this patriot with no country, for
I knew that he had never set foot in Ireland. He recited all the laments for the dead Irish hero as though he
were one himself. He recited them so full of violence
and vengeance that the whole room seemed to reflect
the redness of anger; and I, frightened and mystified,
tried, without being noticed, to cover my ears by hiding
my head in my mother's lap. But I discovered that even
she could be carried away by the desire for the revenge
of past wrongs. I could feel her limbs trembling as I lay
there. The Rosary seemed particularly inappropriate
after this kind of evening. I would look at Smiley through
the spread of my fingers and wonder if his prayers were
for mercy or murder.

From the love of such a literature, from Smiley's increasing knowledge of the history of the persecution
of Ireland, arose a sense of bitterness and hatred of the
persecutors of a country he had never known. He hated

the English so much that he had no time to love anything or anyone else. I, who had been taught by my
grandfather not to dwell on bitterness, made good
friends with many Yankee children. I preferred them to
the lace-curtain Irish. They were sharp and shrewd,
but honest and generous if they became fond of you.
My greatest friend was a Yankee. Betty came often to
the house. Her home was my second home, and her
mother, a woman of great wit and wisdom, was as good
a friend as Betty. Betty called for me one day when
Smiley was sitting on the porch. When she told him her
name, he swung his cane at her and ordered her off
the porch, telling her no good Irishman would allow
an Englishman to set foot in his house. Betty was puzzled, and I was bewildered.

When I went home after school, Smiley met me on
the corner. He sat me down on the wall and for one hour
presented a lecture on the persecution of the Irish by
the English, beginning with Strongbow and concluding
warningly, "You will soon learn there is no end to it,
for wherever there is an Irishman there is also an
Englishman to persecute, whether it be on Money Hole
Hill or in Boston or in Timbuctoo. You will see, Mary
O'Connor."

When I told my mother the whole episode that evening, she said, "The Irish persecute each other. It is
with your own that you will suffer the greatest pain. My
father, John O'Sullivan, used to say that his son, Smiley,
should have been a Sinn Feiner in Ireland. There he
could have found an outlet for his nationalism. In-

stead," she added, "he fights windmills, standing on
street corners reciting revolutionary Irish ballads, shouting Irish songs in barrooms, smashing heads to prove
how strong an Irishman he is. It is a great waste, a
great waste."

My mother worried more about Smiley than all the
others. "His great spirit is becoming his great shame,"
she would say. She would beg him to do something
with his voice, but he would do nothing. She herself
got him a job singing between acts at the playhouse
in the city. The playhouse was one of the most important social institutions in the city, well attended by the
Yankees and prominent lace-curtain Irish. Smiley was
very successful for as long as he pleased to be. He had
tremendous charm, and he was witty. Soon he grew
tired of singing "The Lost Chord" and "Alice, Ben
Bolt." "It's a bowlful of sugar I'm pouring out for
them, surely. Every night the same limp thing with
the words different, that's all — no tune, no melody, no
fire, nothing but something a jellyfish could be singing
better." My mother understood how he felt and stopped
urging him to continue. We would laugh ourselves
into silliness over his imitation of Miss Sparks, who sang
with him, doing "I Dreamt I Dwelt in Marble Halls."
He would drape himself in a tablecloth, clasp his hands
in front of him, pucker his lips primly, and in a whis-
pery voice do a perfect imitation of a refined ladylike
voice.

Smiley could not just give up the job. He was too
much of an O'Sullivan not to end in style. He waited

for a first night when the theater was crowded with all the respectable Yankees and lace-curtain Irish. Coming out from the curtain, he announced that he would sing the national anthem. The people in the theater rose, a little annoyed by being so disturbed. Ladies clutched at their gloves, men bent over to retrieve programs, and Smiley began "The Wearing of the Green." The people were so astonished that they remained standing until he got to the middle of the song. As they sat down, some brave ones struggling into wraps and going hastily up the aisles, Smiley sang as loudly as he could the last part of the song. He bowed, smiled, stepped behind the curtain. That was the last time he ever sang in public for money. My mother was secretly amused, but my father was furious.

The year I was to attend school, through some mysterious cause I became almost blind, and was required to lie quietly in a dark room with soaked bandages over my eyes. My Uncle Smiley was very good to me. He would spend hours in the dark room reciting poems and telling me stories. He was a perfect companion because he was always gay. My illness made him gentle, and it was then I saw the side of him that was admirable. He talked to me about the great imagination of the Irish and their wonderful speech. He referred constantly to a mysterious *Book of Kells,* talked with great excitement of the culture of the Irish in the old days, and how, if he had lived then, he might have been a great scholar. He told me of his great curiosity as a boy and how, there being no books to learn from, he would

take books from the public library and copy from them
the poems and stories he liked, to have something to
read. He had copied complete the whole of two vol-
umes of Irish history.

It was during that time in the shade-darkened room
that I learned there was Irish poetry of love as well
as of hate. He taught me two poems, one a poem written centuries before, translated from Gaelic, which he
taught me to say as well as he did. I had to learn how
to sound every word properly before I was allowed to
recite it to my mother. It was a poem about a cat, and
Smiley would put my cat, Rainbow, in my arms while
I was learning it, to get, as he said, "the proper feel
of the poem." The poem was "Pangur Ban." I can
still say it in the voice of a child, incongruous with the
meaning of the words.

> I and Pangur Ban, my cat,
> 'Tis a like task we are at;
> Hunting mice is his delight,
> Hunting words I sit all night.

I would sit in the dark room feeling the warm softness of Rainbow against me and, with her purring
providing the background, recite softly and richly.

> 'Gainst the wall he set his eye,
> Full and fierce and sharp and sly;
> 'Gainst the wall of wisdom I
> All my little wisdom try.

When I was able to see again, my Uncle Smiley, after
solemn promises to my mother, was allowed to take

me to Boston. We were to go on the excursion train, returning the same day. I was given two dollars by my father, who had at first strenuously objected. It was my first trip away from home and my first ride on a train. I sat on the green plush seat, hiding my excitement behind a great dignified air. My Uncle Smiley at one time had worked in the Maintenance Department at Harvard College, and the pilgrimage was not to Boston as I had thought, but to Cambridge and its literary shrines. I saw almost nothing of Boston except the crowded station.

We took the subway directly to Harvard Square. The subway fascinated and frightened me with its long dark tunnels and red and green lights winking like mysterious eyes in the darkness. We visited a great many places in Cambridge, but I remember only the glass flowers and Longfellow's House. I did not understand at all the reason why my Uncle Smiley took me to visit Cambridge until we were on the way home and then I was still puzzled by his motives. While we were there, he entered completely into the spirit of it all. He behaved, as he said later, like a midwestern tourist seeing America first. When we climbed the steps of Craigie House, I felt sure there would be a holy water fount to bless oneself reverently before entering. My Uncle Smiley behaved with great decorum, removing his cap, nodding politely to all the remarks of the guide. We stayed a long time in the study. Smiley sighed over its air of a scholar's retreat, muttering under his breath that this way, standing and looking, was no way to get the quiet feel of the place. "You should sit at the desk and be trying to make a poem yourself." I wondered at his obvious respect, for I knew Longfellow was no Irishman. When we left the quiet street, Smiley said to me, "No matter, good or bad, he was a poet, and there are not many of them in this country. There's only a few that have the courage to stay out of the hay and grain business." He jerked his head back at the house. "Himself was one."

I am sure he took me to Longfellow's house because of himself, but the visit to the glass flowers was solely for my benefit. It was a conventional thing to do, and I felt its conventionality. They were pretty, but I felt a kind of horror at such artificiality. As Smiley said, there was no one who'd want to be making a poem over them. The other museums seemed as dead; all I remember of them is the huge skeletons of prehistoric monsters suspended in the center of a room and a small glass cage on the side with a puny skeleton that was dwarfed by the rest. Holding my Uncle Smiley's hand, I spelled out the three letters printed on the card: M A N, Man. After that, we visited no more museums. Smiley was seized "with a great thirst," and so we went back to Harvard Square. He drank only one beer, and though I knew his need for more I kept silent, hoping that he would not get drunk and leave me helpless and lost in a place filled with museums full of dead things and houses that belonged to dead poets. All the time I kept thinking of the subway and the long train and I longed for the safety of the kitchen and my mother standing in the doorway with the welcome in her eyes.

Smiley took me safely home. I was tired and sleepy

on the train, and as the wheels clicked rhythmically
their reassurance that I was going home, Smiley recited
a poem to me that summed up as he said the whole
visit. It was a poem by an Irishman — "a poet who had
no fine house dedicated to his memory, a poet who had
nothing but the shelter others offered him while living,
and no shrine but the heart of his people now that he
is dead. It is the memory of the people who keep Irish
poetry alive, for it is not written down elsewhere," he
told me. "Now you take this one," he said, meaning
Longfellow. "He lived in a fine house and he had
plenty, but for all that he never wrote as fine a poem
as the poet who wandered the roads and had no place
to put his head. Nevertheless, Raftery knew better
what it is to be a poet, and so he wrote better poetry.
You can't be as respectable as Longfellow and write
good poetry. There are times when there has to be
a curse in it." His whole speech had turned into a kind
of meditation, and he was not directing his remarks
to anyone but himself. All the way home, he recited
poems to himself and generalized on poetry. Through
a mist of sleepiness, I was only vaguely aware of either
the poetry or the commentary. I was falling asleep
while he recited. The last thing I remembered was the
clicking of wheels rhythmically melting into the words
of the poem, repeating over and over the first lines of
a poem he recited.

> I am Raftery the Poet,
> Full of hope and love,
> With eyes that have no light,
> With gentleness that has no misery.

There were no more excursions with my Uncle Smiley. He grew worse and worse, and as he did I grew more and more fearful of him. There was nothing anyone could do for him. He came less and less frequently to the house. Soon the only word we had of him was my father's indignant reports to my mother, who was unable herself to find him. He hid from her because he feared her thoughts of him. My father would come home on Saturday and tell how he had seen Smiley at John the Harp's, "flopped on a table without a sole to his shoe or a penny in his pocket." He disappeared completely for six months. We heard various reports, one that he was living with hoboes down by the tracks and had taken to begging. My mother did everything to locate him, but with no success. Then one night my father came home with the news that he had seen Smiley again. He had been standing at the bar in John the Harp's when Smiley had lurched up to him so drunk that he had not recognized my father.

"He was begging all right," my father said. "He hauled out of his pocket the medal he received during the war. 'Look, mister,' he said, 'a purple heart with two stars and three bars! Couldn't you spare a drink for a hero?'" My mother's face crumpled up into tears. "My God, why didn't you bring him home, James?" My father looked shamefaced. "Well, Mame, I didn't think it would do you any good to see him. He's too sick for you to take care of. Let the Veterans' Administration take care of him." My mother never said a word, just went down the hallway. We heard the door slam. My father did not try to stop her. She found him lying in the gutter in front of a beer parlor with his head cracked open, where it had struck the stone. She brought him home. but there was no help for him.

I remember the last time I saw him, crawling down the long, dark hallway, retching and insensible to all but the agony of a stomach aflame from the denatured alcohol he had drunk. The American Legion gave him a great funeral with a military burial. My mother, lost in grief as I have never seen her, lay on the bed the whole day with her face hidden from the light. When I came up to the bed, hesitating before her grief, she pulled me down to her and said, "It is the same with all of them. I grieve for them all." It is the only time I have seen her when her religion brought her no consolation.

Say Nothing About the Wakes

I REMEMBER sitting miserably on a haircloth sofa with the prick of it needling my bottom, listening politely to the grown-up conversation of my Aunt Josie and her husband. The room was dark and dim, lace curtains hung at the window, green wallpaper accentuated the gloom, and heavy-legged furniture, plushy and hot, added to the ponderousness of the room and the conversation. I kept my eyes fixed on the picture in a tremendous gilt frame, the only bright thing in the room. I could not wiggle because of the haircloth, and because of my Aunt Josie, who kept a sharp eye on me and used a sharp tongue. "Well-behaved little girls do not wiggle, Mary O'Connor." I hated that "well-behaved" as much as I hated all her well-advised remarks. "Little pitchers have big ears," she would say coyly, putting her finger to her lips, silencing my mother, who always spoke freely before me.

It was a hot, sticky day. The glass of iced lemonade was dripping uncomfortably, falling in spots on my starched dress. The mystery of the picture was beginning to pall; the haircloth was scratching too viciously for me to wonder or even care why a lady dressed in a nightgown was standing in a boat surrounded by water lilies. Slowly and silently, the tears began. They ran tickling down my cheeks and tasted salty when I licked them with my tongue. Suddenly my mother noticed, "God bless you, child, and what is the matter?" I sat there waiting for a breath. It came out in a sob, "I want to go home." My Uncle Tim, quite deaf, held his hand to his ear. "What does the child say?" I shouted at him, "I want to go home!" My Aunt Josie, shocked and startled by my audacity, led me out of the room upstairs to the bedroom and left me there with the words, "Until you learn to behave, you should be by yourself." She sailed out of the room and back to her "guests."

Soon I heard the strains of the victrola. It was John McCormack singing, "A Little Old Town in the Old County Down." I punctuated the sentimental music with my sobs. I knew that my mother would have to sit it out for fear of Aunt Josie's disapproval. I hated everything in the room, the Sacred Heart that hung over the bed, the ruffled curtains, the silver hairbrushes, the graped legs of the bed. I got up, walked slowly to the legs and began to kick. With every breath John McCormack took, I kicked as hard as I could. The demonstration worked. I walked home between my mother and father, clutching their hands, safely away from the scolding voice of my Aunt Josie, a woman of righteousness and rigidity.

My Aunt Josie looked and acted nothing like her

sister, my mother. She was lace-curtain, and had a secure place among the Irish on Money Hole Hill. Tim and she, as she said in her tight-lipped way, were comfortable. They owned their own house and he was successfully established in the hardware business, which was the sole subject of his conversation. My father had a great respect for him. "A good solid businessman," he would say. My mother, taking advantage of Tim's deafness, would mutter when Josie was out of the room, "A good solid bore."

Aunt Josie had married Tim when she was thirty-two. The marriage had produced one child, a doll-like girl looking more china than human. They had bought a house on the Hill soon after their marriage, for "social reasons." "When you're in business," Tim would say, "you have to make contacts." Aunt Josie had worked very hard at respectability and achieved it in all its stuffiness. Everything in her house was exactly the same as in the other houses on Pearl Street. Her daughter acted and pleased exactly as the other little girls on Pearl Street. My Aunt Josie never visited Irish Parish, where she was born. She was loyal to her sister, but not to what she stood for. She was determined that she would make my mother lace-curtain. She was a strong woman and, in many ways, a cruel one. She was the only person my mother feared, for some reason that I felt unaccountable.

When Aunt Josie came to visit us, which was not very often, those visits were a source of terror to my mother. She would spend all day cleaning the house, trying to elevate her plain table by much polishing to the status of a marbletop. I used to sit on the bed and watch her desperate attempts to do her hair in a modish way. It would always end up in a fuzz of untidiness. Exasperated, she would slam the comb on the bureau, muttering, "Now what difference does it make at all, and why do I do it?" I knew exactly how she felt, though: if one could only walk into the room confident and sure that there was not a spot or speck showing.

Aunt Josie, always so confident and sure in her own "style," as she called it, characterized a hanging slip, a loose hair, a knot in the shoelace, as "shanty," and felt that when those lapses were remedied, the transformation from shanty to lace-curtain had begun. Consequently, she was always yanking or pulling at my hair ribbon, retying my bows, hauling at my frocks, commenting on my mother's lack of silk dresses, or staring at her hands that were roughened by dishwater. "Mame, how many times have I told you that you should wear rubber gloves when you wash dishes! Look at my hands. Dishwater never touches them." She would hold up soft, pudgy hands covered with rings. "Indeed," my mother would say after she had gone, "dishwater never touches them, and her with a hired girl."

Before Aunt Josie's visits, we were all cautioned, "Say nothing now, for God's sake, about the wakes." But my Aunt Josie always knew, and delivered herself of a long tirade against them. "If it was someone respectable, it would be all right, Mame, but any old

Harp, no matter who he is. You'll never have any style," she would conclude, preening herself.

Although we lived quite near my Aunt Josie, I rarely played with my Cousin Ann. The desire to was certainly not strong, for Ann was a refined little girl who never dirtied her dress. The times that I visited their house, she played primly under the shade tree in the back yard, giving a perfect imitation of her mother. I drank gallons of weak tea, talked myself tired about the state of her tidy children, her mythical husband, and his business. I was never allowed to touch any of her things. "Your hands are too dirty," she would say coldly.

Once, with a great spurt of generosity, I had gone over to her house myself. My mother had given me all the equipment necessary for a lemonade stand. I looked forward with tremendous pleasure to the game which consisted of selling one glass of lemonade and drinking the rest of the cool, over-sugared drink yourself. My brother Michael and I used to play this game all during the hot summer. Ann, surprisingly enough, was more than willing; but when everything was ready, she said it was not quite proper to set up a stand in front of the house, or to sell drinks. We settled down with all her little friends, exact replicas of herself, and played her game of tea with my lemonade. All the joy of being a grown-up entrepreneur was gone. I hated her doll-like charm which belied the strong will behind it. I felt exactly as helpless as my mother did before Aunt Josie.

Ann and I went to the same school. At school she never associated with me, moving gracefully among the other pretty, clean, lace-curtain children. During the Al Smith election, I wore his button to school and was fairly massacred by the Yankee children. One Yankee girl, the daughter of the bank president, knocked out my two front teeth. It was an epic battle. None of the lace-curtain children came to my rescue. They were horrified by my lack of refinement and discretion. As Aunt Josie said to my mother after Ann had reported the scene: "It's better, Mame, to keep politics to yourself. What if he's not elected?" That was the only time my mother flared up against Josie. "Let them keep it to themselves, then, pushing and shoving it into your face every chance they get! I tell you, Josie O'Sullivan, it is not your kind to be giving me lessons. My children will be honest if they do lose two front teeth for it. There comes a time when a man should fight, and not slink away for fear of losing business." Aunt Josie was not stopped by that, though. As long as she came, she corrected my mother's politics. My father always agreed with her. "It's not ladylike, Mame, for a woman to be attending political meetings," Aunt Josie would say. My mother never answered; she just went on attending them.

One Sunday, Aunt Josie and her family came to dinner. My mother sat at the table heaping generous helpings of food on our plates. I sat next to Ann, whom I could see surreptitiously wiping the silverware under the table. My brother Michael was excited at the prospect of going fishing in the morning and was begging permission of my mother to go out and catch night

crawlers that night. I could see Ann shudder. My Aunt
Josie said, "That is not proper dinner conversation,
Michael." He looked at her resentfully.

After dinner, Tim and my father were smoking
cigars in the living room; my mother was washing the
dishes in the kitchen. I walked down the long hallway
looking for Ann. One of the bedroom doors was closed
and I could hear voices behind it. I was just about to go
in when I heard, "But mother, she's so dirty and —— "
It was Ann's voice. "Yes, I know she is, but you must
be generous, Ann. After all, she is your cousin." "I
don't care. I won't play with her and I want to go
home. I don't like any of them. The silverware was
greasy." There was nothing Aunt Josie could do or say.
She had produced this child.

I went to the end of the hallway and sat down. There
was so much I could not understand. How could anyone not like my mother, and how could anyone speak
against her? Was I dirty? I examined my hands. They
were a little dirty. I went to the bathroom and started
washing them; for an hour I soaped them and washed
them over and over again, trying to change their brown
to the milk-whiteness of Ann's. When my mother found
me, I was crying over the hurt within me. When I told
her, she said nothing; but I never played with Ann
again.

On Memorial Day we all went to the cemetery to visit
my grandfather's and uncles' graves. My Aunt Josie had
seen to it that all the family graves were tidily kept. My
mother helped pay the ten dollars a year for this, but she

was not much concerned over the matter. She had been more concerned when they were living. However, we used to visit the graves on Memorial Day. I can still remember jumping out of bed eagerly to discover the weather, for the state of weather determined whether there would be a band or not. I was much more concerned about the band than about the dead.

We would all start about ten o'clock in the morning, the entire family, and all the O'Sullivans. My mother had usually forgotten to buy a plant for the communal grave. Not to be outdone by Aunt Josie, who always came bearing a many-blossomed plant, large and ornate, I would be sent scurrying over to Bill Zuchini's for a last-minute purchase. I always bought pansies. Somehow their gentleness was appropriate to my grandfather. We would march up Dwight Street to Saint Jerome's Cemetery along with groups of others, all bearing flowers. I would be allowed to place the flowers on my grandfather's grave. I remember the exact place where his grave is, the plain gray stone bearing the words, "John O'Sullivan 1838–1922," and below, "His wife Johanna O'Sullivan 1840–1890 R.I.P."

We all used to kneel then and say our prayers for the dead. I can still remember the soft sod sinking beneath me and the criss-cross lines the grass made on my knees. I never said my prayers very fervently because I had always a great fear that the ground might give way and I would land in the grave. My Aunt Josie always rose with red eyes; my mother masked her grief. I knew what pain it caused her to visit those graves. She would,

as she said, "much rather have lit a candle in the church
for them." She felt helpless and hopeless praying at the
graves.

The band would march through the Forestdale Cemetery first, stopping to place flags on the graves of all the
soldiers. They would then come across the street to
Saint Jerome's. I stood at the gate watching them putting the flags on the graves of my uncles. They played
taps over the graves the year they both died. I had a
great lump in my throat going home Memorial Day that
year.

But the occasions for communal celebration with
Aunt Josie were rare, and since my mother had very
little to do with her circle, we soon saw less and less of
her. She gave us up almost entirely after my mother's
visit with her to one of the women's clubs to which she
belonged. She was to bring my mother as a "guest,"
which amounted to the rest of the club "looking her
over" for possible membership. The preparations for
that visit were endless. My father saved enough to buy
my mother a complete new outfit for a birthday present,
and so that Aunt Josie could feel quite assured that she
would be presentable. I can still remember the dress
and coat — they were blue and the coat had a brown
fur trim. My mother came in to me before she left,
spinning around on her heel so that I could see the
whirl of the skirt. Her eyes were sparkling more over
the new clothes than over the prospect of the club. She
did look beautiful, and the face matched the young picture of her. Aunt Josie came, yanked a bit here and

there more out of habit than necessity. When my mother came home that night, I heard her grumbling in the dark. "Dullest thing I ever attended. That fat Mrs. Fitzgerald up there banging on the desk. 'Ladeez! Ladeez! Who will second the motion?' They spent the whole damn evening considering silly things on something called an agenda. Not a good bit of talk did I have at all." I could hear her anger as she struggled to get out of the warm dress. "Chicken patties and peas! It's half-starved I am. I'm going to have a bite of something." She was not elected to the club, but the next time Aunt Josie came, my mother showed her the gold medal she had received for being the most popular member of a club she had belonged to when she was a young woman.

Aunt Josie more and more cultivated the middle-class Yankees who lived near her, though when she was with us she had not a good word to say for them. The side of them my mother and I liked she never saw. Both she and her husband picked up their worst traits, their stinginess, their hard-headed business methods, the ways of the Yankees that had made them owners of the mills in Irish Parish and family-proud with nothing but a shopkeeper's ancestry behind it. Aunt Josie never admired Mrs. Beaton, who, in the midst of poverty, sat with her ten children and quietly read Dickens to them. The Beaton family was too large. It really was not quite refined to have so many children. She and Tim were the imitators of those whom they secretly despised and secretly felt humble before, and the detractors of their

own people whom they could openly and safely snub.
Insecure before the Yankees, they secured themselves
against the shanty Irish with a position that only money
can buy.

My mother never understood Aunt Josie; she understood her sister Hannah much better, perhaps because
Hannah was more like the rest of the O'Sullivans. Aunt
Hannah had been the most beautiful girl in Irish
Parish, fair-haired, and blue-eyed. She had spent her
young life sitting on the living-room sofa, beautifying
her small delicate hands, and making fun of my
mother's "bucky" friends. She did not work, turning
her nose up in disgust at the thought of the mill. She
sewed beautifully and had the finest clothes of any girl
in Irish Parish. She modeled them after the clothes she
saw on the ladies of Money Hole Hill. She walked the
streets of Irish Parish with the air of a queen. She had
no use for Irish Parish and the people in it; she had eyes
only for the Hill. When my mother went to dances at
the Hibernians', she would occasionally steal one of
Aunt Hannah's delicately embroidered and freshly
laundered shirtwaists, slipping it back into the drawer
when she returned. When Hannah discovered the
mussed blouse, there was a great scene, Hannah dangling
the blouse in front of the guilty one, shouting about the
sweat and "bucky" smell of it.

She waited patiently for a Yankee from the Hill, for
she would have no Harp "plugging away in the mill for
his whole life, sweating to make someone else rich."
Her patience was rewarded and she married into one of

the oldest and wealthiest Yankee families on the Hill. No one ever knew how the marriage came about, for Hannah never mentioned it until it was an accomplished fact. The man, Charles Dickinson, was never seen until after they were married, and then only rarely. She kept the whole thing to herself because the marriage was outside the Church, as well as outside of Irish Parish. She moved to the Hill, and there was, in the early days, absolutely no effort to bring her family into her new circle. She appeared in Irish Parish only for her mother's funeral, with great show and display. My grandfather never mentioned her name without the adjective "poor," something I could not understand, for I knew she had lots of money.

The first time I saw Aunt Hannah she was coming down the long hallway, fancy in furs and feathers, tossing her head from side to side trying to throw off the distasteful smell of a tenement. She addressed my mother, ignoring me completely, saying to her, "How do you stand this dreadful dark hole? It smells of fish." My mother said nothing, but led her into the living room. She had absolutely no envy of Hannah, and felt no resentment toward her. Aunt Hannah had just dropped in casually, but those casual visits became more and more frequent. Somehow, my mother was a mecca for all the unhappy O'Sullivans. No matter how different their lives from hers, they all came to her in time of need. And time of need for all of them lasted until they were dead.

Gradually, Hannah began to talk to my mother.

They would sit in the living room, Hannah nervously rocking back and forth in the big leather rocker, revealing, cautiously at first and then more and more openly, all of her woes. I used to play with my dolls quietly in the corner, listening to her sharp tongue, bitter in its recital of the past and the present.

She had not been accepted, of course. It was an old, old story: the bitterness of her father-in-law and the arrogant attitude of the women, who had relegated her to her "proper place" the minute she set foot in the door. She occupied with her husband a suite of rooms in the family home on Washington Avenue. Her husband, out of deference to his mother, had seen to it that she received the proper education for a lady. She was refined and polished into a proper nonentity. She would describe with bitterness the scenes of humiliation at the dinner table when she was waited on by people she had known all her life in Irish Parish, people whom she had never cared about, but whose small, dark rooms belowstairs she was warned without provocation against visiting. She was cautioned to lock her jewel case because "Irish maids steal anything they can lay their hands on." "God knows," she would say to my mother, "I had no desire to remain Irish, but they saw to it that I could be nothing else."

Inevitably by her marriage to Charles she became a First Congregationalist, though she herself desired to be nothing. Every Sunday morning she was required to attend the service with Charles in order to fill the family pew. She listened to the ravings of old Mr. Dickinson at the dinner table against the Papists and listened to tirades about the ammunition that the priests kept stored in the cellars of their churches. None of these things, she told my mother, meant anything to her until she realized that all the remarks were subtly directed at her. She had been ready and willing to accept their ways until she learned that she was not going to be allowed to do so.

"My God, the first party they had after I came, I heard them telling how they were going to have an Irish woman in their drawing room, and I saw the shock on all the faces when I entered. They looked at me, the way you'd think I had a tail." My mother listened silently to Aunt Hannah, never counseling or warning. She told my father later, "There's nothing to say or do but listen. That is the only reason she comes. She wants a sympathetic ear." My father cautioned my mother constantly against advising rebellion. He had only one desire — to keep out of the affair. My mother would laugh rather bitterly at his fears. "I have no need to counsel rebellion; Hannah's heart is filled with it; but she'll not run off with the chauffeur. She's too clever for that. There are other ways. She'll find them, though I could pray that she wouldn't."

As the years passed, we saw her constantly. We even went to the Dickinson house to visit her, passing through the darkened corridors with a look into the elegance of the drawing room and the library as we walked. I remember holding my mother's hand and climbing an immense staircase, heavily carpeted, with rows of stern-faced pictures lining it. I smelled the smell of that house and it was the same smell of death that I had been so conscious of in the museums at Cambridge. We would go silently along the corridor until we came to Hannah's suite. The six rooms were done in what she casually referred to as "the French style." Miserable as her life had been in those rooms, she still could not quite give over the satisfaction to her pride that "the suite" afforded. Her drawing room, where we had tea, was "pink and gold" and filled with delicate chairs that I used to be afraid to sit on, thinking to myself that they would not hold the weight of a mouse. Instead, I would sit on a footstool whose gilded claws fascinated me and later became symbols of those visits. I remember sitting stiffly in the midst of all that elegance, holding a dainty cup of cambric tea as carefully as though I were holding a bubble, and watching my Aunt Hannah, as pink and gold as her room, gracefully pouring tea into the pink-flowered cups. She looked as though she were born to it. I remembered my grandfather's definition of a beautiful woman as "fine and foxy [red-headed] and every freckle as big as a dollar," and found it wrong because Aunt Hannah's beauty contradicted it.

While my mother and she talked, I would study the painting of Aunt Hannah that hung over the mantel. She sat on a white-and-gold chair, her beautiful hands resting quietly in her lap. It was a serene picture, the delicate face calm and quiet, but slightly flushed with the triumph she had accomplished. That picture must have existed in the dreams she had had in Irish Parish.

Aunt Hannah used to accompany us to the door when we left. The three of us would descend the staircase, Aunt Hannah explaining what she called "the Rogues' Gallery," as we went. "The first one is old John Dickinson," a grim face with a stern slit of a mouth. "He gave a load of manure to the foundation of Harvard College." She was deliberately scurrilous in her remarks. "That one there was his wife." The face was equally grim, equally intent on duty. "Those two are the plaster saints of the family. They keep the candles going in front of them every night. This one here" — the costume had shifted, but the face was the same — "hunted witches and bitches." My mother would interrupt, "For God's sake, Hannah, watch your tongue." She recited the roll of Dickinson saints contemptuously, annihilating their sanctity in one sentence. "There is one picture missing, one of Edward." That was all she said. I wondered who Edward was, and why his picture was missing.

The last picture was that of Charles Dickinson, the man she had married. From the nineteenth century on, the faces had begun to change; they were still grim, but more hearty and healthy, with a full-blooded, port look. The thin line of the mouth was replaced by a pouty lower lip. More and more they began to look like the people I saw on the streets of Money Hole Hill. Charles Dickinson's face was gentle, but there was a weak look to it. It was the only face that attracted me, for it had a look of rebellious despair and he seemed to have an eye that saw beauty without a price. I liked him, though I never saw him. I could understand now why he had married Hannah. As we walked down the staircase, the stony eyes of those portraits seemed to follow me. It was always with great relief that I reached the door and the street outside without ever meeting any of the portraits face to face.

After a while, I no longer went with my mother to visit Aunt Hannah. She was pregnant and self-conscious about it. My mother left me home until the pregnancy was over. She went regularly once a week, and braved specialists, nurses, and disapproving Dickinsons to assist at the birth. I remember the night she came home after the birth. She had been gone two days. Her absence, though obvious, was left unexplained. When she came in the door, I sensed immediately that she had seen trouble enough, so I did not bother her. She sat at the kitchen table, trying to eat, her face twisted with fatigue and sorrow. She sat looking straight ahead. At last she spoke. "It is over," she said; "two days and the marks of her heels in the floor boards to remind her. She cursed every living thing until it is a wonder God did not take the child from her. Perhaps better if he had, for there'll be nothing but pain and sorrow in that house over him."

My mother was right. Hannah had done everything to prevent the conception of this child that the Dickinsons needed to carry on the name. That was one of her ways of repayment. When it was assured that there would be a child, she had spent her time wishing for its death, cursing its conception, bitter and vengeful against everyone. She never entered her husband's bed again. That did not matter. Charles Dickinson had his son. Aunt Hannah had almost nothing to do with the child. She saw him only at his bedtime. He was "going to be a Dickinson."

Once she smuggled him out of the house and brought him to visit us. I remember him standing against the side of the house, stiff and shy, watching my brothers play — painfully aware that he did not belong. I took him by the hand and led him into the house. We walked down the long hallway and I felt the tenseness in his hand. It was not that he didn't belong; it was that he couldn't. I felt sorry for him in a grown-up way, for he seemed so lost to any world of reality. After that visit, we never saw him again. He was "farmed out" as my Aunt Hannah said bitterly, sent to a boys' school in New York where she could not reach him. She saw him on holidays, and then only in the presence of others.

After the child's birth, Hannah no longer concealed her hate for the Dickinsons. She no longer spoke only to my mother. There wasn't a person on Money Hole Hill who didn't know. My mother used to say "it's a kind of insanity." She made public every skeleton in the Dickinson closet, trying to destroy the thing that was most priceless to them, their family heritage. It was during this time that I discovered why Edward's picture did not hang with the rest. She told my mother the story, and, in her bitterness, did not stop with my mother, but published it for all the eager tongues on Money Hole Hill to turn over.

"I went to the Dickinsons the month after I was married." There was a sigh in her voice which disappeared as she told the story. "I used to hear the noise at night, and, frightened, I would wake Charles to listen with me. 'Nothing but mice in the walls, Hannah. It's an old house.' That was the only explanation I got. I asked the others, but got only sly, concealed answers. I tell you I smelled a rat and not a mouse. One day I went to the third floor by myself. One of the doors was locked. As I was hunting for the key, I found myself trapped by Mother Dickinson. She was looking like one of the portraits. 'What are you looking for?' she asked. I faced up to her. 'Why is this door locked, and what are the noises I hear in the night?' I demanded. Her face changed in an instant as those plain concealed Yankee faces can. She twisted my arm and held me, glaring into my face. 'You are never to enter that room, and you are never to ask questions of anyone about the noises you hear, do you understand? I will kill you, I swear, if I ever find you here again.' She turned and left, and I went weeping to my room, in anger, though, not fear.

"Finally, one day I was going down the hall on my way downstairs when I looked up the third-floor staircase. There stood a man. My God! I could never describe him. He came down slowly. He had the Dickinsons' eyes, but they were not stony, they were mad!

I ran down the stairs. He came after, softly, for he did not want to be discovered. I don't remember what happened, but they were all in the drawing room having tea when I fainted in upon them. There was a scene all right, a good one for their noses to look down at. Of course, I was accused of freeing him. In ten years he had not been out of the room, living in his own filth and dirt — they shoved the food in at night and locked the door quickly for fear he'd get out. It was his shouting and screaming and hammering on the padded door that I heard at night. I've told them that if they do not put him in an institution, I will. They wouldn't like that, the Dickinsons with their fine house and fine ancestors. No, they wouldn't like to have that broadcast, not at all."

When she finished her story, she looked bitterly and defiantly at my mother. My mother looked out the window at the mulberry tree in the yard. Her face was curiously abstracted, I noticed, and not at all as mine was, I am sure, full of fear and horror. She turned back to Hannah and said, almost in a whisper: "That is wrong. You will do yourself harm as well as the Dickinsons. It is better to say nothing. I tell you, Hannah, I have been praying for you now since this marriage, and my prayers have been that you would forget bitterness and resentment. It is yourself you are ruining entirely, not them at all. You will find a day when you can no longer live with yourself if you continue this way."

Aunt Hannah did not listen to my mother, but continued fostering the hatred within herself. She contrived all ways she could to hurt the Dickinsons. She completely forgot her own pride in order to break theirs. She thought to shame them by shaming herself. The change took place gradually. At first it was a loose pin in her beautiful hair; soon it was a missing shoelace, then mismated shoes — gradually the complete disintegration of her beauty took place. Her nails that she had spent hours manicuring in Irish Parish became dirty and unsightly, her hair colorless. She lost her teeth; and her once round chin became sharp and pointed, wagging vehemently as she spoke the bitter word. There was soon nothing left of the pink-and-gold picture that hung on the wall.

Her personal appearance was the greatest change for many years, but we soon began to notice a difference in her talk and personality. Her parodies which had once been amusing became horrible to hear. We dreaded to see her come, for we knew that we would not only hear the same tale, but that it would be more painful with every repetition.

One Sunday evening I was staring out the living-room window, when I saw Aunt Hannah turning the corner. I could tell by the fast pace which had replaced the usual loose shuffling that she was excited. I called to my mother: "Here comes Aunt Hannah." I took a kind of perverse pleasure in the announcement, for I knew it would disturb her. My brother Michael groaned and reluctantly left his chair. Eddie put down his violin and rushed to the kitchen, shutting the door behind him. Only my mother and I were left in the living room. We heard Hannah moaning as she opened the front door. It was a kind of incoherent groaning which became clearer and clearer as she climbed the stairs. I looked at my mother, who for the first time in my life sent me away. "Leave the room," she said, and I left. I sat with my brother Eddie in the kitchen.

Through the closed door, down the long, dark hallway, we could hear the sharp cry of grief, over and over, "My son! My son!" Suddenly my mother called sharply, "Edmund." We rushed down the dark hallway to find her struggling with a madwoman. Eddie and my mother held her down while I ran wildly down the street to fetch Doctor Martin. For months, she lay in my mother's bed staring blankly at nothing. My mother would say, "Who could have known that one who had cursed so bitterly at his birth would weep so bitterly at his death?" I used to sit by the bed watching my Aunt Hannah when she was getting better, remembering the shy, slim little boy who did not seem real, wondering how he died; for no one ever mentioned the cause of his death.

When Hannah was well again, she used to ask me to read the papers to her, especially the social columns. I would read, halting and stumbling over "soirée" and "invitation," pronouncing the unfamiliar names only by her prompting. When the name Dickinson appeared, her eyes would brighten. "Read it again," she would say. I would read, "Mr. and Mrs. John Dickinson held a Sunday afternoon musicale in their home

July 25th. The eminent composer musician, Charles
Duncan, played some of his own compositions. The
guests included ——" Then I would recite the names
of all the eminent Yankees on Money Hole Hill. When
her mother-in-law's death was announced, she chuckled,
"I will outlive them all."

Lying there in bed, she made her plans for the future.
All the grief over her son was forgotten. I used to come
upon her talking and mumbling to herself. She
dreamed as successfully now as she had in the old days
and she put those dreams into effect. In time, by sheer
stubbornness, she did outlive them all, and through
clever legal manipulation fell heir to the house and all
the property.

The Dickinson name was dead, borne only by an
O'Sullivan. Aunt Hannah lived for some time in the
old home, keeping it all open, occupying the place of
old John Dickinson at the huge dinner table, still as
filled with fury against the dead as she had been against
the living. The name itself was the family and she
took her revenge on that. She began to be known as that
"eccentric Mrs. Dickinson." Children taunted her,
grown-ups talked of her. She became a Money Hole
Hill "character." Her story was whispered to all new-
comers. People thought her crazy, so did I; but she
would look slyly at my mother and say: "Exactly, that's
fine. Let them say it. It suits my purpose." Gradually,
she grew more and more "money-mad." We would see
her driving through the streets of Irish Parish in her
archaic buggy, parking in front of the Dickinsons'

blocks where she went to collect the rents. She would trust no one else to do it. She gave up all relations with lawyers, and refused to bank her money, keeping it hidden in cubby-holes in the big house.

Her generosity to us disappeared completely, and instead of the elegant gifts that I used to receive from her, she would send a pair of dark brown cotton stockings or a ten-cent penwiper. Her miserliness became notorious, and the salespeople would shudder when they saw her coming, with her green shopping bag on her arm. Her beautiful costumes of the past were gone, and she appeared on the streets of Money Hole Hill wearing old John Dickinson's hat and fur coat, with a pair of men's boots on her feet.

She finally closed up the big house and moved out into the chicken coop. There she lived with a pack of dogs that she kept to protect her money. She starved the dogs, as well as herself, to keep them ferocious. I went once to see her in the later days. She had moved her white-and-gold furniture in with her. The whole wall of the chicken coop she had lined with the Dickinson ancestry, and in the center of the line of portraits she had placed her own picture.

I looked at them all and then at herself long and hard. There was no longer a Hannah O'Sullivan. That hung on the wall. The old woman, shuffling down the long chicken coop to throw a log into the wood stove was Hannah Dickinson. Her face, grim, lined by bitterness and hate, should have hung last in the series of Dickinson portraits.

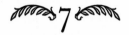

7

He's Your Son, Too

I REMEMBER seeing a slim, dark-haired boy standing on the second-floor porch, swinging my cat Rainbow back and forth by the tail. Despite the knickers, he seemed like a very old person to me, and I feared doing what I had to do. With the pain heavy in me at his harming the animal, I rushed toward him, begging him to stop, for I knew that he was working up momentum preparatory to slinging Rainbow over the porch rail into the alley below. He paid no attention to me, but continued swinging her back and forth, widening the arc with each swing. I screamed for my mother and my brother Eddie, knowing they were my friends and would stop this fearful persecution. He turned to me when they did not answer, laughing and showing his teeth. In a fury I sprang at him, biting and scratching. With one push he threw me to the side of the porch. The cat's pitiful cries blended with mine. I crawled over the porch toward him and, as he turned, sank my teeth into his leg, biting as deeply as I could, clutching the leg with my arms, intent on only one thing, to hurt him as badly as he was hurting Rainbow. He dropped the cat, and, screaming with pain, started to pull out my hair. When my mother appeared, I was still biting, and he, raging, had sunk his teeth into my arm. That was my brother Tabby.

That night I sat in the big leather rocker, rocking Rainbow back and forth, one arm badly bitten. I was glad of the pain, for it alleviated, as only physical suffering can, the terrible pain I felt inside. Tabby sat in the corner, his leg up on a chair; and I could smell his hatred, so animal was it. For months after, he persecuted me. He would have beaten me except for my mother. Instead, I would find special toys mysteriously broken, obstacles in my way so that I tripped over them. I finally fell over one in the hallway and broke my arm. Then the persecution stopped, and we almost became friends.

Tabby was a legend in our house from the day he was born. Of all of us, he caused my mother the greatest pain at birth, and continued to do so during his life. My grandfather used to tell me how Tabby had screamed night and day for the first year, until my mother and everyone else in the house were in despair. My mother took him to the doctor to see what was wrong. The doctor handed him back, saying, "He's a fine healthy baby. He's just cross." He became known throughout the neighborhood as a "cross child," and was nicknamed "Tabby" because he was constantly fighting and scratching like the cats he hated.

Tabby led the gang, and under his guidance it terrorized the neighborhood. Most of the games he organ-

ized depended on persecution for their success. My
mother fought Tabby's violence until the end, though
in a sense, after she had witnessed one of his early cam-
paigns, she knew he was already lost.

Across the street from the school was a dark, sinister-
looking house. Its front faced the schoolhouse, its back
the alley behind our block. Attached to the side of the
house was a long covered passageway with a long flight
of stairs that led from the alley up the hill toward the
school. None of us dared to use that staircase because
of Tabby's violent stories about the old man who lived
in the house with nothing but a parrot to keep him company. I, who was terrified by the stories, went only once
through the dark, dank passageway, feeling sure that at
any moment Mr. Gamzoo would appear at the head of
the stairs with a great carved knife in his hand. Under
Tabby's leadership the gang would torment the old
man by teasing the parrot that sat, usually, in the back
window, calling out, "Polly wants a cracker." Tabby
and the boys would mimic him until the parrot beat its
wings against the cage in fury. Then Mr. Gamzoo
would appear at the window and silently remove the
cage. No matter how much he was persecuted by these
boys, Mr. Gamzoo said nothing. That infuriated Tabby.
He wanted "to hear the old man squeal."

At last he hit upon another method. He lined up the
gang after they had stamped their way down the passageway, making as much noise as possible. They all
began to chant, "Mr. Gamzoo,you dirty old Jew! Mr.
Gamzoo, you dirty old Jew!" Within a few minutes,

the parrot took up the refrain, mimicking the boys in its cracked, rasping voice, saying the words over and over, until the window was quietly closed and the shade pulled down. This sport became Tabby's great pastime. After school at three-thirty for weeks the boys stood outside the house shouting their chant, laughing at the parrot's response until the tears rolled down their faces.

One afternoon I joined in the chant and was standing there feeling more and more satisfied with the warm glow of hate. At that moment I saw my mother coming down the alley from the store. I ran to meet her, thus separating myself from the rest, for I knew she would be angry. She pushed me aside roughly. There was pain and terror in her face. She walked through the crowd of boys, who fell silent when they saw her. Only Tabby, in front of the rest, unaware of her presence, lost in the ecstasy of hate, was still chanting his malediction. Swinging him around to face her, slowly and deliberately she began to shake him. When Tabby was out of breath, she took him by the arm and led him up the passageway to Mr. Gamzoo's house. The rest of us escaped in silence.

When Tabby came home, his face was red and swollen from tears, but it was still defiant. He went immediately to his room. My mother said nothing about what happened, but when I came into the kitchen after supper, she was furiously rattling pans. Whatever she had said to Tabby kept him quiet for a week, but it was the kind of quiet that is brooding on hate. He concealed it carefully from my mother, but behind that mask of silence he was carefully organizing a new campaign against Mr. Gamzoo. Three months later, a furniture van drew up in front of his house, and Mr. Gamzoo moved, taking the parrot to remind him that hate is a contagious thing. My mother suspected what had happened. I saw her looking at this boy whom neither words nor blows could change.

The only person who could do anything with Tabby was my brother Eddie, who overindulged him. We had a picture of Eddie and Tabby on a pony, taken when they were eight and six respectively. Eddie, his head shyly turned away from the camera, had his arm protectively around Tabby to prevent him from falling; Tabby was smiling full-faced into the camera. That protection of Tabby continued until Eddie had to save or sacrifice himself entirely. If Tabby did something wrong, Eddie prevented the spanking. Eddie, confined to inactivity by the heavy brace on his leg, would sit on the sidelines doing Tabby's homework while Tabby played baseball in the lot. Everything that Eddie received was turned over to Tabby. Once Eddie, perched on a stool at Bill Zuchini's eating a college ice my Uncle Smiley had bought for him, looked out to see Tabby, pathetic and forlorn, his nose pressed up against the plate-glass, looking in at him. He never forgot that scene, and he did everything to prevent Tabby's relegation to the place of outsider.

I remember Tabby chiefly as a young man, for he was eight years older than I, and for the most part, except for the cat episode, he ignored me. What I knew of him as a child, I heard from my family in the form of the "Tabby legend." My mother had to go to see the principal at school more often for Tabby than for all the rest of us put together. I remember the fury with which she used to set out "to hear another complaint." It was not the complaints that infuriated her so much as the mystery of this child. She never could understand what made him what he was. She would come home after each one of those visits with the same words ringing in her ears: "A brilliant child, Mrs. O'Connor, but perverse. No one can do anything with him."

At sixteen he left school without graduating. This was more than my mother could bear. She talked to him, fought with him, did everything to prevent what she considered a catastrophe. Finally she gave up. I remember her remark: "My God, I chased my brothers all my life to get them to school, and now I have a son who is going the same way." My father heartily agreed. "He's an O'Sullivan from head to toe. He'll never be any good." My mother turned on him in fury: "You forget that he's your son, too, and you sitting there since the day he was born, wagging your head over him, but not understanding any better than I do what devil is inside him. A lot of help you've been, complaining all the time that it's Eddie and I who spoiled him." My father would glare back. "It's the two of you all right, and the bad examples he's had in front of him every day — drunken bums. Between all of you, he's ruined."

After Tabby left school, my father was determined

on one thing: he would put Tabby into the mill. But Tabby would not go, and there were great scenes and fights. My father would say: "The mill is not good enough for you. The pool hall, I suppose, is better." All this behavior produced in Tabby was a fierce resentment toward my father. So intensely did they hate each other that they could not sit down at the same table.

When Tabby came home drunk one night, it was the finish for my father. After that Tabby was tolerated, that was all, and in the darkness I could hear my father berating my mother over the son "she" had produced. The worst scenes occurred because Tabby used to lie in bed mornings and refuse to look for a job. I would hide in the closet to keep out of the violence of those scenes that produced nothing but more bitterness.

Tabby finally got a job, a good one; but he never turned any of his money in at home for board as was customary in Irish families. Instead, he spent it on clothes and Polish girls. In the early days he never went out with any Irish girls. He could not bear the shanty Irish; "dumb flat-footed Harps," he called them. He went out with the Polish, as my father said, "because he could put on a big front."

I remember going up to Mountain Park with my mother and father to see the fireworks. On our way through the pavilion, we stopped in at the dance hall and sat in the chairs behind the railing that marked off the slippery floor. The orchestra was sitting in an arch at one end of the hall; a great crystal ball cast colored light that splintered as it glanced off the shiny floor.

They were playing "Me and My Shadow," and I leaned my chin on the railing, watching the slim young figures two-step by. My brother Tabby was the best dancer on the floor, his sharp, shiny shoe pointing gracefully as he spun. I waved to Eddie, who was sitting across the hall, smoking a cigarette, moodily watching the dancers. That night, Tabby won a loving cup. It stood in his room and became a symbol to my father of the futility of Tabby's life.

Tabby dressed elegantly in the jazzy clothes of the period. My mother half-humorously called him "the Sheik of Araby." She would spend hours ironing his shirts so that there was not a crease or wrinkle in the collars. Tabby was out every night; and wherever he went, Eddie went with him. Eddie would follow him into the men's room at Mountain Park, trying to per-suade him not to drink the gin that Tabby carried in his pocket. The evening usually ended with Eddie hold-ing Tabby up on the lurching trolley car as it made its last trip. He would sneak Tabby into the house quietly so as not to waken my father, undress him, and put him to bed. Sometimes I used to hear them, on Saturday night especially, Tabby very sick and drunk, Eddie, very tired and irritable, trying to quiet Tabby as they came in the front door.

Tabby eventually lost his first job, got another and lost that almost immediately because again he did not report on time; then the old familiar battle began again. Eddie would give him part of his pay, lend him his best shirts; my father would attack both of them furiously. There was no peace in the house with Tabby and my father in it together. When the neighbors began to talk of Tabby's drunkenness, shaking their heads — "You remember her brothers. It's bad blood, bad blood" — my father would stand no more, and Tabby left. He left for Boston, the stronghold of the lace-curtain Irish, determined that he would become a member of the world my father valued so highly.

My brother Eddie used to go to visit him, coming home with glowing reports of Tabby's success. My father never believed a word of it. He considered Tabby a four-flusher of the first order. After a while, Tabby started coming home on weekends, dressed in beautifully tailored suits, bringing expensive flowers for my mother and expensive cigars for my father. My father accepted them grudgingly. Tabby bragged that he was working up to the managership of a big automobile sales service. He earned, he would say, with a grand flourish, seventy-five dollars a week. He would show my father his stuffed wallet to prove it; but no matter how hard things were at home, he never offered a cent. He was generous with grand presents, but never with money. After dinner we would all sit in the living room while Tabby told of his exploits.

"I met Judge Mahoney last week," he would say, proudly watching my father's face, "through Bill Murphy. You know the Murphys, Ma. They live in that big house on Washington Avenue, Bill went to Holy Cross and Boston University. He's a lawyer in Boston, and what a practice he has! We go around together all the time; as a matter of fact, he's introducing me at the K. of C. next week." He would settle back complacently. His voice still held the huffy note that I remembered as typical of him. He would puff out the words, trying with bluster to make them sound more convincing. "Judge Mahoney's buying a roadster from me for his daughter. I met her last week at a dance at the Hotel Bradford."

My father would never say a word during all this talk. Tabby would grow quiet, pick up the Sunday newspaper, shaking his foot nervously all the time he was reading. With a gesture of irritation, he would throw the paper aside, saying, "Come on, Eddie. Let's go out!" We all knew what that meant, but there was no stopping him. Eddie would go with him to the hotel cocktail lounge. Tabby would stand at the bar, one foot up, and loudly order, "Scotch and soda." They would have one, two, three. Then Eddie would try to persuade Tabby to come home, but he always failed. Tabby would talk loudly of his connections, his job, his money. He would set up the whole bar and then try to fight with the whole bar for not believing his "success story." He would come home without a cent in his pocket, pulling the big dealer's car to a screeching stop in front of the door.

The stories about his jobs were all true. Whatever organization he joined, he always rose rapidly. My father claimed that this was because he was a liar. "He could sell a car without wheels," he used to say. He was, without question, a good talker. "He's got the Irish gift of gab," said my mother. "Sure, and he could talk his way out of hell." He was smart and shrewd, except when he was drinking. He never went to any but the best places now, and he was never seen with Polish girls any more.

He was full of promises that he never kept, though as he told my mother of the washing machine or coat he was going to buy her, he meant his words sincerely. My mother would say, "He can talk himself into it and out of it just as fast." Despite her anger with him, in the early days, she would never allow us to speak against him. She and my brother believed in him better than he ever believed in himself. My father would come home with the tales that Tabby had told in bars, indignantly reporting, "Mame, you are now a graduate of Mount Holyoke and I went to Holy Cross." As the years went by, Harvard replaced Holy Cross. At first it was Tabby himself who had gone to college; but, as the drinks went down, he endowed his mother and father, in one casual sentence, with degrees.

I used to listen to him those Sunday afternoons when he talked of the people he met and his "in" among the lace-curtain Irish in Boston. I used to tire quickly of his talk, for it was not conversation but a monologue with the *I* of it most prominently featured. The Irish imagination, which had created my grandfather's fantasies, was now solely used for the creation of status. Unlike my grandfather and my uncles, he had no use for books. When

Eddie refused to go out with him on Sundays, Tabby would look contemptuously at the book Eddie was reading, "God, how can you stand that stuff? Milton, Shakespeare, they're all as dead as doornails. You'll never learn anything from those phonies."

My father would agree with him for once: "I tell you, Eddie, you'll ruin your mind with the stuff you're reading." Both my father and Tabby had the lace-curtain Irish distrust of the intellect set to any other purpose than the making of money.

The longer Tabby lived in Boston, the more lace-curtain he became. He joined the K. of C. That gave him a standing on Money Hole Hill he never had had before. He bought a set of golf clubs and practiced on Sunday mornings in the back yard, driving the golf balls up against the side of the house, until the constant thumping nearly drove us all crazy. But he became skillful at the game and was invited to play at the Country Club.

One weekend, he drove up for my brother Eddie and my mother and me to take us to Boston. It was the weekend of the Fourth, and I went rather reluctantly; I was afraid of Tabby's ugly drunken moods, moods that were occurring more and more frequently. He took us for Sunday dinner to the Parker House, explaining all during the meal how exclusive the place was until my mother flashed out at him: "Well, perhaps then I should be washing the dishes instead of eating from them. Perhaps that's what you think." He paid no attention to her. After dinner we went to the Public

Garden, and my mother and I went for a ride on the swan boats. Tabby went for a drink, Eddie reluctantly following him. We swished around the little pond, neither of us enjoying the ride for worrying over Tabby's disposition after the drinks; for we knew there would be more than one. When we got off, we sat on one of the benches waiting for them to return. I watched the pigeons mysteriously circling one another, hating their pompous chests and dignified gait. They lifted their feet and set them down the way a fat woman in shoes too tight for her lifts and sets her puffy feet down. They walked exactly like Aunt Josie.

My mother rose. "We'll go and see if we can find Eddie." Just as we walked over the bridge, we saw the two of them coming toward us. Tabby was drunk, but not yet drunk enough to forget about us entirely. We walked across Charles Street to the Boston Common. The Fourth of July speakers were on the platform. I could make out the uniforms of the American Legion. The loudspeakers were blaring. The mayor was speaking of the great heroes of the past wars "who had died to bring America freedom and equality." As we walked up the path toward the benches around the bandstand, the rhetorical voice followed us.

When we came near the benches, we saw the great crowd collected. In the center of the crowd was a Negro. He was standing there silently, leaning his hands on a black tightly furled umbrella. Tabby pushed forward to the center, saying in a loud voice, "What's he been up to?" A surly voice from the crowd spoke. "Damned

Nigger's been trying to tell us how to run our country.
We been telling him to shut his trap, or it's back to
Africa for him." Tabby shoved his face into the
Negro's. "Look, shine, we don't like Jews or Niggers
in Boston, see; so you'd better breeze, before you get
hurt!" The Negro never moved his hands. "I'm as
free as any of you. I have a right to speak, same right
as those men down there." He waved his hand in the
direction of the platform. The voice was still blaring,
winding up his speech with "We hold these truths to
be self-evident, that all men are created equal."

Tabby had the man by the collar when a great red-
faced policeman strode through the crowd. "What's
all this, now? What's all this?" When he saw the Negro,
he said, "Oh, so it's you again. If I run into you on my
beat again, I'll put you where you belong. I told you
before to keep that big mouth of yours shut." The
crowd laughed in triumph. Tabby said to the policeman, "You tell him, officer." The officer glowed. "He's
nothing but a troublemaker shouting about equality.
The trouble with these birds is they think that the
world owes them a living." He waved his club at the
Negro. "Now get out of here, and don't come back, or
I'll put you where you belong!" The Negro walked
down the path with dignity, the sullen eyes of the
crowd following him.

When Tabby came up to my mother, she looked at
him, on fire with anger. "And who do you think you
are to be pushing people around, I want to know?"
He said soothingly, "Oh, Ma, you don't understand

these things. We're having a lot of trouble in Boston
with Jews and Niggers." "And," my mother said contemptuously, "exactly who is 'we'?" Tabby looked at
her surprised. "The Irish, of course." My mother
glared at him. "You and all the rest of them are a great
tribute to the Irish, I can tell you that. If I had enough
strength in my right arm, I'd lay a clout on you that
would knock the bully out of you." She seized my hand
and left Tabby standing there. We took the train home.
Tabby didn't come home for six months.

When he did come home, he never mentioned the
incident. He told us then that he was trying to get into
Boston politics. My mother said, "You're welcome to
them. I guess it's where you belong all right." He never
said anything in front of my mother again, but when
she was not around he used to talk.

One Sunday, he appeared looking white and ill. My
mother put him to bed and called the doctor. He told
her that Tabby must stop drinking. "He's in bad
shape, Mrs. O'Connor. He'll be sick a long time. Perhaps he should go to the hospital. It will be a lot of
work for you." My mother said, "Let him be. I'll take
care of him." My mother assumed complete responsibility for him. He was in bed six months. She bought
cigarettes for him and the best of food. When anyone
protested, she would say, "He's my son" — that was all.

All during the early part of his illness he was quiet
and still, but as he got well the bluster reappeared in
his voice and he grew impatient with the family. He
used to protest when my mother would say, with bit-

terness, "Where are all those fine friends of yours? Not
one of them has come to see you." Tabby would answer, "Who the hell would want them to come to this
dump?" When he was well enough to go back to Boston,
my mother told him what the doctor had said. He
brushed her aside. "No one needs to tell me what to
do. I've been cooped up six months without a drink.
I saw you watching Eddie like a hawk for fear he'd
sneak one in. I'm going down right now and have one,
and to hell with you and your advice!"

In six months, Tabby was himself again with plenty
of "money and guff," as my mother called it. He had
another good job; the white linen suits and expensive
cigars appeared again. He was now "in" with the "big
shots" in Boston, politically "in." He was still selling
cars, but he would talk of running up to the State
House and visiting "the boys." He called all the state
senators by their first initials and talked of political
favors as though they were bonbons. "Look, Eddie, if
you want a good job, you come to Boston. I'll speak to
T. P. about you, and you'll be sitting on top of the
world."

With his rise to political favor, we noticed a change
in his attitude toward the Church. He had gone before,
ducking in and out before and after Communion, standing at the back of the church, one foot in the vestibule
and one foot in the aisle inside to insure attendance
at Mass. Now, though he still did not attend regularly,
he spoke of the power and influence of the Church.
He talked constantly of Father Coughlin and what a

brilliant mind he had, but he never dared to turn Coughlin's radio talks on in our house because of my mother. Though he had not an ounce of religion in him, he sprang furiously to the defense of the Church, using his fists on anyone who said a word against it. He bought *Social Justice* regularly every Sunday morning when it was distributed in front of the church.

He hated the Yankees, while he secretly envied them, and moved up to Beacon Hill so that he could give Pinckney Street for an address. My mother once said to him bitterly, "You'd be taking your hat off to the Haydens, too, if you met one on the street. For all your talk, you're just like the rest of them, wishing you'd been born on the Hill."

He had no love or respect for the Irish spirit or tradition and used to speak of my grandfather as "that crazy old coot," but what he did respect in the Irish was what he called being a "go-getter." He identified that spirit with being Irish, and could never see that the Irish were simply imitating the shrewd, successful Yankee businessman, whom they supposedly disliked. Nothing pleased him better than to tell of how an Irishman had beat a Yankee in business methods. He despised gentleness of any kind, identifying it with weakness. Eddie's dreaminess and idealism he indulged only because he had loved Eddie from childhood. Anyone else who was not exactly like Tabby, living according to his beliefs and way, he identified as "crackpot." He would talk personalities at the table until my mother would crack her palm on the table. "Enough!

They do you no harm. Sure, and you wouldn't understand the soul of any man unless it had a hundred-dollar bill plastered across it."

No one in our family had any realization of what was happening to Tabby. As time went by, he drank more and more, became more and more belligerent and more and more lost. I was sitting in the front room one Christmas Eve with nothing but the colored bulbs of the tree lighting the room. The whole room was filled with deep quiet. Sitting on the sofa, looking out into the crisp clearness of the night, I wondered alternately which was the star of Bethlehem and which large package under the tree was mine. The whole family was out, and I sat there on the couch with the warmth of the room shadowing me, watching the pattern of color that the lights reflected in the window. Suddenly I heard a car screech in front of the house. I knew it was Tabby before I heard the clatter of leather heels on the stairs. Instinctively, I ran and hid, for his footsteps were the loud, hard ones, those of the belligerent, drunken Tabby. I hid behind the red portière and watched him.

First he rattled around the house looking for someone to talk to. Finding no one, he flopped full length into the chair beside the tree. He lay there for a while. I looked at his tense, red face. The eyes were dilating. The peace and quiet of the room excited him into violence. He yanked at the lamp chain. The lamp did not light because it had been disconnected to make room for the cords of the tree lights. In a fury he reached behind the tree, pulling and tugging at the cords. He lurched and fell, the tree smashing full length on top of him. I could hear the shattering of the delicate birds of paradise that I had wrapped and unwrapped so carefully each year. He shoved the tree aside, staggered to his feet and pushed on the overhead light. He only glanced at the tree, carefully examining his hands for cuts. Brushing the broken bulb fragments from his clothes, he went out the door. I could hear the clatter of his heels down the stairs and the slam of the car door. He was gone. I came out and sat down in the middle of the room, surveying the scene. Everything was smashed and shattered; the peace, the quiet, the beauty, the warmth. When my mother and father came home, I was still there quietly contemplating the lost peace. All visions had fled in one flash of violence.

No one escaped Tabby's violence. He needed a victim every minute if he were to achieve his kind of happiness. When Eddie started playing his violin, he would turn on the noisiest music, partly to drown out Eddie's playing, partly to disturb Eddie, who was sensitive to the slightest coldness.

Whenever my other brothers went out with the girls, Tabby would spend his time ribbing the boys in a coarse way. Every Sunday we had at least twenty people to dinner at our table. We never knew a gloomy New England Sunday. There always was gaiety and laughter befitting a holiday. The company was usually made up of relatives and friends of my brothers, for there was a standing invitation at our house for all our friends.

One Sunday we were all seated at the table, behaving with great politeness, for my brother Michael, exactly sixteen, had brought his first girl to dinner. I remember how amused we all were at Michael's slicked hair and careful manners. They both sat at one end of the table: Michael, as shy himself, trying to ease her shyness by urging quantities of food on her. Tabby came in from Boston and with great show of good humor sat down at the table. He swallowed the conversation at the table in one gulp and started on the usual tale of his own prowess. He had just been promoted to sales manager, and every pore of him gleamed with success. The important people he had met dangled in his conversation like scalps around an Indian's belt. In the midst of this recital, he looked down the table and saw the new face. It was a pretty face, but that did not interest him. He waited only for the name, "Yvette!" He mouthed the name. "Yvette — Frog," he stated complacently and went back to his dinner. I remember sitting there feeling the slow burn of shame creeping over my face. There was no scene: Yvette never came back to our house; Michael never brought another girl home when Tabby was there.

The fights Tabby got into became more and more violent, and we all dreaded his visits more than ever. As time went by, he began to lose whatever standing his bragging and pocketbook had brought him. His stories became more puffed up then. As his position went down, his tales grew larger and more fabulous. He rubbed shoulders with all the great of his imagining. The mayor called him in, begging him to do some campaigning for him. "I was too busy," Tabby said casually. His violence grew as his status diminished. Hitherto he had kept most of his fighting for the bars. Now if any man made an innocent remark about the Irish, or criticized the Church, Tabby would spring at him, "So you don't like Irish Catholics." He always lost those fights, so he soon began to look for people to fight and win over. He turned on his family then, and I used to shake with fright when I heard him coming. The only person that he feared was my mother. After he had administered a few beatings at home, my mother took charge of the situation. She would hear him coming; all of us would be dispatched out of the room. Tabby would come roaring up the stairs, and she would meet him at the door. From the living room I would watch her facing him down. He would swing uneasily from one foot to the other while she looked at him. Her eyes penetrated the mist and fog of his drunkenness until, as though hypnotized, he would turn quietly, walk down the stairs and leave.

I used to weep for Eddie in those days because he was the one who felt most deeply what was happening to Tabby. He berated himself and everyone else for Tabby's faults, but he never blamed him. My mother, who had treated her brothers in whatever state gently and tenderly, had gradually become as cold as ice toward Tabby. Whatever her brothers had done, they had not been this kind of bully. Tabby stood before her as a violent antithesis to every principle that she

stood for. His attendance at church made her wild
with fury. "It's a wonder God doesn't strike him dead
for daring to set his foot in the door of any church." His
political principles she considered completely traitorous
to every one of her own. "He's sold himself out," she
said. But she never turned him out. "He is my son."
"He's a mystery to me," she would say, speaking her
thoughts aloud. "God knows I brought him up, fighting myself to keep that very devil that's in him out of
him." Sometimes I would catch her in the bedroom
looking at Tabby's picture with Eddie, shaking her head
and sighing; and when she wept in her bed at night,
I knew that her sorrow was over Tabby. But despite
all her sorrow, she never let Tabby win. Toward the
end, she would say, with an insight from the pain he
caused her: "The lost are the most pitiful. The lost
are the worst."

Tabby finally married, something my mother had
half-hoped for and half-hoped against. "I wouldn't
wish him on anybody," she would say bitterly, at the
same time hoping that some woman would marry him
"and straighten him out." Tabby did not marry a
strong woman. He married a shy, gentle girl, and he
loved her in his own way. For months after the marriage he did not drink. He still told stories and talked
the same, but he did not drink. Eddie, glowing, would
say, "You see, he's a good guy. He's all right. Just give
him a chance." Tabby was trying, and he had a sympathetic audience in his wife. He acquired a good job and
everything was serene. There was to be a child, the first

grandchild. My mother was delighted, and more than interested; but she never interfered with advice or visits. The child was the cause of Tabby's downfall. When you had a first child, you had to have a drink. When you had a first child, you had to brag about it, and finally you had to knock someone down to prove that your child was the best one ever born. "All very natural," my mother told him bitterly.

The child and wife interested him until the newness wore off. Then the old story began — drinking, bragging, fighting, accusations hurled at the wife "for trying to make a monkey out of him, for tying him down." Soon all his pay was being spent at bars "buying drinks for the boys." His wife never complained, but when my mother saw her, she interfered. She brought the baby and the wife to our house. I watched the wife come up the steps, her lips grim and her face gray with hunger. Slowly the story came out of sleepless nights of waiting, trembling, the beatings, not enough money to buy food, and her broken pride. My mother said brusquely, "Never mind your pride. Eat. You have nothing to be ashamed of, but I have. I produced him." She fed the wife with love and food until the grayness and grimness were gone. I, a little jealous, used to watch her rocking the baby and singing to it the songs she used to sing to me. The singing was now even more of a keen.

We all waited for Tabby to come. My mother never spoke of him, but I knew she was waiting too. I used to see her kneeling at night beside her bed, kneeling sometimes for hours, praying for what she called "guidance." Then she stopped. We all knew that she had decided what to do. She got a separation for the girl and legally adopted the child herself. Then Tabby appeared, full of savagery and indignation. My mother opened the door to him. He stood there undisturbed and undaunted this time. He started to bluster. "What the hell business have you got ——" That is as far as he got. She struck him full across the mouth. The mark of her fingers spread, sealing his mouth with red. "I am striking you for the blows you have struck. I have prayed God to keep me from the thing I am doing, but I know there is nothing else I can do, for if He cannot change you, can I? I will care for you when you are sick, I will bury you when you are dead, but from this moment on, you are no longer my son." She shut the door; he went out to the car. I could hear the voice of my brother Eddie weeping quietly in the corner. My mother turned to him, "Edmund," she said, "remember you are weeping for me as well." She went into her room. I crept into my brother Eddie's arms trying to quiet the terrible tears of a man.

Olagon! Olagon! Olagon!

I REMEMBER first the eyes of my brother Eddie, soft and
sad. I had been dreaming, and woke with the choking
fear of a child who sees in the darkness the terrifying
visions of his dreams filling the room. I remember the
familiar objects of the room, dreamily distorted into
forms and figures that moved menacingly from every
corner. In my half-waking, half-sleeping state, I moaned
softly for fear of letting the threatening figures know
I was there. As though from a great distance, I heard
footsteps coming down the long, dark hallway. Fearing
another horror, I screamed myself awake just as the
light went on and a pair of brown eyes looked down at
me. The face was indistinct, but the eyes were shining
and clear. I felt all my fear drain slowly out of me, as
the eyes drove away the devils of the dark. That was
my brother Eddie, whose love covered me like the
gentle wing of a bird.

Infantile paralysis left Eddie marked as only the af-
flicted are. It set him off from the other children and
left him alone. It was this loneliness that made him
turn to me. At first it was just the comfort of comfort-

189

ing me; but soon I became, without knowing it, a comforter myself. I shared with him the things he loved best, books and music. I was born on the note of his violin, and I grew up with Eddie forming that note into a melody. Every evening after supper he used to play the violin. I would slip out of the room, following down the long, dark hallway the notes of his music. I would slide quietly into the big leather rocking chair, sitting there in the dark parlor, rocking in and out of a world that existed only as long as a slender, pale boy drew his bow across the violin. The notes would rise singing and joyful, and I watched his long, slender fingers dancing up and down the strings. The notes would fall grave and quiet, and again I was seized with the loneliness and sadness that I felt the first time I heard the violin. On rainy days I would stand at the window, looking out into the dark, listening to the rain falling gently outside, accompanying the thin notes of the violin like a slow, steady dirge.

Eddie played for himself and the man who had written the music. He could not play for anyone else. He tried to play as though he had written the music. I watched him, the violin held firmly under his chin, his fingers skipping and steadying, and his face full of the joy of creation. It was when he was playing that his face came most alive. At other times it was a face that was covered with dreams. It was that face that appeared in his high-school picture, dreamy, sensitive, the lips almost trembling. The moment anyone else came into the parlor, Eddie would put the violin down and snap the case shut; and with that snap his face would take on its mask of abstraction.

Becoming a member of Eddie's world was not easy. He had carefully closed all the doors of communication between himself and the rest of the world. I had first to prove to him my desire for communication. I did this by a clumsy but ardent imitation of everything he did. Since he played the violin, I too must become an accomplished violin player. I used to take his violin into the bedroom when he was at school and, tucking the pillow under my chin, try to hold it as he did. The bow was too big and I could not reach the end of the violin, but I would patiently scratch away at it for a half-hour, not understanding why it was that no music ever came out. I did this for many weeks until my mother could bear with the noise no longer. One night at the supper table she said, "Edmund, Mary wants to learn to play the violin. Why don't you teach her? She's been scraping away at it by herself every day for two months." This episode opened the first door.

With great patience, Eddie started to teach me. He borrowed a small violin from his teacher and began. He would place my awkward fingers on the violin, showing me how to finger it properly. Trembling with eagerness, I would draw the bow awkwardly across the strings with a horrible scraping result. For months I struggled, playing scales in my room until the whole family was crazy with the sound of my practicing. Eddie finally asked me to stop. It was torture for him to hear me. He would turn my hands over in his, looking at them and saying: "I don't understand it. Your hands are made for playing, but you can't play." Then he started me on piano. That was as bad. I thumped with the ardor of a great pianist, but the result bore no similarity to the desire. Eddie consoled me by telling me that my inability to play was caused by not seeing well. "You'll have to be content with being a good listener, Mary," he would say. All my daydreaming was in vain.

When I was nine years old, Eddie gave me an opportunity to create in a different way. He bought me a set of pencils and several leather-bound notebooks and told me to write. I was much disturbed, I can remember, because I had nothing to say. I would sit for hours looking at the blank page, trying to think up something impressive enough to put down. I wanted desperately to say something profound and grown-up, but all I could think of was a statement I had heard. "The wings of a bird are covered with night." I put that down: I looked at it, trying to make something out of it; it stared back at me in all its black and white order. I turned it around, "Night covers the wings of a bird." Then like a flash the right way came to me. "The wings of a bird are covered with darkness," I wrote, very proud and pleased with myself. I took it to Eddie, apologizing, "Of course, I know it's not true." Eddie laughed without unkindness. "It's perfectly all right, Mary. In the world of imagination, anything can happen. I don't mean you to write for me. Write for yourself. Put down anything you think, feel, or see." We went to his room. He showed me then his own notebooks. As I sat in the middle of the bed listening to him read, I could hear the pigeons in the eaves rustling and cooing softly. He read: "Do right, be right, see right, think right, and say what is right, not because someone tells you to, but because only by the road of righteousness can you be happy." I did not understand a thing he was saying, but I was as impressed as he was with his own words. He went on: "He that loves much, much is forgiven unto him. To love greatly is to be great." "This is Latin," he said, reciting, with what I thought a much more beautiful pronunciation than any that I had heard in church, "*Timeo Danaos et dona ferentes.*"

This was the beginning of my intellectual education by my brother Eddie. I was nine. He was nineteen. Everything he wrote he read to me, though it was years before I understood what he wrote. When he discovered that there was a desire in me similar to his own, he began to foster it. I, who had never been able to read much because of my eyes, began to feel a tremendous longing to read, because of the great learning Eddie had from books. I knew Eddie obtained his books from the library because I used to walk down to the corner to meet him coming home from there carrying his weekly supply. Wanting to be like him in every respect, I set off one day to find the library. It was a long walk, and I, terrified of the strange streets and people, felt millions of miles from home. Finally a man showed me the way. I looked at the huge stone building, feeling the weight of it breaking down my last bit of courage.

I walked into the main library and was directed downstairs to the children's room.

By this time I was so confused that I desired only one thing — escape and that as quickly as possible. I seized the first book I could lay my hands on and started out the door. A shrill, sharp voice called, "Little girl, exactly where do you think you are going with that book?" In the hushed quiet of the library the voice sounded like the trumpet of doom. I had to take the book now. Miserably, I did all the things directed, filling out cards, signing statements, thinking all the time of Eddie doing the same thing. When I finally escaped with the solemn injunction, "Due in ten days," ringing without any meaning at all in my ears, pride began to replace fear; and I found my way home on the strength of that pride. I was sitting in a corner on the porch, still trying to fathom the mysteries of *Water Babies,* when Eddie came home from work. I was in tears over it, for I could not believe that a book from his library could be so disappointing. He took the book from me and said, "I will get books for you, Mary, if you want to read and if the doctor says you can." He was really pleased and proud of me, and I heard him saying to my mother, "Imagine going way down there by herself after a book."

Some evenings Eddie read aloud to me, and lying on the couch, crunching on peanut brittle, I would watch him as he read, his face changing with the meaning of the words. The lamp on the dining-room table would cast a half-shadow on his face; and as he read, I studied his face, marked with shadows that no lamp cast.

As I grew older, I became Eddie's constant companion, going everywhere with him. We would go out in the evening together, walking and talking. He did not hesitate to speak of anything before me. He would drink beer and I would listen, wide-eyed, to his talk. He was no longer a Catholic. My father called him an "atheist," and would point to the books, saying, "That's the cause of it, too." I used to shudder at the word, feeling with all the strength of my being that God would strike Eddie dead, remembering the priest's violent denunciation of "godless atheists." Eddie could not be one. Such people existed only in some remote place where prehistoric animals existed.

But Eddie was one. I remember sitting in Bill Zucchini's smelling the musky odor of fruit, sipping the sweet taste of the soda, trying not to choke in my fear at Eddie's words: "There is no God." For weeks I kept silent before his tirades, but one night I got up enough courage to ask him, "How do you know there is no God?" He explained at length to me and then said, "How do you know there is a God?" I looked at him, shocked and startled. That had never occurred to me. I sat there quiet, silently saying Our Fathers and Hail Marys as rapidly as I could for my own and Eddie's salvation. I could hear the ceiling cracking as Eddie talked.

At ten o'clock I said weakly, "I think we should go home, Eddie." He looked at me, saw the fear and pain in my eyes. "I'm sorry, Mary, truly I am. I thought you would understand." I shook my head. I lit candles for him every time I went to church, but Eddie never came back to Catholicism. After that, though he still talked freely, and though he still brought home books to me, he was careful of what he taught me. My mother would tell him sharply at times, "Don't push the child beyond her understanding. You're making an old woman out of her, Edmund."

One evening we went out canoeing on Hampden Pond. It was a great lark, for I had never before been in a canoe, nor at Hampden Pond. The small pond seemed like the ocean, and we, sitting in the center of it, contemplating the universe. The sky was clear and starred. Eddie let the canoe drift while he studied the sky. I was searching for a word to describe what I was feeling when Eddie spoke. "It is a fearful thing to contemplate infinity." I looked at him. He went on, "Beyond all is infinity, the only thing that really exists." "Is God infinity, Eddie?" I asked.

He answered quickly: "No. God is the puny name that man has given the infinity he does not understand. Once the moon was God, then the sun, now infinity. What is all that but naming the unknown and then, in the excitement of finding a name, thinking you are a great fellow, so God must be like you: a fine fellow, with a small brain and a lot of nonsense in it, a fine fellow made in the image of yourself." He said bitterly, "I could think up a better God."

I never said a word, too fearful of this blasphemy

in a small canoe, in the midst of the ocean, with the eye of infinity staring down at us.

I tried to shift the subject. Eddie did it for me. "Einstein is a real God, one who can draw a circle around the universe!"

I knew the name, a name, in my mind, attached to a fabulous person, a person who had done something no one else could understand. I knew he was great, and I coupled him with the great men our schoolteachers always talked of.

"Isn't he something like Henry Ford?" I asked tentatively.

Eddie just laughed. "What is Henry Ford? — a man with lots of money. That's no criterion for greatness. Henry Ford understands Fords, Einstein understands the universe."

He launched then into a discussion of Einstein's theories. I understood very little of what he said. I sat there, the canoe rocking gently, listening to my brother Eddie's voice weaving in and out of infinity, and wondering how the light of a star could curve and carve such a beautiful path to this world.

Eddie had great difficulty with my father, who never understood what Eddie was doing. My father looked suspiciously at every book and every friend that Eddie brought home. When Eddie refused to play the violin any longer, my father moaned about the money he had wasted on his musical education. Eddie gave up the violin because he felt he could not play it well enough. Everything he did he wanted done perfectly. He still played for me occasionally, but he refused ever to appear in public again. My mother understood Eddie best of all, and she was completely undisturbed by his books or his friends. What she feared was his desire for solitude. She used to urge him to go out, but Eddie had no desire to go. He preferred staying at home with my mother and me. We used to sit around the dining-room table, the three of us, and talk, Eddie urging my mother to tell her stories and sing to us. Those were peaceful evenings.

What pained my mother most of all was that there was not enough money to send Eddie to school. All his teachers, everyone who knew him, said he was brilliant and should have training; but there was no money. Instead Eddie had to go to work as a clerk in the City Yards. Every Friday evening he came home with his pay envelope unopened and handed it to my mother. I knew my mother's pain at having to take it, but it was an absolute necessity if we were to be housed and fed. Eddie became one of the main supports of the family. "He is being sacrificed like the first-born of every Irish family," my mother used to say, sacrificed as she too had been sacrificed.

None of this had made Eddie bitter; he used to shrug his shoulders and say nothing when my mother sorrowed. Instead, he tried to educate himself. He had a book list, obtained from one of the boys who had gone to college. He read with avidity through the whole list. His dreams of being a mathematician gave way before other dreams, none of which reached fruition. I used to watch him sitting in the living room, his leg slung over the arm of his chair, chewing his fingernails in his excitement over some new idea he had discovered in the book he was reading. But in leading his family's life, Eddie began more and more to have no time for his own. When the lay-offs at the mill turned into permanent lay-offs, Eddie took on complete responsibility for the family.

One day my mother came home very much excited. There were to be Civil Service examinations for a fine job at the library. It was exactly suited to Eddie. He would be ordering books for the library and doing other work there. My mother was not very clear about the job. She had heard of it from Mrs. Fogarty; and since it had to do with books, in her mind it was perfectly suited to Eddie. "Doesn't he know more about books than anyone on the Hill?" We all agreed. Eddie was secretly excited, too. He hated the work he was doing, "pushing a pencil" all day. He took the examination, came out the highest on the list, but was not given the job. The head of the Board of Aldermen had a brother. My mother was told that Eddie didn't have the right connections. "Connections!" she shouted. "Connections! I thought it was brains you were looking for." It was the same with everything Eddie tried for. My mother swallowed her pride and went begging among the lace-curtain Irish to establish the proper connections for Eddie, but they never connected. "Wasting himself, that's what it is," my mother would say bitterly. She fought long and hard for him. When she could not make the proper political connections, she fell back on religion.

My father had been out of work two years; my brother Eddie was the sole support of the family. A mission had just been started at the Saint Jerome's Church. My mother and I made the mission for the intention of both Eddie and my father. I prayed that my father would get a job so that Eddie could be released to live his own life. My mother prayed for Eddie's freedom, which was tantamount to praying for a job for my father. She also prayed that Eddie would find a position more suitable for him. She prayed for a recognition that he had not received thus far.

We would start out at six-thirty every evening for the church in Irish Parish. As we approached the church, I could see the scenes in the stained-glass windows, illuminated from inside: Christ preaching the Sermon on the Mount, a long, lean figure with one finger pointing to heaven. When we arrived, the church would be filled with women praying for jobs for husbands and sons. It was right in the middle of the depression; the mission was more than well attended.

At seven o'clock promptly the service began. Everyone in the church rose and sang, a thing that was unusual and most exciting. I could hear the voice of one of my mother's friends, pitching and tossing from one key to another, high above the rest. After the song, with a great rustling noise the congregation settled on its knees; then the priest began the litany. It was the litany to the Blessed Virgin. "Queen of Heaven," the

priest began. The people answered, "Pray for us."
"Star of the sea." "Pray for us." "Tower of Ivory . . .
House of Gold," on and on, my imagination leaping
from one visual image to another. My mother had
had a great struggle with her conscience over asking
God and the Saints for something as materialistic as a
job, but had settled the problem by saying, "If you
don't eat, you can't pray." I looked at her during the
litany; she was completely absorbed in the beauty of the
prayer.

When the litany was over, the visiting priest came out
of the vestry, genuflected before the altar, and ascended
the pulpit. I did not listen to the sermon; and unlike
my mother, who was quietly saying the Rosary, I did
not pray. I became absorbed in a study of the church,
which I did not know as well as my own. It was the
church where my mother had been baptized and con-
firmed. The plaster saints, ablaze with color, fascinated
me. On one side of the altar was Saint Patrick with his
gilded miter and brilliant green robes. In his hand he
carried a staff topped by the green shamrock. Under his
foot was the snake he had driven from Ireland. On the
other side of the altar was Saint Jerome robed in the
brown habit of the monk. He was looking down at the
Christ-Child in his arms.

When the Passion father ended his sermon, he
reached into the box where the people had dropped
their petitions. There were petitions for a holy death
and petitions for an easy birth. There were petitions to
cure drunken husbands and wayward sons, but the

greatest number of all were petitions for employment. After the mission had been going for a few days, there were many small slips of paper glorifying God for jobs received. Oh, how I prayed that my mother and I would be dropping one of those in! I could see Eddie's face when he learned that God had created a job especially for him. "Then surely he would believe," I would think. Exalting over this daydream, I would rise at the end of the service and sing with the rest as loudly as I could:

> Holy God, we praise Thy name.
> Lord of all, we bow before Thee . . .
> Infinite Thy vast domain,
> Everlasting is Thy reign.

My mother and I would walk home silently, both of us full of the conviction that before we got home both Eddie and my father would be well taken care of by divine intervention. My father did get a job, but it lasted only two weeks. Eddie went on "pushing his pencil," adding up figures on the cost of cement.

One night Eddie came home and said quietly: "It's all up now. I'm through at the Yards this week. They're economizing." The last was said bitterly.

We were sitting at the table and Eddie stared at his plate after the announcement. There was no need to expand. We all knew what it meant. This was the last thing that could happen. I did not dare look at my mother. We all finished our dinners silently and retreated, leaving her in the kitchen by herself. The sound of her dishwashing was the only noise in the house. At first it was quiet, then it grew louder and louder. When the loud, deliberate rattling of pans was more than Eddie could bear, he got up and went into the kitchen. I followed him and took up a towel and began drying the dishes. My mother was raging against something she could not formulate. Eddie tried to talk to her. She remained silent. After the dishes were done, she put on her hat and coat and went out, never saying why or where she was going.

We all sat in the living room trying to avoid talk. Eddie and I immersed ourselves in books we did not read. Michael twiddled nervously with the radio. Only my father sat glumly, making no pretense, staring into blank space. I watched Eddie's face from behind my book. It was no longer the face of the young, dreamy Eddie. It had a bony look about it and the mouth was a straight hard line. It was the first time I had seen anything cruel in that face. About ten-thirty my mother returned. She came into the living room and said, "You'll go to work tomorrow, Edmund, at the city employment office. It's a clerk's job, seeing the unemployed and filling out blanks on them. God knows it's no better than the last one, but it's something, anyway." With this plain statement of fact she left the room without further explanation. Eddie went to work the next morning. It was only months later we learned that she had gone to the biggest of the lace-curtain Irish politicians and almost by force obtained the job for Eddie. In later days it became an amusing tale, but that night my mother saw no humor in it.

The job was a miserable one. All day long the unemployed formed a line before Eddie's desk, waiting patiently and impatiently to be interviewed. Eddie would come home the first weeks with no spirit left in him. "Just a long procession of woe," he would tell my mother. As the months went by and the unemployed mounted, Eddie became more and more violent in his response. The women would come in begging W.P.A. work for their husbands. "My God!" Eddie would say, "it's bad enough to see the men broken down by this, but when the women begin to come bringing their kids to prove how desperate they are, I could go out back and cut my throat." My mother tried to console him, but her efforts were feeble. She suffered through every case he recounted just as he did.

It was during this time that Eddie fought most violently with my father over politics. Eddie grew more and more antagonistic to the moneyed Hill. He had never before felt any personal bitterness. Now he talked of the mill owners in a way that made my father leave the table, muttering to himself the old cry that he knew all those books would never come to any good. Eddie would shout after him, "Just come down to that place for one day and see what has happened to those people who depended on your fine, upright Haydens for a living." Even my mother, who had always been vocal about the Hill and all its injustices, found herself restraining Eddie. Most bitterly of all, he began denouncing the Irish on the Hill. His denunciation was bitterest of all against "the dirty politics of the cheap

Irish politicians living respectably on top of the heap through lying and deceit. You don't find them pushing pencils, listening to tales of woe all day. No, they sit in their offices and arrange things for the unemployed, getting rid of petitioners, people they've known all their lives by sending them with a useless note to us, asking us to do all we can for them, knowing full well there's nothing we can do, hoping to keep votes with that easy trick."

My mother worried over Eddie. He could neither eat nor sleep, and at night I used to hear him prowling restlessly around the house. One night I heard my mother talking to him, trying to find out what was the matter.

His answer was violent. "I tell you I can't sleep. I spend all night trying to figure out what is causing all this. I can see those people all night waiting desperately to be heard. It's the injustice I can't stand and the despair. I tell you, Ma, that I look at those people all day and then come home and see Pa sitting in that chair by the window. It's the same thing all over again, desperation and despair; and why? — that's what I want to know."

My mother said quietly, "You'll never find out this way, Edmund. There's no answer that can be found in rage."

His answer was still violent: "What else can you do but rage when you find yourself caught like a rat with no way out of the trap?"

"Well, Edmund, we're all trapped. In the act of

being born, we are caught, but there's a way out of this trap. I know that better than you do. There's no trap that can hold you so long as you have courage. There's only one thing that can cage you, and that's yourself, with your mind creating locks no keys will fit. It is then you have to fear. I've tried to bring you up to see that, Edmund. None of this matters. You can be hungry and cold and have not a stitch to cover you, and you'll mind it all right. You'll feel the bitterness of the chill, cold wind and the pain of hunger in your belly and the shame of it all, and you'll cry out against it all; but there's nothing to that when you are seeing it all with a spirit that has windows that sees beyond it. I tell you, Edmund, I've seen far worse than this in the warped spirits of those who are trapped and tortured by their own minds. You forget too easily what you have seen. Go to bed, Edmund, and remember your grandfather, who saw worse things, things that you, I pray, will never see, and still kept always before him the hope that his own would learn the truth of his hope. The war that goes on in you can have only one result if you are the child of my vision. You will learn through hate that you can live only through love."

Eddie listened, but he did not learn. Gradually the cruel lines about his mouth deepened. He no longer played the violin or read in the evening. We soon began to fear his coming home as in the earlier days we had feared my father's arrival. I would hear him coming up the stairs and go into my own room. I used to eat with my mother after the others had finished, for I could not

bear the silent dinner table. Where before there had
been wit and wisdom, now there were only Eddie's
constant complaints. Up until this time he had not
attacked my mother, but now he was as violent against
her as he was against my father. The slow hatred began
first with the people he saw at the employment office.
He used to tell us how he would go to the houses in
Irish Parish to investigate their claims, prowling around
their houses to see if they had hidden any luxuries —
opening iceboxes to make sure they had as little food
as they claimed, refusing to give employment to anyone
whom he found in John the Harp's having a glass of beer.
There was no more suffering or sympathy for them.
They were lazy buggers trying to put anything they
could over on him. He took special delight in telling
how he trapped them when they tried to get an extra
week's work by lying. Soon people we had known all
our lives began complaining to my mother about
Eddie's behavior, asking her to intercede for them. All
who had known the old Eddie were shocked by the
change. Jerry Hogan told my mother that he was worse
than any snooping Black and Tanner that he'd ever
known. "It's the God's truth, Mamie, you've reared a
son with the heart of a black and bloody Englishman."

My mother finally decided to speak about what she'd
been hearing. Eddie came home one Friday evening
with a black look on his face. I watched my mother at
the stove serving his food. He began to complain about
the "stinking fish," a food he detested. "Why in hell
do I have to eat this stuff? Here I am the only one in

the house bringing in money and I get this shoved into my face. I tell you I'll bring home meat for myself and cook it myself next Friday — you and your damned Catholicism and your prayers to a God that has no ears."

My mother interrupted. "I've never fought with you over your beliefs, Edmund. You had the choice open to you. I never interfered with your leaving the Church. It was your own will. But there will be no attacks on what anyone in this house believes. Is that clear to you, or am I having to tell my own son that he's acting the part of a jackass? What makes you think a bit of money gives you the right to act the tyrant in this house, filling it with a meanness and cruelty that is driving all the good from it? Take it all and go join with those on the Hill. It's there you belong with your coldness and cruelty."

My mother's outburst made Eddie worse than before. We were spared none of his resentment. Every mouthful any of us ate had the look of stealing from his pockets. My mother refused his money and instead began going to the W.P.A. with a wagon for beans and flour, but Eddie insisted on giving her his envelope.

One evening Eddie brought home a friend, a man named Kirkpatrick whom he had just met. He was a tall, shuffling fellow with sandy hair and face. I disliked him at once, for I was feeling more and more painfully my isolation from my brother Eddie. The face of this man was, as my mother remarked later, "like a fish," with loose, full lips and drooping eyes. He was very amiable, making good conversation with my mother

and father, telling witty stories, flashing out with sharp
barbs. His whole quality was brilliantly negative.
Later, I sat on the porch with him and Eddie listening
to him discourse on philosophers and writers whose
names meant nothing to me. Eddie was listening carefully, noting names that he should read. There was
something in the caustic way of the man that made me
think of an animal licking its wounds. I watched him
shifting nervously about in his seat, using his hands to
dramatize what he was saying. Soon his restlessness became obvious to Eddie and they both went downtown to
Kirkpatrick's room.

My mother was disturbed by Billy Kirkpatrick, and
after they left she asked me what he had been telling
Eddie. I could not reproduce the conversation, but I
remembered its carefully restrained savagery. That
night Eddie came home drunk for the first time in his
life, and I heard my mother helping him up the stairs.
Every night after that, I would lie waiting for the
dreadful stumbling return of Eddie. One night I got up
about eleven and went into the living room and found
my mother sitting there in the dark waiting for him.
She had done this ever since the drinking began, and
I knew that the disintegration of the child, who was the
flower of her vision, was killing her hope. She never
said a word to him — she had ceased fighting with him,
realizing somehow that this was something that could
not be fought with words. Late at night, I would be
startled out of my sleep by her incomprehensible moaning and mourning cries that could not be put into the

words of the day. Shivering with the terror of those cries, I would slip into bed beside her, trying to comfort her so that the ceaseless moaning of her sleep would end.

Eddie was never violent or boisterous in his drinking. He was what was much worse, grim and silent. Kirkpatrick soon became a fixed member of our household, eating and sleeping there. My father hated him intensely and would go out whenever Kirkpatrick stayed. There was, for all his sinister quality, a great charm about the man; and though his verbal brilliance did not dazzle my mother, I could see why Eddie had taken to him.

He talked a great deal about the Irish in a biting, witty way. His attitude toward them was mixed. At one moment he would twist his stories so that they appeared like the stage Irishman of the vaudeville show; at another moment he would be off on a long tirade against the English and the need for a strong Irish nationalism. I used to listen to his running verbal battle with my mother, who was fighting this man tooth and nail to save her son.

"Now, Mrs. O'Connor, you take Pat and Mike and look at them squarely, two good-natured, dumb Harps willing to shift from one to another depending on who has the price of a drink — stupid, clumsy, carefree louts. The Parish is full of them. 'Books did you say, Mr. Kirkpatrick? It's not books that's troubling me, but where is the price of me next drink is what I'm thinking hard on!' They'd sell the *Book of Kells* for two good slugs of John Jameson's whiskey."

My mother never answered him in his own terms, but would take another line. "I'm certain you're seeing the thing squarely, Mr. Kirkpatrick, distorting none of the facts. But what I'd like to know is, is it Pat and Mike you're talking of or yourself?"

Mr. Kirkpatrick would smile slyly at her. "Well, to tell you the truth, I'd make a better bargain than that, Mrs. O'Connor. It's true what I say. It's the way the Parish is now, full of drunken loafers living on relief. You're living in a dream world like that misty poet dreaming of 'a romantic Ireland that's dead and gone,' seeing it all by the light of the moon. There's no more Johnny O'Sullivans in the Parish. They're all up on the Hill, kissing the boots that kicked them for the sake of a dollar and a calling card. The ones below there aren't smart enough to make the Hill, that's all."

"And what about yourself? I can't see that you're flourishing."

"Oh, I'm just a spectator of the great Irish *débâcle*, that's all. As long as I have a drink under my belt, even I can stand Pat and Mike."

"And what would you do with Pat and Mike, Mr. Kirkpatrick, and with Mr. Pat and Mr. Mike that's on the Hill? Roast one to feed the other? Or would you be as you are now sitting in Kerry Park, forever gazing at the water as it goes over the dam, and using the sharp side of your tongue as you watch it go? You're like the man forever watching someone else digging the ditch — no use to the man digging, no use to the other spectators, and no use to yourself. A sharp tongue should have a sharp purpose."

"Oh, now, Mrs. O'Connor, I could have a purpose. I could be their jub-jub boy leading the parade on Saint Patrick's Day and a fine golliwog it would be, plastering the shamrock on every barnside in the United States. Oh, and they'd follow me, too, from the Parish and the Hill like they follow any priest or politician that is willing to pipe them over the top of the dam. There's power in their numbers and their constant begetting. They'd follow the leader, all right, to the top of the world and jump off, so long as he went first. I've been telling Eddie over and over what easy game they are. He could lead them — even I could if I hadn't cohabited with so many whores."

Even Eddie recognized the savagery of the man, but he went on seeing him and reading the books he recommended. He no longer read to learn, but to verify his conviction that Billy Kirkpatrick was right.

My mother spoke to Eddie for the first time, telling him that she thought the man vicious and vain.

Eddie turned on her furiously. "Call him what you like, but he's got more brains in him than the whole stupid gang in this house."

"That may be," my mother answered, "but that brain is twisted, and you will know it one day. To your own sorrow you'll find following the leader is not a game. At any rate, do not bring him here again, for I cannot bear to see my son listening to a man who talks out of a pit of bitterness the like of his. I warn you bring him here no more, for I cannot sit by and watch the poison of him spreading through you."

Eddie flung out the door. "If he's not welcome here, neither am I."

Eddie came home that night and in a drunken stupor packed his clothes. My mother did not go out to him, but I, who had spent the night weeping in the dark of my room, went out and asked him, trembling with intensity, not to leave us. In tears I could not say all the things I had planned, but could only repeat over and over between my sobs, "Remember, Eddie, remember!"

As an answer he flung me violently into the corner of the room, mocking me. "Remember, Eddie, remember! And what have I got to remember but the whole stupid lot of you hanging around my neck since I was seventeen, dragging me down to your own stupid level! Remember, remember! I'll remember that all right."

My mother stood in the doorway listening to him. She spoke quietly: "And you'll remember, Edmund O'Connor, a woman who had two sons who left her in violence and with nothing in the solitude of the dark night to remember but their violence. It is the same with both of you. You are now at one with Tabby. Creators of rage and a hate that I pray God will destroy you before it destroys others."

As the sound of Eddie's steps receded in the dark street, my mother wept, rocking back and forth in her woe.

The following week we moved. It was May, and I went out for the last time to sit under the lilac tree that grew by the side of the house. The air was filled with their odor. I picked one, burying my face in its color, trying to blot out everything that had happened since the first day I had smelled them. But the sound of the movers, reminding me of change, filled my ears with the awareness that the past and the present cannot exist together. I rose and went into the half-empty house staring down the long, dark hallway at a past that was changed, utterly changed by the present.

We moved to School Street, which was the boundary street between the fringes of the Hill and the Parish. My father went back to the mill, doing odd jobs, earning enough to keep us from complete want. My brother Michael was the only untroubled person in the house, making new friends, investigating the new neighborhood. I spent most of my time in the house reading and brooding, antagonistic to a place that I had not lived in before, longing to go back to the home whose every sound was familiar. I used to walk up there at night by the old tenement trying to look in the windows and see what strangers had taken it over.

The move back even to the fringes of the Parish was no triumph for my mother. Tabby and Eddie were gone. My grandfather was gone. The O'Sullivan boys were gone. There was no return to what had been. We had lived on the Hill. My father no longer talked about it. He drew the curtain. His retreat was complete. In the Parish the faces I had known as a child no longer existed. Strangers replaced them. Only my mother remained as a symbol of what might have been. But even she had changed. She laughed seldom, she sang no more, but what was worst of all, she never mentioned the past nor the people who had created it. She never spoke of her father or her two sons. She never looked over the walls of the present. In the evening I would watch her sitting in the kitchen reading the paper, but neither birth nor death interested her now.

I used to meet my brother Eddie walking with Billy Kirkpatrick. He never stopped or spoke. My father used to see him in John the Harp's drinking. We knew that he had lost his job and was living with Billy Kirkpatrick.

One evening during the first winter in the new house, I was overcome by the loneliness I felt for the past. When I could bear it no longer, I went out, determined to find Eddie and bring him home. I took my sled and told my mother I was going sliding for a while. It was only six-thirty, but the streets were already dark, lit only by the feeble glow of the scattered street lights. The runners of the sled I pulled behind me made no sound in the snow; only my own footsteps echoed in the empty streets. I went down into the Parish, for I knew the old wooden boarding house where Billy Kirkpatrick lived. It was behind the playground set back from the street and surrounded by high bushes. I left my sled out on the street tilted up against the bushes and went up the path quickly. I was frightened by the dark, sinister-looking path, but having come this far, I was determined not to give up. Instinctively, I tiptoed into the house and up the stairs of the dark hallway. At the top of the staircase was a door with a light shining under it, and I could hear voices of men talking. I hesitated on each step carefully, trying to eliminate the creaking by creeping slowly from one to the other.

When I reached the top, I could distinguish Billy Kirkpatrick's voice and was about to knock when I heard a loud harsh voice surging out into the dark hall.

"I've told you, Eddie, ever since we were kids what a damn fool you were. Never able to fight — always letting the other guy beat you. Christ Almighty, you've got to use your fists if you want to get anywhere in this world. They're all out to get you first, you've got to be too fast for them."

Billy Kirkpatrick's slow, drawling voice interrupted. "Brains, not fists, Tabby. You'll get nowhere with your fists."

"What do you mean get nowhere! Look at me! I'm on top, seventy-five bucks a week, a car, plenty of clothes, and why? Because I know how to fight, by God. If you scare people, you can get anywhere. Make 'em so damned scared, they're afraid to say no. Sure, you've got to have a good line, too, but you've got to have a good strong fist behind it. I wouldn't have this job if the boys in Boston thought I was a lily, I can tell you that."

I heard Eddie's voice quietly ask, "What are you doing, now?"

"Oh, odds and ends, odds and end, working for some of the political big shots. Plenty to eat, plenty to drink — no worries — no one around to nag me the way Ma did. I'm doing better than I ever did in my life. . . . Jesus Christ, you can't even drink, Eddie. Look at him;

he's as white as a ghost. I'll bet you puke after the next one."

Billy laughed, "He will."

"Eddie was always the lily of the family," Tabby went on. "The rest of us would be out playing baseball and he'd be home tuning up on that damn violin, sawing away on it with a moony expression on his face. All the old ladies liked him, and my mother, God Almighty, he was tied to her apronstrings from the day he was born — even went out with girls who looked like her. You know he wouldn't even shoot craps with the rest of us for fear he'd hurt her feelings. Some sweet return you got for playing nursemaid to the bunch of us."

Eddie said nothing, but Billy Kirkpatrick spoke again dryly. "Well, he's out of that now, but he still wants to be a good boy." I could hear Eddie retching out the window. "Why don't you get him a job in Boston, Tabby? Get him out of this stinking town. I can't take him anywhere but what he's running into that family of yours, and feeling guilty. I've tried to get him to go into local politics, but he's too scared of what your mother would think. God, what a hellion she must have been to get such a hold on her kids."

"Hellion is right," Tabby answered. "I've still got a scar in my back where she stuck a fork in me. She's an old witch, with her songs and stories, scaring the daylights out of her kids. Her old man was as bad. Holding their heads in the air without a dime in their pockets."

Billy Kirkpatrick's voice, still indifferent, asked, "Are you still a Coughlinite, Tabby?"

"Sure I am. There's a smart man for you."

"Yes," said Billy softly, "a man with brains. Knows what the Irish need is a leader. He'll lead them a fine dance, and one day they'll all go up in a puff and Eddie here will be fiddling for them. Yes, a smart man, though a priest. We'll have to join his group, Eddie," he said ironically; "then we'll be filled with the wild glow of purpose. A fine thing for a man." Then he laughed. "With Tabby's fists and Eddie's brains and a keg of whiskey to keep both of you from collapsing, we could go far. But that keg of whiskey would be essential, for neither of you bastards have any guts without it." His tone had changed now completely. He was speaking with slow savagery. "Look at you — two of a kind — fine typical Irishmen! God, you disgust me! Get out of here, both of you, braggart and coward, two sides of the same coin. Get out! You remind me too much of myself."

Tabby's voice, filled with fury, rose. "You son of a bitch, be careful how you talk to me! I'll knock your head off."

Then, I heard Eddie's voice, sobbing with fury, rising hysterically. "I'm not like you! I'm not like you! I'm not like either of you!" The door opened, and I saw Eddie standing over Billy Kirkpatrick, striking him violently, shouting, "I may be a fool, a great fool, but I am not like you." Tabby was trying to restrain him, and he turned on him with equal fury, shouting, I'm not Tabby! I'm not Tabby!"

I, crouched in the dark corner, was trembling with the increasing violence of the scene.

Suddenly a door opened below, and a woman shouted up the stairs. "You drunken bums, get out of here or I'll call the police!"

Before she had ceased speaking, I saw Eddie flash out the door and down the stairs. The other two began fighting each other. I rushed wildly after Eddie. He was gone when I reached the street. I took my sled and hauling it began slowly to walk through the dark streets, too paralyzed to be frightened. Before me was the blackness of the night; behind me, as before, only the echo of my own footsteps.

When I got home, the house was dark. I undressed quickly and went to bed, trying to warm myself so that the trembling would stop. I could not sleep, but heard my brother Michael come in and rummage in the pantry before he went to bed. Later, my mother and father came home. I could hear their voices, and heard my father shaking the stove and banking the fire for the night. I closed my eyes when my mother came in to see if I were covered. I was still cold, but the trembling had ceased. I was somewhat comforted now by the presence of the others in the house. When all was quiet, I heard the City Hall clock slowly striking twelve and on the last note the front door opened. Someone had come in and had gone into the parlor. I was too scared to move, but lay there waiting for the choking fear to subside, trying to form words to call my mother. Suddenly the deep silence of the house was broken by the familiar snap of the violin case.

I dreamed a dream that night, and I was outside the kitchen window of my childhood home. The rain was cold and chilling. Inside, the room was warm. I tried to feel the fire and hear the teakettle. Everyone was there: my grandfather, my mother, my father, my brothers, my uncles, and many red-faced people, prosperous and fat. Even outside, I could hear the stamping and shouting. The din was unbearable: a phonograph was blaring loudly; my brother Tabby was singing a brash accompaniment to it, encouraged by Billy Kirkpatrick, "Don't tread on the tail of me coat! ha! ha! Don't tread on the tail of me coat!" With each "ha! ha!" the red-faced people stamped collectively and raised their glasses high in the air. It was a horrible, unmelodious song, and the spirit behind it was vicious and violent.

Over in one corner I saw my brother Eddie, standing, his violin under his arm, biting his lips with tension. As the din increased, the figures of my mother and my grandfather rose and with slow, sad step went down the long, dark hallway. No one noticed their departure. I called to them, but they never looked back.

Tabby was tugging at my brother Eddie, trying to pull him to the center of the room. He resisted violently. Billy Kirkpatrick was smiling ironically at Eddie. It was then Eddie noticed that my mother and my grandfather had gone. He looked solemnly after them, and raised his violin to his chin. "Give us something Irish," Tabby called. "Let's have 'Brannigan's Pup.' Make it loud."

Eddie looked at him and quietly drew the bow across

his violin. The music was thin and sweet — everything was very quiet. It was a dirge, a lamentation for the dear dead men. It rose and filled the room with the passion of grief. I put my head down on the cold stone window sill and wept. In my ears, in answer to the violin, I could hear the long lamentation of the dead for the living. *Olagon! Olagon! Olagon!* I turned and walked away from the window and on my face I could feel the chill, cold wind blowing from the north.

Afterword

1

Mary Doyle Curran's *The Parish and the Hill* can be read as the fictionalized account of one Irish Catholic immigrant family's difficult, only partial, assimilation into already established Irish-American and Yankee social systems, from the first generation to the third. A record and a fiction, from a particular point of view, about an event that is momentous in people's lives: the change from one culture to another. *Event* is wrong—a process that takes a long time. A change from one culture to another means a change of self: both a death and a birth. New citizenship brings with it a new identity whether people intend it or not.

The Parish and the Hill views the process of change as painful, involving much loss of treasure, in exchange for no proverbial "pot of gold."[1] Mary O'Connor, the narrator, sees many members of her family in desperation. She participates in deaths, in the conflict that leads to the dying of old identities, more often than in happy births of new ones. The narrative ends with a dream sequence.

Appropriate to the tone of the story, Mary O'Connor's dream is a wake, a deathwatch. "Many red-faced people, prosperous and fat" make a din, and stamp and shout. They call for comic, commercial Irish songs—"Brannigan's Pup"—and they march to "Don't Tread on the Tail of Me Coat! Ha! Ha!" The representatives of first-generation Irish America (Mary O'Connor's mother and grandfather) depart and she hears the wail of the

223

dead spirits, mourning their departure, and mourning for the living. The wail is Gaelic, the old language. One of her brothers joins the riotous celebrators; the other is serious and plays an Irish peasant melody, "thin and sweet," as the dead depart. In the dream, first-generation Irish-American culture has died; the second generation, crowding and noisy and celebrant, asserting its new Irish-American identity, is taking over.

In the narrative's terms, it looks as if the "lace-curtain" Irish may be driving out the "shanty" old (I will discuss these terms more fully later). Middle-class ideology, crass competitiveness, money and status values, a threatening Irish-American form of fascism also (the story ends in the late 1930s, when Father Coughlin's *Christian Front* was gaining adherents especially among Irish Americans in the eastern United States)[2] may be replacing the integrity, the human caring, of the older community.

But the dream has another side. In it, Mary O'Connor and her favorite older brother, from whom she has been estranged, are reunited. They both mourn rather than celebrate. As they participate in the traditional ceremony that allows the dead to depart, they are also preparing to take on their own new American identities, which will be different from those of the lace-curtain middle class, and necessarily different from those of their grandfather and mother. The narrative has suggested that they will be intellectuals, a thinker and a poet, in the American world, although they are young, poor, and isolated. They will have to struggle.

It may help to know—as *The Parish and the Hill* does not tell us—that in Ireland, into the twentieth century, wakes were held not only for the dead, but also for emigrants departing for America.

> In traditional wakes for the dead, the relatives and neighbors of the deceased sat through the night and watched the corpse until burial. Among Catholic peasants the custom was a seemingly incongruous mixture of sorrow and hilarity, with prayers for the dead and the mournful keening of old women alternating with

drinking, dancing, and mirthful games. Although real deaths did not occasion American wakes . . . Catholic countrymen at least initially regarded emigration as death's equivalent, . . . traditional countrymen "made very little difference between going to America and going to the grave," and . . . when you left home, "it was as if you were going out to be buried."[3]

The "incongruous mixture of sorrow and hilarity" in Mary O'Connor's final dream, therefore, may not signal a necessary victory for the kind of Irish Americanism she most deplores. The dream recognizes discord and incongruity as traditional wakes recognized many contradictory emotions and impulses in life, while they mourned the dead. In the context of the American wake (any Irish American will recognize the familiar custom), we see Mary O'Connor and Eddie, her brother, finally leaving home to enter their America. The mourning is deep and real, partly to comfort those who are left behind: they have to know they will be missed. But usually the emigrants choose to go, set out—in tears—but careful not to lose their tickets. The home is destitute and can't support them. They have to go.

The dream is Mary O'Connor's American wake. She is about to leave her family—a much more momentous act in the older Irish and Irish-American context than it would be in the present; she is like the emigrating children who, although expected to be broken with grief over leaving their parents in Ireland, were also expected to go. They left because their parents could not support or feed them, because they had no land or work at home; they left to earn money to send back to their parents. Yet, "among the saddest and most popular songs were those which, like the traditional keens, reproached and reminded the emigrants how lonely and miserable their parents would be after their departure. 'Where are our darling children gone,' asked one song heard in County Kerry; 'Will they nevermore return,/ . . . To their fathers and their mothers,/ They have left in misery?' "[4]

Mary O'Connor's dreamed wake is, like the American wakes held in County Kerry where her grandfather was born, a traditional ceremony that looks both backward and forward: a necessary ritual, not necessarily a final death.

2

The Parish and the Hill views Americanization—or assimilation or acculturation—mournfully: as a process in which identity may be lost, is certainly called into question. And perhaps terms like acculturation, or either of the others, suggest too automatic a process. As if, by mutual consent, the host culture eagerly welcomes and accepts, while the newcomer, equally eager, willingly accommodates to an already well-defined benign order. Some mutual consent there must be, if immigration is to take place. But the large influx of European populations into the United States, mainly of peasant and working-class origin and displaced by social changes in their homelands, often made individual histories stressful and tragic in the period between 1820 and 1920, and beyond. Accommodation among immigrants, their children, and the host culture, especially in urban areas, could be uneasy, hostile, distrustful, well into the twentieth century.

This family's founders, Johanna Sheehan (1840-1890) and John O'Sullivan (1838-1922), emigrate separately from County Kerry, probably between 1860 and 1870. They meet again and marry, as they had intended, in Holyoke, a paper- and textile-manufacturing town in western Massachusetts.

Irish immigrants, from the time they began to arrive in large numbers, were distrusted by established Americans. The Irish were thought to be an inferior race. They were poor and had to sell their labor. They were Catholic—a religion thought to be based on superstition and controlled by priests and a foreign power, the Papacy, that demanded absolute loyalty; potentially subversive of Protestant America. They were also suspected of reserving their real loyalties for the Irish struggle for independence from England: they might never put America first. Furthermore, they banded together, lived according to social patterns of their homeland, and were largely unprepared for industrialized society. One social pattern, the use of alcohol and the use of the saloon as a meeting place, was especially offensive to puritan American sensibilities.

After the Great Famine in Ireland in 1846, the Irish who poured into the United States impressed observers as being more like refugees (which they were) than sturdy independent settlers; many were panicked, disoriented, and demoralized by the horrors of starvation and social disintegration from which they had fled.

That some of the Irish turned out to be good political organizers, that the group achieved power in urban machine-politics as they became more settled, frightened other Americans. Nativists feared that the entire character of *their* America would be changed and corrupted. That the country's character *was* changing with industrialization was a reality: immigrants, whose labor was needed, were an effect of change as much as a cause. But they were likely to be blamed, and feared.[5]

The O'Sullivans settled in an urban community with an already established Irish settlement, a specifically Irish tenement section. The Irish who had preceded them there were mainly from their own home county, Kerry. This makes the O'Sullivans typical of postfamine immigrants. The sense of connection to home and neighborliness, desire for kin and regional bonds, familiar speech and customs, generally seem to have outweighed the pull of the unknown for Irish immigrants; in addition, work was easier to find on the recommendation of kin and countrymen than among strangers.[6]

The Irish Parish, Ward Four, which Johanna and John entered, had its Catholic church, St. Jerome's, dedicated in 1858; parochial schools for both boys and girls were established in the 1860s; the St. Jerome's Temperance Society, Holy Name Society, and Ladies' Sodality were founded early in the 1870s. Holyoke was known throughout the western part of the state as a "wet" town with a larger than usual number of saloons and corner "dram shops"—both legal and illegal—in proportion to its population. There was a German Lutheran community and a French-Canadian Catholic one, as there would be a Polish Catholic one somewhat later. All these ethnic communities were largely composed of mill workers, but they lived apart from each other, worshipped separately, socialized with their own, and felt more hostility than friendliness toward each other. The Yankees or Protestant Americans of English extraction would soon be outnumbered by the ethnics (in this, Holyoke was unusual among American towns), but Yankees had founded Holyoke, with capital from Boston, caused the Connecticut River rapids to be dammed, the mills and canals and tenements to be built, where before there had been fields and farmland.

The Yankees, of course, were not all mill owners, managers, or bosses, nor all middle class, but the view from the "Flats" near the canals, and from Irish Parish, was uphill, to higher regions, progressively larger, more impressive single-family houses, and to upper-class Protestant Yankeedom.[7]

Johanna and John, entering the cohesive, supportive Irish Parish community described in chapter 1 in *The Parish and the Hill*, perhaps felt no great stress or continuing pain as the result of emigration from Ireland. Or no more than decent mourning and ordinary homesickness. They found a version of village life continuing, although it was harnessed to the mills and the mills' workday, not to the seasons and the weather.

Their children and grandchildren, responding to the first World War, to the American world outside the Parish, and to the Great Depression, have infinitely more troubled histories. Drunkenness and depression, suicide, madness, xenophobia, compulsive fighting, and, in politics, incipient fascism distort a group of people who begin in spirit and talent. The accommodations of the second generation to the host culture are frighteningly self-destructive.

3

The granddaughter, Mary O'Connor, third-generation Irish American, tells the story. Mary O'Connor, for good reason, perceives Yankee culture as historically hostile to, and exploitive of, her people. The Irish who had preceded her grandparents to Holyoke, she characterizes as innocents, coming to find the mythical pot of gold, and for "the food that could be picked from the trees simply by lifting one hand." They were soon disabused of that notion and found that "they had exchanged the English landlord for the Yankee mill owner."

These innocents become the shanty Irish. They establish their close-knit village-like community with informal networks for mutual support that emphasize kinship and extended family relationships, in the midst of the industrial town that needs their labor but derides or, at best, ignores their society.

By Mary O'Connor's time (she is seven in 1922), the relationship is not so simple. The Irish, no longer innocent, are beginning to leave the Parish in search of better housing and less cramped lives; in search of higher social standing, property, and status. The former immigrants are once again on the move in an emigration from one American stage to another. To acquire standing and status, however, they will have to change themselves. They will have to move from being shanty to become lace-curtain.

The process in which people of one kind change into another, abandon one identity and set of values to adopt new ones, and the casualties it leaves along the way, is the process that troubles Mary O'Connor, who observes it from childhood, and participates in it. Her deepest anger is directed not at the Yankees as a group, but at those Irish Americans who abandon and deny their old identities, their ties to the old community, in a struggle to become "the worst of all, imitators of imitators, neither Yankee nor Irish, but of that species known as the lace-curtain Irish."

Those terms—shanty and lace-curtain—bear closer examination. Both words are derogatory: to be shanty is to be ignorant and inferior; to be lace-curtain—or become so—means you have initial inferiority that you must hide, or for which you must compensate somehow. Both words can have high emotional charges, or still had them in Mary O'Connor's childhood. To the contemporary sociologist, who titles one chapter "From Shanty to Lace Curtain," they have become merely descriptive.

> By the early 1900s, the American Irish as a group were in transition from the position of new immigrants, disparagingly called "shanty Irish" by Yankees of the mid-1800s, to a position of middle-class "lace curtain" respectability. Although the transition was marked by increasing numbers of individual successes, as those of longer residence or personal enterprise moved into positions of financial, political, and social prominence, it was largely a group phenomenon—a product of the settling in of the second- and third-generation descendants of early famine immigrants, who now came to regard themselves, and to be regarded, as acculturated members of an American mosaic.[8]

The O'Sullivans and O'Connors participate in this group phenomenon only marginally and sporadically. Out of a large extended family, only one sister has arrived in the middle class before the Great Depression. In the depression, Mary O'Connor's immediate family—father, mother, and three older brothers—loses whatever economic and emotional stability it had during the twenties. Casualties, who won't or can't make the transition from shanty to lace-curtain, they are part of a sizable minority.[9]

What was shanty? Probably first the one-room dwelling of poor Irish villagers. The roots of the word are Gaelic. In English it means "temporary dwelling" or "hut." Charles Dickens, traveling through New York State in 1841, described how the Irish railroad builders lived:

> . . . with means of hand in building decent cabins, it was wonderful to see how clumsy, rough and wretched its hovels were . . . roofs of sod and grass . . . walls of mud . . . neither doors nor windows; some had nearly fallen down . . . . all were ruinous and

filthy. Hideously ugly old women and very buxom young ones, pigs, dogs, men, children, babies, pots, kettles, dung hills, vile refuse, rank straw and standing water, all wallowing together in an inseparable heap, composed the furniture of every dark and dirty hut.[10]

A memoir in the Holyoke *Transcript* of 1879 described a scene from thirty years earlier, when Irish laborers constructed the dam that provided the mills of Holyoke with power:

> I was through here peddling maple sugar . . . I stopped at one of the shanties . . . first, the man and woman came out the door, then six children . . . then six boarders . . . then a cow . . . then a sow and six pigs came out, all from the same door . . . .[11]

The Irish laborers who had begun to appear in the small hilltowns around Holyoke in the 1850s "were regarded as stupid and dirty, superstitious and untrustworthy, diseased and in despair. They were viewed as beggars and thieves."[12] If these people found work, they might have slept in a farmer's barn, or they might need to construct shanties.

In ports like Boston and New York, reporters had described the "crowded shanties and tenant-houses where newly arrived shiploads [were] quartered upon already domiciled 'cousins' . . . until such time as 'luck' may turn up, or the entire colony go to the poor house or be carried off by fever or smallpox."[13]

Shanty, then, as a pejorative description of a style of life, is derived from superior critical outsiders' observations of a rural, bare-survival existence, devoid of amenities such as plumbing, and in which very poor people are too busy surviving to have learned to give thought to appearances. The assumption is usually that such people have the choice to live otherwise but are too comically ignorant or depraved to change their ways. And, of course, people so depraved, or lazy, must be dangerous. Drinking and fighting are also part of the image: "It's as natural for a Hibernian to tipple as it is for a pig to grunt."[14]

These rural images of shanty life could be transferred to the

Irish sections of industrial towns and cities with relative ease; the immigrants' tenements were also dark, dirty, and dreadfully overcrowded, and the people and their patterns of behavior looked just as uncouth to better-off, better-settled observers.[15] That Irish Americans, decades after the shanties had disappeared, might be eager to escape from this stigmatizing stereotype, is obvious.

One possible escape route was to become lace-curtain. Lace-curtain is sometimes used to describe prosperous, or rich, Irish-American Catholics; the difference it points to, then, is between upper-class rich Americans of Yankee extraction and one kind of newer rich, not entirely accepted by Protestant old families. Ellin Berlin's 1948 novel, *Lace Curtain,* has such a heroine, and uses the term in that way.[16]

More often, lace-curtain means middle class, especially as it points down, to difference from the shanties. Catholicism becomes less a matter of propitiating rituals, like sprinkling holy water to ward off evil spirits, lighting candles, and telling beads, and more a way of organizing people into groups with regular meetings, stated purposes. The priest or teacher might come to dinner, not just bring bad news about the children. Manners and dress have to be attended to, as does the appearance of house and neighborhood. As William V. Shannon writes in *The American Irish,* "lace curtain . . . connotes a self-conscious, anxious attempt to create and maintain a certain level and mode of gentility . . . the complex of lace-curtain values was epitomized in the cliché . . . Ssh! What will the neighbors think?"[17]

This is a great concern of Mary O'Connor's lace-curtain father, who learned it from the Anglicized aunt who brought him up. It does not concern her shanty mother. Shanty—if we think of the rural images and of the crowded tenements—implies that the neighbors are close, and may even be living with you. What they think is less important than whether, or what, you are all going to eat. None of you is in a position to judge the other. Lace-curtain means to be separate enough from your neighbors, and

strange—or estranged—enough to adopt them as a kind of conscience, a control or potential judge, as you are theirs. You become competitors, as well.

While shanty is ramshackle, open, a mixed variety of living
beings in forced intimacy, inhabiting a space intended to serve
minimal practical functions, lace-curtain is structured and confined. The curtain emphasizes boundaries, separations, small
units set off from each other in a larger conformity. The only
important boundary for the shanties, even after they have been
transformed into red brick tenements in Irish Parish, remains the
line that separates them from the Yankee world beyond, and from
other ethnic communities.

The lace-curtains, on the other hand, define and refine boundaries between separate persons, separate families. They begin to
divide the "haves" from the "have nots," the respectable from
the disreputable, the good housekeepers from the bad. They establish categories that can be relevant and have application in the
world outside the Parish.

In Irish Parish "we" means Irish and Catholic. "They" are
the Yankees first, but "they" also includes all other outside
groups. With the beginning of lace-curtainism "we" is the one
group in the one house, behind the curtains, which intends, if
possible, to belong to a new group, sharing the interests of "us,"
the property owners. Such an identification might carry more
weight in the world and precede ethnicity and religion in importance. If it did, then "they" would no longer mean Protestant
Yankees, or Poles or French Canadians, but only those who own
nothing.

Something like that is the lace-curtain hope, and attaining it
involves a realistic appraisal of American life, much self-
discipline, some understanding of economic conditions, and
some luck. The anxiety component is hard to calculate, however;
internal conflict caused by the rejection of the old self, the stern
imposition of a new, may be too strong for an individual to bear.
The repressed, rejected, unsuitable old shanty self may erupt in

self-destructive impulses, or in bursts of outward-directed aggression. Or lace-curtain discipline may seem too harsh from the outset, the game not worth the candle; people may retreat into passivity and simply drift from day to day. Others may mistake appearance for reality—assume that to talk and dress lace-curtain without securing an economic base will be enough. The balances that each individual has to achieve during the process of change are complicated. The possible self-hate, encouraged by an original "bad" image still current in the host society, may be crippling.

From her grandfather, Mary O'Connor has absorbed an image of the Irish Parish of his younger days that seemed to be without stress, more like an idealized vision of a rural Irish hamlet in Kerry: "The people were the same . . . the same gay look in the eyes of these people and there was love among them . . . there was no dissension then. We were all the same, and if a woman made a cup of tea there would always be a friend by to drink. No one ever had to shake a teakettle in an Irishman's house. There was always plenty."

Her father moved the family to the "Hill" when she was four or five: "When we moved, Irish Parish was still at one with itself. Ours was looked on as the first great apostasy; for my grandfather . . . was still considered one of the archangels of Irish Parish . . . we left Irish Parish for less green fields; and we became outcasts from our own race, and aliens among the race of Yankees."

That was *her* first emigration, and there is no going back. The Parish doesn't exist anymore in that unified way (if it ever did) just as the hamlets in Kerry don't. Also from her grandfather, she gets the beginnings of a structure—attitudinal but without suggestions for real action—that might expand the ideal Parish into the rest of America:

> It will do no good to be fighting with [the Poles]. It's what the Yankees may be looking for. They're great dividers of the opposition . . . setting one half of a country against another. You've all seen the waste in that . . . . This country has plenty of room for

all, but not enough if there's bitterness between those who have
nothing but their hands to sustain them. There's enough bitterness between the Hill and the Parish as it is, with the Yankees
looking down on the lace-curtains and the lace-curtains looking
down on the shanties . . . the shanties thinking themselves better
than someone else so that they can have someone to look down
on. It's a disease . . . and if you catch it you're done for . . . for I
see it on the Hill. You'll end up hating the person who eats and
sleeps next to you . . . and it's enough to be hating the right
things.

Implicit in the narrative's emphasis on uniting all outsider
groups (Irish, Poles, French Canadians, blacks, Germans, and
Jews) with the poorer Yankees is an image of a united working
class, living in that new, expanded version of Irish Parish. The
mutually supportive, cohesive community that her grandfather
described to Mary O'Connor was Edenic: "Full of peace till the
time came when the serpent got into the garden and none content
after—all of them making the gold rush to the Hill and trying to
outdo the Yankees at their own game . . . . Trying to prove they
were as good as the next one when no proof was needed." Mary
O'Connor's hoped-for restoration rejects the "gold rush" in all
its versions. Her implied Utopia is founded on her grandfather's
insight: "It's foreigners we all are in this strange country . . .
and who is to prevent its bursting into a thousand pieces, one
piece dividing against another if we do not make peace with one
another?"

4

In *The Parish and the Hill* the men's behavior is more self-
destructive, more passive-aggressive, generally more violent and
ineffectual than the women's. The uncles, who were World War I
heroes, degenerate into alcoholism: Uncle Patrick kills himself in
depression, and Uncle Smiley picks fights in bars over Irish nationalist issues and is observed panhandling and cadging drinks

before his alcoholic death. Both began with talent for music, literature, and history; neither found a place. The other five uncles disappear, although for years the police brought them home, drunk, on Saturday nights to their sister's house.

Mary O'Connor's two older brothers degenerate; one is a bully, the other seems too weak to assert himself. Both drink, and Tabby, the bully, exploits women. He beats and abandons his wife and child. In general, the men behave as if they had no choice; they are controlled by forces in them and around them that they do not understand. Their behaviors, in the context of the narrative, conform to certain notions of Irish character, determined by Irish history, but working differently in men than in the women.

Young, single Irish Catholic women emigrating from Ireland to America were escaping from male domination as well as from poverty. Most of them, in accord with their culture's pattern, desired to marry—a severely restricted choice in Ireland. If they achieved marriage in America, gender expectations, brought from the village, made the man the economic provider, the woman responsible for home and children.[18]

Obviously there would be many variations and exceptions to these patterns under American conditions,[19] but if a young woman did achieve marriage in America, as many did, she had at least one concrete experience to prove that independent action could achieve the goal it aimed for. After marriage (if the man did not desert the family or die early as many did),[20] she may have had greater power and independence in her expected sphere in America than she would have had in rural Ireland. Or than the man, thrown into the American labor market, could experience. So the women might be less conflicted in living out their choices and responsibilities, more sure of themselves as capable of decisive action, even under adverse conditions, than their male counterparts.

The fates of the men and women in *The Parish and the Hill* suggest this speculation. The word fate seems appropriate because it appears so often in the works of writers dealing with Irish culture and history. One contemporary historian, Kerby A. Miller in *Emigrants and Exiles,* asserts that even in postfamine Ireland,

> a traditional Irish Catholic worldview—with its emphases on communalism as opposed to individualism, custom versus innovation, fatalism versus optimism, passivity versus action, dependence versus independence, nonresponsibility versus responsibility—remained prevalent and continued to shape attitudes towards social phenomena.[21]

The Irish-American sociologist and priest Andrew Greeley takes fate back to ancient Celtic culture, and suggests that attitudes or sets of mind from pre-Christian Irish culture have survived in Irish Americans: "In a number of different studies using quite different measures, my colleagues and I have found that this unique blend of fatalism and hope persists two and a half millennia after that first trace of Celtic religious culture . . . the Irish have the highest scores on hope and also the highest on fatalism."[22]

According to William Shannon, Irish history "rubbed into every Irish mind a primitive tragic sense" and encouraged "among many Irish a sense of themselves as a fated race."[23] An acceptance of fatedness, of lack of control over one's own destiny, may—at least—be characteristic of worldviews formed in peasant societies, like the one the grandparents had known in County Kerry. Many immigrants from Ireland defined their emigration as a tragic exile, a fate thrust upon them by British oppression, and not of their own choosing.[24]

John O'Sullivan never voices such a sentiment, although he remembers green Kerry with affection and reflects that he may have left the best part of himself there. He left, following Johanna, whom he could not have hoped to marry in Ireland; he had been a landless farm laborer, and she a smallholder's daughter, for whom a marriage had been arranged by her father. At the time in Ireland, daughters had become "closely guarded property" often exchanged for an adjoining field by their fathers. Farm laborers in Munster, which includes Kerry, were among the worst housed and worst paid in all of Europe.[25]

Thus they left of their own volition, and John O'Sullivan was glad enough to accept the "dark mill" that allowed him to feed his family. Nevertheless, the model he presents to his progeny is less activist than fatalistic: he senses the coming of change—and not for the better—but accepts it, as he does the coming of his own death. Just as he cannot change the nature of his sons—in his words, "dumb beasts" who "fight for the love of fighting"— he cannot act against the

> something else that I cannot say, though I feel and know it. It has something to do with all of us and not the boys only. It's a wind from the north and who knows when it will stop blowing? Perhaps Mary O'Connor here will be the only one who will not feel it chilling her in her sleeping and waking—or it may be even colder then—who knows? Well, let us pray that none of us here will be welcoming it.

The speech does not suggest that the child, singled out and listening "here," will have choice. She may escape disaster, but if it comes, it will be like a force of nature, something to be endured rather than actively fought. For a model of active resistance against social and individual evils, Mary O'Connor must turn, as she does at her grandfather's death, to her mother.

Mame O'Connor, so closely identified with her father O'Sullivan in the text and in her daughter's perception, is also the daughter of Johanna. Johanna left her home in Kerry alone, and in secret, to escape her father's domination. Like many country girls, she could not read or write: she left a note written for her by the schoolmaster to tell John O'Sullivan that he could find her among other Kerry people in America. About half the post-famine emigrants from Ireland were young women like Johanna, setting out to find jobs and independence, possibly a husband, in America.[26] Women making such decisions, even if they felt the pain of exile from the homeland and accepted a general sense of human fatedness, gave *their* daughters a model that suggested women could act at least to change their private fates. Although Johanna's life was used up in childbearing (she bore seventeen children), her daughters, Mame, Josie, and Hannah, and her granddaughter Mary, appear to take more control of their lives, and to make more significant choices—if not always happy ones—than do her handsome, talented, and hard-drinking sons and grandsons. In other words, the male characters in the narrative seem more inclined to accept old John O'Sullivan's prophecy of coming doom—the "cold wind" that can stand for the breakup of community and family, the loss of connection and coherence—as a fixed fate than are the women.

If fatalism, a sense that the events of one's life are foreordained and that the life will probably be tragic, is, as various writers have suggested, a strand in the Irish perception of reality, the decline of so many characters may be more comprehensible. The men in the narrative appear to initiate very few actions in their lives. They *react* to circumstance, often with rage or by drinking, but moving out of the family apartment, or moving back in, appear to be their major decisions. Tabby's move to Boston and his subsequent rise through jobs and marginal political payoffs are based on lies and fantasy; they go nowhere. The men are caught in economic limitations, traps; but they do little that is realistically conceived to escape from them. It may be significant that the union man who organizes James O'Connor's mill (and influences Mame more than James) is a Scot, not an Irishman.[27]

A sense of doom does, in a way, dominate the narrative from the beginning. The first tale, told by an old Irish woman in chapter 1, concerns the O'Sullivans. It tells of their past glories in the Old Ireland, of their castles of gold and silver, their fairy gold, their dealings with spirits and the devil himself. No one knows how they lost their treasure—they may have hidden it from the English, or lost it to the Sidhe; but the young ones wander the world, seeking it still. The story goes that one girl looked for it in dreams. She lifted a rock to find only dung. It concludes that fairy gold cannot be found in America. And Yankee gold, at the foot of Money Hole Hill, the teller asserts (shuddering), is not something *she* would touch.

One could read the story as a parable, especially since at the end the speaker warns John O'Sullivan to seek no gold in America. He, of course, does not; he seeks only daily bread for himself and his family. But those O'Sullivans who still yearn for the fairy gold, the castles of gold and silver (say, poetry, music, philosophy, beauty, as well as power and riches), and lift up rocks, as if in dreams, to find it, will not do so. It isn't there. They will have dung instead. Thus Smiley and Patrick, Eddie and Tabby, in their various dreams and alcoholic nightmares. If you find Yankee gold, as Josie and Hannah do, and as Tabby tries to, you will be tainted too, but differently. And if you look for no gold at all, like Mame O'Connor and her father, you may be well advised to stay in Irish Parish.

I have suggested that the women make more significant choices than do the men. They choose husbands. For Irish women of their background and generation (like Johanna), this was new freedom of action, a liberation. With the husband, each one chooses a fate, but within limits we see each one working actively to control at least some part of that fate.

Hannah, Josie, and Mame O'Sullivan all marry men above them on the social scale. The first two by conscious design and with purpose. Hannah marries into an old Yankee family, the town's aristocracy. Her Irishness has never meant anything to her; she wants money, beautiful things, freedom. The Dickinson family treats her with contempt; she is humiliated in every way because she is Irish. When she finally has a son, he is taken away so that she cannot contaminate him. Yet she has beautiful clothes, furniture, *things,* and lives in a mansion. That she outlives all the Dickinsons and inherits the fortune is a planned triumph of will, but by then she has gone mad: turned into an ugly, crazy Yankee. She has found the pot of Yankee gold.

Josie marries a respectable Irish hardware-store owner. She

has one child, the cousin Ann, whose doll-like snobbery makes Mary O'Connor feel dirty for the first time. Josie is the survivor in the family; she makes the most realistic choice. She chooses property, gentility, and a carefully planned rise to home ownership; she acquires standing in the community by joining the right clubs and by avoiding her old Irish acquaintances. All her emphases are on outward appearances; she is always critical of her sister Mame's dress, and especially critical of shanty actions. The Yankee gold she finds is a set of values that will admit her to the middle class and make her inoffensive to proper Catholics *and* Protestants. That it makes her hardhearted toward her dying father and all others is irrelevant to her.

Mame O'Connor, whom I have called an activist, marries a skilled worker who has denied being Irish in order to learn his trade. James is a good provider and steady, but unadventurous and dour. He disapproves of most of Mame's ways (he is in Aunt Josie's camp), as she disapproves of his—his conservatism, his lack of working-class identification. There is much dissension between them, some good-natured, but some serious enough for him to occasionally leave for a boarding house.

He hates her drunken brothers in the house; he believes she does not keep the children clean and in order. Mame laughs at his strictures and discounts them; she is enormously busy. She attends almost every wake in Irish Parish, asserting that all the Irish are related; she comforts the bereaved, feeds the hungry (Yankees included), tends the sick, lights candles for women in labor, collects and corrects her brothers and sons when they stray, cares for her father as he becomes feeble. She is active in her ward's politics, bringing in the vote; she is the one to walk the picket line when her husband is ashamed to do so. She baptizes one brother's nine children (after washing them) while their father is nowhere in evidence and their Lutheran mother "at work." She is saving their souls, but also making them Irish. On many public and private occasions she defends French Canadians, Poles, Jews, and blacks—especially against her son Tabby's aggressions; at the height of the depression she goes out to demand and get a job for Eddie from the ward boss. She continues to light candles and make intentions for work for her husband as well.

Much of the time, Mary O'Connor accompanies her mother, and much of the nursing, some of the dying, happen in the family apartment; Uncle Patrick's first suicide attempt, and Uncle Smiley's last agony, take place there. Partly because of her mother, Mary O'Connor witnesses things usually kept hidden from proper middle-class children.

Mame O'Connor is also warm and loving; she sings Irish songs, and she loves company. She is shanty enough to contradict a pretentious priest. Toward the end of the narrative, when she is facing defeat, she sums up her position, which is not that of critic only:

> Would you be as you are now sitting in Kerry Park, forever gazing at the water as it goes over the dam, and using the sharp side of your tongue as you see it go? You're like the man forever watching someone else digging the ditch—no use to the man digging, no use to the other spectators, and no use to yourself. A sharp tongue should have a sharp purpose.

All of her activities have a purpose, as her sharp tongue does, but it may be important to note that in most of her activities she acts informally, alone. Except for her connection to the Democratic party, which she breaks off after hearing a racist speech by a Boston politician, and to her church through ritual observances, she is joined to no organization or group. Her husband has joined the AFL (American Federation of Labor), giving in to her nagging to do so, but if there were women's political groups, she has not considered joining one. Her activities are based on the ethos of Irish Parish, in which family is related to family in an informal network; she opens this network to include new neighbors and other groups, but does not change the concept. And, as I have already suggested, informal village self-help is not enough, although it may do a good deal. It will not produce social change, or provide work during the depression, when the O'Connors are reduced to cutting down their attic beams for firewood.

To shanty Mame O'Connor, most formal organizations seem lace-curtain, regimenting, controlling, and dishonest. The club meeting to which Josie invites her is an alienating experience; she hears the ladies follow their dull agenda, no one tells good stories—they make small talk—and the ladies' food leaves her still hungry. The situation is genteel, repressive, and incomprehensible to her. She is also not invited to join.

When Tabby, in search of easy success, joins the Knights of Columbus and takes up golf, his family is not impressed. They have no concept of structured leisure, any more than they have of genteel organizations for self-advancement. While shanty men drink and fight, men like James O'Connor go out quietly for a drink with friends, or stay home; he improves himself by reading *The Atlantic Monthly*. Evenings are spent around the table, reading and telling stories or gossiping or entertaining a neighbor; their formal company is family or, at James's lace curtain insistence, they entertain the Yankees with whom he works.

In general, they reject the idea of making "connections" through social or organized activities. In Mary O'Connor's view, the canny politicians, who work for their own and their associates' advantage in the name of the Irish, against other ethnic minorities, are grasping lace-curtain strivers. Mame O'Connor still lives in the shanty—and Christian—assumption that connection exists: one is born connected to others and lives by nature in connection among them. But going to the political boss to beg a job for Eddie deeply humiliates her shanty pride.

She welcomes the unionization of her husband's shop and is on good terms with the organizer; when she walks the picket line in James's stead, she becomes a public scandal and enjoys it. At this point one might expect a change in consciousness; we know from other women in fiction and actuality that the experience could change one, make one stay active in the union. Here it seems to have been a one-time experience, no conversion: "instinctively she took the side against the powers that be and came out strong for unions. She learned all the phrases from Hugh and dinned them into my father's ears''; yet the one incident is the last one. She leaves it to the men. She has crossed the line of gender definitions, entered the male world, only to take her husband's place, not to occupy a place of her own. To become a Mother Jones, she would have had to lose her husband (as that woman from County Cork had); and Elizabeth Gurley Flynn moved from militant Irish revolutionary parents into a political career. Mame O'Connor in Holyoke is activist within traditional female limits. As a model for her daughter, or her sons, her activism will need to become organized. The familial and informal connectedness between persons that she asserts and honors cannot, at least on the evidence of this family's experience, build a strong enough system inside industrial society, and against lace-curtain pressures, or shanty drunkenness and drift.

Mame O'Connor doesn't worry about "what the neighbors think." She worries about her neighbor and tries to lessen hardship wherever she sees it, within the limits of an informal, woman's sphere. Her daughter, Mary O'Connor, will have to find additional ways of dealing with the larger economic and social systems, as the Irish Parish of her early childhood—segregated and poor but mutually supportive—has dissolved. The active mother has given her a good start. Mary O'Connor, however, may have to equip herself with ideas and theory—learning phrases, instinctively, and dinning them into a husband's ears— as her mother did— is *only* a start. Husband and children and family responsibilities, finally, have limited her mother's choices.

The free choice to marry, which I called liberating for young Irish Catholic women at a particular moment in history—and which some attained by emigrating to America—looks different by the time Mary O'Connor has grown up.

5

Who will Mary O'Connor be, who is she? A child growing up in the midst of the strains of family dissension and dissolution, economically moving downward not upward, seeing death and loss of pride, humiliation, around her. She experiences more violence than children are supposed to. Her brother Tabby breaks her arm when she tries to keep him from killing the cat she loves. She sees her father beat her brother with an iron poker, and forbid him the house. Tabby will later beat her, and beat her brother Eddie.

Her mother and her Aunt Josie fight bitterly over putting the grandfather in a nursing home (the lace-curtain solution to approaching death). Her mother and father fight over her. Her uncle almost kills her when he turns on the gas to kill himself. Her other uncle berates her friend, a little girl with an English name, and tells her she must hate all the English. Her Aunt Hannah lies sick in their house, moaning and groaning, for months, and berating the Yankees. Hannah's little boy dies and she grieves endlessly. Mary O'Connor gets her front teeth knocked out when she wears an Al Smith button to school (in support of the first Irish-American presidential candidate) during the 1928 campaign. She sees her brother's half-starved wife and baby, and she watches her mother slap him across the face, telling him, "You are not my son." She has watched Uncle Smiley crawling and retching, down the long dark hall, in his death agony. She has been mysteriously blinded for a part of her childhood, and her brother Eddie is crippled by infantile paralysis.

She saw her grandfather die, and her uncles sitting in a row with the other drunks in the park. She heard her brothers discussing their mother, calling her a "hellion" who has destroyed them. She has picked up coal along the railroad tracks when they could not afford to buy any, and seen her father reduced to traveling the countryside, an itinerant laborer, like the early "shanties" looking for pickup jobs.

She doesn't know what she looks like: her mother tells her that she is the angel in the picture on the wall, but part of her doubts it. She is dressed, in her childhood, in black serge bloomers and other people's castoffs; her mother doesn't care about appearances. She compares herself to the dainty lace-curtain cousin, all blonde and pink disdain, who thinks their silverware is greasy. There are candles burning all around their house, for dead souls and women in labor and people in trouble, but her brother Eddie tells her that there is no God. Not a good background for growing up smoothly into adulthood and identity.

She is the youngest, the watcher and recorder, who draws conclusions. The one who will have to write it, put it in words, try to make some order out of conflict, and salvage some good if she is to survive.

She tells us she is born at the moment she sees her grandfather and recognizes that there is another person in the world, separate and lonely like herself, but ready to accept and comfort her. They become constant companions—he in his second childhood, she in her first. From him—the former unofficial king of Irish Parish— she absorbs a positive vision of human and communal possibilities, better than what she sees happening around her. He tells her about a world in which everyone had a place, lived in performing fixed functions: hard work in the mills for the men and hard work for the housekeeping women, but consistent and effective. After work they told the old stories, sang the old songs. Saturdays the men went to the tavern and "leapt high in the dance"; they brought home Porter for the old woman, but no one was hurt by these habits. The spirits of the dead and other pagan spirits were closer than the Yankees; beings moved from one world to the other mysteriously, but candles and holy water and decent confessions, faith and respect, could keep them in their proper world. They enriched your existence and kept you aware, also, that the human world connects with others, is not all in our control.

The positive characteristics Mary O'Connor absorbs from her mother were discussed earlier. But she gets good influences from her other relatives, too, not only examples of defeat and conflict. She can pick out the saving graces. Uncle Patrick taught her music—first took her to hear *The Magic Flute*—and trained her ear to classical music. He taught her to distinguish between sentimental lace-curtain Irish ballads and the real thing sung in a wild gypsy voice without training. She admired his silent fight against alcohol and depression as she listened to his hundreds of records with him late at night.

Uncle Smiley, before he degenerated, taught her Irish poetry. Some of the violent nationalist poems frightened her, but he also taught her two poems of love. She learns to love language and rhythm and cadence, the sound of the voice in recitation, from him and from her grandfather. Smiley takes her to visit a poet's house in Cambridge—Longfellow's—and admits that even Yankees can be poets, if not as authentic and passionate as the Irish.

Her father's lace-curtain coldness is mitigated by his steadiness, and later, when he tells her his story, she can understand him. Her brother Eddie, an autodidact because there is no money for schooling, discusses his ideas with her, inspires her to want to read. He gives her a first notebook and tells her to write—for herself, not for him. She begins to play with images in writing, making discoveries about how words fit together. As a shanty child she admits to no real influences from school and teachers, but Eddie teaches her to use the library for herself.

There are six formative images or scenes in the novel that may be seen to define what Mary O'Connor is to be. Each is derived from a family member other than her grandfather, who still presides behind her total conception of herself.

As a little girl she brings home the holy water from church for her mother; Mame O'Connor requires it for propitiating the spirits, spreading good intentions. She also distributes it to her neighbors. Mary becomes "a hawker of holy water" with specialized equipment: funnel, demijohn, and wagon for deliveries. This is a version of spreading good in the world, half-pagan, Catholic, peasant, and shanty; in some way Mary will continue to do so or try to, although her equipment will change.

When she plays the role of priest to the Yankee children, giving them communion and wearing her mother's apron—reciting "I am the ghost of thy father"—she is doing what Patrick (who had wanted to be a priest) might have done, but again with modification. She is a girl playing a male role and she is ministering to Yankees; she will commune with them in later life, too, and minister to them as well as to Catholics, but not in the official lace-curtain church.

When she recites the two "poems of love" that Smiley has taught her, she becomes formally a poet, assumes that role. The first poem, "Pangur Ban," was written in Gaelic by an Irish monk-scribe in exile from Ireland in Austria.[28] Pangur Ban is the name of his cat; Mary holds her cat, Rainbow, when she recites it. The important lines are "Hunting mice is his delight,/ Hunting words I sit all night. . . . 'Gainst the wall of wisdom I/ All my little wisdom try." The cat is "sharp and sly" in his trade, as she will have to be in hers, but the poem asserts that "in peace our task we ply." A peaceful, scholarly, and solitary writer, taking delight in his work: part of a desired and desirable identity. The monk's example indicates that the trade can be carried on in exile from the homeland.

The other poem is also a translation from the Gaelic, "I am Raftery" by Anthony Raftery, who lived in the eighteenth century.[29] He was blind, as Mary O'Connor had been blinded temporarily. His lines are "full of hope and love,/With eyes that have no light,/With gentleness that has no misery." Partial blindness can keep one from seeing too much misery; hope, love, and gentleness are characteristics she has been surprised to find in poetry, but they are those she most desires. She can accept this identity as poet; Irish without belligerence and chauvinism or fighting. And Raftery was poor, a wanderer. That all these images are male (a peddler, or hawker, is traditionally seen as a man) complicates the girl-writer's assumption of her identity. In the text she will have only one real female forebear.

Another male forerunner, or ancestor, is mediated to Mary

O'Connor through Eddie, in a half-comic, half-solemn scene, as all these images are half-laughable and half intensely serious, the way aspirations look if placed against the realities of ordinary, troubled daily life. Eddie takes her, for the first time in her life, out to the center of a local lake in a boat. They contemplate the stars and Eddie tells her about infinity and Einstein. She asks if Einstein is something like Henry Ford (the kind of hero she has heard about in school: a lace-curtain aspiration). Eddie answers: "What is Henry Ford?—a man with lots of money. That is no criterion for greatness. Henry Ford understands Fords, Einstein understands the universe." Although she does not understand his further explanations, she sits, "the canoe rocking gently, listening to my brother's voice weaving in and out of infinity, and wondering how the light of a star could curve and carve such a beautiful path to this world." The theories of the Jewish physicist and pacifist, combined with a sense of the beauty of the universe in peaceful isolation with a loved person who is also a teacher and mediator, adds to her previous self-images that of the learner of new doctrine, suitable to the new world. It can reassure her that the new world will not be limited to the aggressive lace-curtain Irish-American one, which she has seen tainted by anti-Semitism. It will be universe-directed, all-inclusive.

Finally, there is one prophetic female image that Mary O'Connor also absorbs. This one is not as positive or comforting as the preceding masculine series, but has to be viewed as of equal importance. It frightens her as it impresses her, unlike the other images cited. It goes with her mother's first reassuring identification of Mary O'Connor with the picture of the angel on their wall at home. The occasion of this image is an entertainment at the orphanage Brightwood, which looks like a prison to the children. The high point of the entertainment is one of the youngest orphans, dressed in a prisoner's striped suit, weeping as she sings to the assembled company:

If I had the wings of an angel
Over these prison walls I would fly.

I would fly to the arms of my darling,
And there I'd be willing to die.

The little girl had been crying because in the excitement of the
performance she had wet her pants—again a half-comic image as
well as a pathetic one. When she leaves with her mother, Mary
O'Connor feels all the orphans' eyes on her, "staring resentfully
at this intruder who had a home and wore her father's name."

So on the one hand, she is made aware that her father provides
more than discord between himself and her mother, in the total
structure. "Home" and "name" are important stabilizing ele-
ments, as one feels oneself growing into an identity that includes
homelessness: the hawker, the exiled monk, the wandering poet,
the Jewish scientist in exile as well. Yet little girls who aspire to
male roles in a society that defines them primarily as future wives
and mothers, active in their traditional sphere, may feel that they
need wings to escape the prison of gender definitions. There is no
more Irish Parish in which the woman's role seemed coherent,
wise, important, as free as the man's while both were inside the
Parish's system.

The weeping, and the willingness to die, that go with the song
are like the weeping and the wailing at the American wake; new
identities and new roles are not taken on without grief and regret
or risk: the old self *does* die painfully. The spirits of the old world
need to be convinced that the emigré, or escapee, mourns them if
they are not to haunt the newly living. Mary O'Connor's
flight—which she prepares for throughout the text—cannot be
joyful, told as it is in terms of stressful and tragic dislocations and
preceding emigrations and immigrations.

That the identity images include not a single one of a sexually
active, childbearing woman and that the narrative as a whole—
which, after all, takes a young girl from childhood to late
adolescence—mentions no sexual initiation, no stirring of romantic love in Mary O'Connor, must be taken into account. The
narrator has excised that strand of development for a purpose. A

deep reading would bear out the fact that she is attempting an escape from sexuality as she has known it, as well as from gender definitions, in order to accomplish her flight and become a writer.

The girl orphan singing about yearned-for flight, and the two Gaelic poets, exiled monk and blind Raftery, are identities that pose problems as they offer hope to Mary O'Connor inside the novel. Mary Doyle Curran's language and imagery often suggest still another model, unknown to her character Mary O'Connor. Stephen Dedalus, in Joyce's *Portrait of the Artist as a Young Man,* undertakes his celebrated flight into exile from Ireland, vowing, in male pride and self-assertion, "to forge . . . the uncreated conscience of my race."[30] For the Irish-American woman writer, herself aspiring to creative flight, his example provides inspiration, but further complicates gender identity.

It is my suggestion that if we turn from the American wake that ends the book back to chapter 1, and read the vision of Mary O'Connor's remembered Irish Parish with the sense that it is also a vision meant to guide the future, we can read it as evidence of a flight accomplished.

6

I will not try to tell *who* the Mary Doyle Curran, who told the story of Mary O'Connor and remembered her vision of a green Irish Parish in a Massachusetts mill town, was: I would only be fitting her into some other text of my own. But I can tell something of her surroundings, and circumstances, as they relate to *The Parish and the Hill.*

She was born in 1917 in Holyoke—called the "Paper City" then—and created by Boston capital on the pattern of Lowell and Waltham. She died in Boston of lung cancer in 1981.

She was born Mary Rita Doyle, the daughter of working-class parents: Edward, an Irish-born woolsorter in the Farr Alpaca Mill (long defunct, but then, and into the 1930s, considered to be

a paragon of stability), and Mary Sullivan, his American-born
wife.

The father's trade was skilled, considered exclusive, conferring
special status, and was—as *The Parish and the Hill* also makes
clear—not ordinarily open to Irishmen:

> The wool-sorters were in fact rather a guild than a union, an
> exceptionally aristocratic group . . . a special caste and their or-
> ganization a kind of club. Most of them English by birth, they
> nourished a tradition of days, when the master wool-sorter went
> to work in a high hat, as much a gentleman in his way as the mill
> owner in his. Until long after 1903 the difference between a skilled
> wool-sorter and an ordinary wage earner was never questioned.[31]

Mame O'Connor in *The Parish and the Hill*, of course, sharply
questions the difference and denies it; that would have been
Mary Curran's position. Her politics at the time of *The Parish and
the Hill* were progressive.

Her mother never worked in the mills, as French-Canadian,
Polish, and German wives might have done. Except in the most
dire economic circumstances, Irish mothers did not work outside
the home. Girls were expected to work, if there was need, until
they married. Grown-up unmarried children lived at home; they
either paid board or gave back the whole pay-envelope, usually to
the mother. Pocket money would be returned to them. Mary
Doyle's situation deviates significantly from the pattern: when
she was old enough to work, the money she earned went into a
fund for college.

The Irish-American mother's effect on her children has been
variously discussed[32] and has figured prominently in literature
from James T. Farrell and Eugene O'Neill to Elizabeth Cullinan.[33] Specifically about Holyoke, Constance Green wrote that,

> Unless there was no other possible breadwinner the mother of an
> Irish family did not work in the mills, as was frequently true of
> other nationalities. Hers was the rôle of home-maker, and hus-
> band and children alike bent every effort to maintain her in it. In

consequence the Irish family had a unity and dignity which neither poverty nor prosperity could destroy.[34]

Inside the family, the mother could have a good deal of power,
dominance, and independence; participation in church and political activities, kinship and communal responsibilities could have
added to independence.

On the other hand, the pattern in Ireland had been one of
female subservience to men and gender segregation. At least one
writer suggests that "both male dominance and the bachelor
group ethic persist as an influence on Irish family life even into
the 1970s," and contribute to women's dissatisfaction in marriage, and heterosexual relationships.[35] Mothers and wives of her
mother's generation in Mary Curran's published and unpublished work are sometimes active, independent, *and* nurturing,
sometimes troubled and destructive. Crowded quarters for large
families, mixed parental feelings about incessant childbearing (although children were obviously valued) no doubt encouraged
ambivalences in both daughters and sons: some of that ambiva-
lence appears in Mary Curran's manuscripts.

Mary Curran in an interview[36] said her mother believed in
"the eternal values" and in education for her children. She often
reminisced about her mother as a cook: each member of the family was served his or her favorite food at meals when the money
available made that possible. And each of the Doyles apparently
had finicky tastes: one meal could include lamb chops for Mary,
beef for the father, ham for someone else. Mary herself became
an excellent cook and valued that skill. Like her mother, who she
said fed the more needy families in their neighborhood—
especially the children—she took pleasure in providing food for
hungry people, in shared feasts. And her pies and clam chowders
were authentically New England's, produced without recourse to
cookbooks.

"My Mother and Politics" printed in *The Massachusetts Review*'s
"Woman: An Issue" in 1972[37] gives a straightforward, joyful ac-

count of young Mary Doyle's mother's involvement in Democratic politics in Holyoke and suggests that the mother was ulti-
mately a strong positive model for her daughter, who valued and
praised her mother's wit and native intelligence. In that piece,
Mary Curran quotes from a letter from her aged mother, "P
Eisenhower better get down to L Rock and quit playing golf."
And I want to quote here the note written by mother to daughter
in August 1948, just after publication of *The Parish and the Hill.*

> I am darn hot, how-ever I received your book and thanks, have
> read it, and sure got a big kick reading it . . . will be at your place
> about 1:30 or 2 so don't make no dinner . . . then we can talk as
> [your brother] is very anxious to talk over your book so you can
> just here [sic] what we think about it.

I'll risk the statement that these were two women who continued
to have qualities and interests in common.

Mary Doyle was the youngest child, an only daughter. There
were four older brothers, one of whom became a pharmacist. She
was the first in her family to attend college, and graduated in
1940 from the Massachusetts State College, now the University
of Massachusetts in Amherst. A friendship with Mary Ellmann
began during these undergraduate years. She commuted, still
living with her parents, until her senior year, when, apparently,
her father pulled up stakes and pushed her into exile: he moved
to a nearby small town with her mother. The parents sold all their
household goods—including their daughter's bed— and from
then on lived in furnished quarters, too small to house grown
children. They had never owned a house, a fact of life for many
working families in America, then and now.

Mary Doyle worked her way through college, and wore her
one skirt until the seat was too thin to be worn without a coat to
cover it. She was for years a waitress at a restaurant that still
exists outside Holyoke. She worked in the library. She spent a
year as pay-clerk in one of the sheds in the Farr, her father's mill,
which no longer needed him. In that job she learned to know the
French and Polish women mill workers, who may have been

more shanty than she was at the time. Earlier, she had been on
WPA (Works Progress Administration), getting on the rolls when
her father could not, and had taken a paid course, learning to be
a housemaid. The young women students, most of them laid-off,
sophisticated, and tough mill hands, recited their creed in unison
each morning:

> I will always speak politely
> I will always be neat and clean
> I will always answer the telephone courteously
> And above all I will never answer back.[38]

Training as a maid, she recapitulated the experience of thousands
of young Irish women in America during the nineteenth century;
by 1850 housemaids were known as "Bridgets."[39] When she left
for the State University of Iowa, where she would take a Master's
degree in 1941, she had thirty dollars in cash and the promise of a
job waiting tables in a boarding house in Iowa City. In 1942 she
did something perhaps more typical for women of her generation
than going to graduate school had been: she married a fellow
student from Massachusetts and became a "war bride." The
groom, already in naval officer's whites, was on leave; she would
spend part of the academic year 1944–45 in the East, living the
life of a navy wife, which, especially when they were transferred
South and she was appalled at the treatment of black people,
didn't suit her.

At Iowa she worked with Norman Foerster, René Wellek, and
Austen Warren, all eminent professors; Austen Warren became
her thesis advisor for the dissertation, "A Commentary on the
Poetry of Gerard Manley Hopkins" (1946); the late Eleanor
Blake Warren became an equally valued friend and mentor.
Sometime during an Iowa winter, while her husband was at sea
and she awaited his letters anxiously, she began a piece of writing
that would become *The Parish and the Hill.* But I will let her tell that
story in her own words from an unpublished fictionalized account of those years, written (I think actually dictated) perhaps in
the early 1970s.

Iowa City, drenched in a soft coal smoke, was dreary beyond
words. I was lonely and frustrated; so I buried myself in books. In
the spring I was plagued by leaf hoppers staining the pages of the
books I was reading. In the fall and winter I was plagued by sub-
zero cold and frozen mice who tried to nestle next to me for
warmth. The dreariness of the town grew, and by Christmas the
Santa Claus in the window of the drugstore rocked back and forth
laughing in insane jollity. I used to go to the drugstore because
they sold Dunhill pipes, and also it was such a comfort to talk to
the man behind the counter about pipes. It brought me closer to
John.

Finally, I began to ignore Iowa City and its *Germelshausen* world.
I moved between the apartment and the library like a sleepwalker.
But when there was a full moon and the brightness woke me, I
wept. One night, after I had finished my dinner at the local diner,
two fellows whom I knew only by sight came up to me, the blond
one more aggressive than the dark one. He asked me, "How
about coming to see the rats run?" I knew they were both in
Psychology. Partly out of desperate loneliness, I said "Yes." I did
not recognize the invitation as a "pass." We went deep into the
basement of the heavy grey Psychology building and into a large
room devoid of anything but cages and mazes. They led me directly to what the blond fellow called "his experiment." The rats
were frantically running the maze to get at the food. They were
ugly and crazy with frustration. I was horrified by them. "Just
like people," the blond fellow said. I protested. Both of them,
Behaviorist psychologists, scorned my protest that people were
different. I had been brought up a Humanist, and I knew people
behaved differently from rats. They smiled at me condescend-
ingly. "Frustrate people sexually, reduce them to starvation, and
they behave no differently than rats," the blond fellow said, looking at me as though I were a two-year-old child and hadn't seen
the light. Then he reached into the maze and hauled out a pant-
ing, frenzied white rat. "Here," he said, holding the rat towards
me, his own arms displaying scars of rat bites, "hold it. You'll get
over a very important neurosis." I stepped back and said quietly,
"I prefer the neurosis." They walked me home, and I did not
return the blond fellow's advances. When we reached the door of

my apartment, I turned and said, "Thank you for walking me home." The blond fellow handed me a book. "Here," he said, "read this," and he turned abruptly away. I looked at the title (when I got inside), *Frigidity in Women*. Suddenly there was a flash of lightning and a roar of thunder. The lights went off. I stood there in the darkness and vowed not to read the book. However, I found a candle, got into bed and started reading. By four o'clock in the morning, I had every symptom in the book. I was wretched. It never occurred to me that, of course, I had not seen John for almost three years. I had to do something. I reached for an available notebook, which said Alexander Pope on the cover, and I began to write to comfort myself. I created a warm, totally illusory grandfather, gentle and full of love. I wrote almost forty pages. At eleven that morning, I was exhausted. I had exorcised the rats, freed myself from phoney frigidity and had had a genuine catharsis. I put the notebook in a drawer and forgot about it.

The next day, I did what I usually did. I read through *PM*, paying special envious attention to pictures of war brides and babies, reading through and cutting out interesting recipes. I had a shoe box full of them, waiting for peace. I had my daily letter to write to John, and a letter of my mother's to answer. I wrote to her very rarely because it seemed to me that all I did was lament.

Mona Van Duyn and Jarvis Thurston, who were also teaching and studying at Iowa at the time,[40] remember hearing the "Grandfather" piece read aloud by Mary Curran at a writer's group meeting, and that the piece was met with praise and encouragement. Also with amazement, because it had been expected that Mary Curran would read something more scholarly, perhaps an excerpt from her dissertation. She was not a regular member of writers' workshops or groups, apparently, and at least to these friends had not presented herself as a novelist or poet. Another friend, Luther Allen, who attended her wedding and knew her well during an earlier semester, recalled that her main interests then were politics and classical music, besides the literature she studied.[41]

The unpublished passage seems to me a powerfully imagined

account of how a young woman, talented and intelligent and already committed to marriage *and* professional training in a male-dominated world (if she had woman professors at graduate school, their names are not remembered) might first repress her own creativity, then require extreme emotional stress and anger to release it. I find the passage a fascinating, rich and comic, also sad, text about sexual attitudes, symbols, guilty fears, aggressions, and woman's creative work. An open text that can be read in a variety of ways, according to one's system and ideology. I recognize the woman—*girl* one would have been called then—too. She is partly a Mary I knew; she is one of us and many of us. I think I have shared the process, the ambiguities, described here.

Mary Curran was in and of her time. She had assumed that her life would include marriage (she was divorced in 1952, and did not remarry) and children. The war probably helped her to her first teaching jobs at Iowa; war and postwar ideology, however, encouraged women to think of themselves and their work as supportive of men, secondary, even as some women were finding satisfactions in living alone, having independent work. Satisfaction in a life without husband or children was not easy to admit; it probably meant a dread disease. Women coming of age in the 1940s felt pressured, often, to accept their duty: to seek personal fulfillment in marriage, creative fulfillment in childbearing. It was hard work for some. Admitted failure could cause self-doubt, guilt, humiliation.[42]

A working woman, a college teacher, she supported herself for thirty-five years. She taught at Wellesley, at Queens College; later she was professor of literature and director of Irish studies at the University of Massachusetts in Boston. She started an Irish studies program while at Queens. She found it hard to combine teaching and writing; her list of published work is not long. During the 1950s she spent time at Yaddo and the Huntington Hartford Foundation and became friends with Josephine Herbst, Babette Deutsch, Paolo Milano, Saul Bellow, and other writers; the novels written then and in the 1960s remain in manuscript. She left a body of unpublished work—completed novels, many poems, drafts and revisions and plans for new projects, and she had expected to return to writing, to work more systematically, on retirement. In 1979, the year she published four poems, she was planning a new book, although she had been troubled and ill and could not work consistently.

A poem, in her own hand, is headed "*Final Poem*, 4:50 A.M. May 22, 1978, written in N.E. Medical Center. To My Father, a Grand Man." Such specificity of date, hour, place, isn't usual. Most of her finished manuscripts are not dated. It is tempting to assume that like the grandfather she created, she had heard the presences coming and was prepared. To assume such a liminal experience would take us back to Irish Parish. But the assumption would not be true. The word "Final," so portentously and imperiously underlined on the sheet of yellow paper, is an instruction to the typist: this was to be the last poem in a completed series. She meant it to end a manuscript, not a life. She had plans.

If Mary Curran didn't resolve the contradictions in her life—in many women's lives—she was well aware of them. As a teacher she enabled her students; intellects and lives were changed in her classes, and students became lasting friends throughout her teaching career.

She was unusually sensitive to disabling circumstances and conditions under which others might suffer, perhaps because she knew disablings, and physical disability, firsthand. Her awareness of damaging class and race and ethnic antagonism, awareness of oppression and brutalization of women by men, of men by other men and institutions that have power over them, inform the matter of *The Parish and the Hill;* of sexist attitudes at the workplace, or inside marriage, she was surely aware. She had always suffered from weak vision and was legally blind, using a cane to guide herself, during the last ten years of teaching. She was a hard drinker; the "curse of the Irish" caused episodes of depression, breakdown, and hospitalization from which recovery and reestablishment became increasingly difficult. Some of her very last dictated and unpublished writing is extraordinary.

To return to the contradictions, I can only guess at defining them as I read in—or into—the text, *The Parish and the Hill.* There stands Mary O'Connor in the doorway, one parent pulling at her in one direction and one pulling in the other: "Full of pain and panic I wondered why neither would cross the threshold. With the clear logic of a child, I realized that I could not go both ways." She had welcomed the civil rights movement,[43] the anti-war movement, and the women's movement; her commitments had been clear enough since *The Parish and the Hill;* in her will she took a last step in the same direction:

> Proceeds from any publication [of *The Parish and the Hill*] after my death shall go to any creative project in the arts for American Indians, American Chinese, American Blacks and Puerto Ricans. . . . The use of these funds as stipends to recipients should not be tied to any university. Candidates should include persons who have triumphed over severe emotional psychoses and those who are handicapped; said persons to be given special consideration but not to take precedence. There should be no age limit after twenty-two years of age and awards shall be restricted to women. . . .

Anne Halley
Amherst, Massachusetts

Acknowledgment: For help generously offered and given, I thank Luther Allen, Hannah French, John Houton, Shaun O'Connell, Werner Sollors, Jarvis Thurston, and Mona Van Duyn.

NOTES

1. All quotations in the text, unless otherwise attributed, are from *The Parish and the Hill*, (Boston: Houghton Mifflin, 1948; rpt., New York: The Feminist Press, 1986).

2. Information about the Irish in America, unless otherwise attributed, is in Stephan Thernstrom, et al., eds., *The Harvard Encyclopedia of American Ethnic Groups* (Cambridge, Mass.: Harvard University Press, 1980). For information about Coughlin, see also John F. Stack, *International Conflict in an American City* (Westport, Conn.: Greenwood Press, 1979). Also, Chapter 15 in William V. Shannon, *The American Irish* (New York: Macmillan, 1963).

3. Kerby A. Miller, *Emigrants and Exiles* (New York: Oxford University Press, 1985), 558.

4. Miller, *Emigrants and Exiles*, 562.

5. John Higham, *Strangers in the Land* (New York: Atheneum, 1963), *passim*.

6. John Bodnar, *The Transplanted* (Bloomington, Ind.: Indiana University Press, 1985), 65.

7. Information about Holyoke is in Constance M. Green, *Holyoke, Massachusetts* (New Haven, Conn.: Yale University Press, 1939), *passim*.

8. Marjorie R. Fallows, *Irish Americans,* (Englewood Cliffs, N.J.: Prentice-Hall, 1979), 45.

9. Miller, *Emigrants and Exiles*, 499–506.

10. Quoted in Andrew M. Greeley, *The Irish Americans* (New York: Harper and Row, 1981), 76.

11. Quoted in Green, *Holyoke, Massachusetts,* 43.

12. Marcus Lee Hansen, *The Immigrant in American History* (New York: Harper and Row, 1940), 161.

13. Quoted in Edward Wakin, *Enter the Irish Americans* (New York: Crowell, 1976), 41.

14. Quoted in Wakin, *Enter the Irish Americans,* 58.

15. Fallows, *Irish Americans;* Higham, *Strangers in the Land;* Shannon, *The American Irish, passim.*

16. Ellin Berlin, *Lace Curtain* (Garden City, N.Y.: Doubleday, 1948).

17. Shannon, *The American Irish*, 142–45.

18. Bodnar, *The Transplanted*, 80–81.

19. For married working women, compare Gerda Lerner, *The Female Experience* (Indianapolis, Ind.: Bobbs-Merrill, 1977), especially, "The Working Mother Keeps House," 134; and "How to Live on Forty-Six Cents a Day," 290; also "The Woman Revolutionary: Elizabeth Gurley Flynn," 419.

20. Shannon, *The American Irish*, 37.

21. Miller, *Emigrants and Exiles*, 428.

22. Greeley, *The Irish Americans*, 19–21.

23. Shannon, *The American Irish*, 9.

24. Miller, *Emigrants and Exiles, passim.*

25. *Ibid.*, 407–12.

26. *Ibid.*, 407.

27. I'm aware that there were many *actual* Irish men involved in the labor movement; *see* Thernstrom, *The Harvard Encyclopedia of American Ethnic Groups,* for examples.

28. Complete text can be found in David H. Greene, *An Anthology of Irish Literature* (New York: New York University Press, 1971), Vol.1, 11.

29. *Ibid.*, 282.

30. James Joyce, *Portrait of the Artist as a Young Man* (New York: Viking Press, 1965), 253.

31. Green, *Holyoke, Massachusetts,* 216.

32. Greeley, *The Irish Americans;* Fallows, *Irish Americans, passim.*

33. Relevant texts include Farrell's *Studs Lonigan* trilogy; O'Neill's *A Long Day's Journey into Night;* and Cullinan's *House of Gold.*

34. Green, *Holyoke, Massachusetts,* 370.

35. Fallows, *Irish Americans,* 101.

36. *Boston Post,* August 1948.

37. *Massachusetts Review* 13 (1972): 147–51.

38. Compare Lerner, "Friendly Counsel for Domestics" in *The Female Experience.*

39. Wakin, *Enter the Irish Americans,* 54.

40. Interview with poet Mona Van Duyn and her husband Jarvis Thurston, former professor of English and chair, Department of English, Washington University, St. Louis (now retired), September 1985.

41. Interview with Luther Allen, former professor of political science, University of Massachusetts, Amherst (now retired), September 1985.

42. Betty Friedan's *The Feminine Mystique* (New York: Norton, 1963) is still the most easily available text for the ideology.

43. Andrew Goodman, one of the three civil rights workers killed in Philadelphia, Mississippi, in the summer of 1964, had been a student in her writing class at Queens College. He wrote a poem in that class published in the *Massachusetts Review* 6 (Autumn/Winter, 1964–65).

BIBLIOGRAPHY

Bodnar, John. *The Transplanted.* Bloomington, Ind.: Indiana University Press, 1985.

Casey, Daniel, and Robert Rhodes, eds. *Irish-American Fiction: Essays in Criticism.* New York: AMS, 1979.

Fallows, Marjorie R. *Irish Americans.* Englewood Cliffs, N.J.: Prentice-Hall, 1979.

Glazer, Nathan, and Daniel P. Moynihan. *Beyond the Melting Pot.* Cambridge, Mass.: MIT Press, 1963.

Greeley, Andrew M. *The Irish Americans.* New York: Harper and Row, 1981.

_____. *That Most Distressful Nation.* New York: Quadrangle, 1972.

Green, Constance McLaughlin. *Holyoke, Massachusetts.* New Haven, Conn.: Yale University Press, 1939.

Greene, David H., ed., *An Anthology of Irish Literature.* 2 vol. New York: New York University Press, 1971.

Greer, Colin. *Divided Society.* New York: Basic Books, 1979.

Handlin, Oscar. *Boston Immigrants.* Cambridge, Mass.: Harvard University Press, 1959.

_____. *The Uprooted.* New York: Grosset & Dunlap, 1951.

Handlin, Oscar, ed. *Children of the Uprooted.* New York: Braziller, 1966.

Hansen, Marcus Lee. *The Immigrant in American History.* New York: Harper and Row, 1964.

Higham, John. *Strangers in the Land*. New York: Atheneum, 1963.

Lerner, Gerda. *The Female Experience*. Indianapolis, Ind.: Bobbs-Merrill, 1977.

Miller, Kerby A. *Emigrants and Exiles*. New York: Oxford University Press, 1985.

Scott, Bonnie K. "Women's Perspectives on Irish-American Fiction." In *Irish-American Fiction: Essays in Criticism* ed. by Daniel Casey and Robert Rhodes. New York: AMS, 1979.

Shannon, William V. *The American Irish*. New York: Macmillan, 1963.

Stack, John F., Jr. *International Conflict in an American City*. Westport, Conn.: Greenwood Press, 1979.

Thernstrom, Stephan, et al., eds. *The Harvard Encyclopedia of American Ethnic Groups*. Cambridge, Mass.: Harvard University Press, 1980.

Underwood, Kenneth Wilson. *Protestant and Catholic*. Boston: Beacon Press, 1957.

Wakin, Edward. *Enter the Irish American*. New York: Crowell, 1976.

Warner, W. Lloyd, ed. *Yankee City*. New Haven, Conn.: Yale University Press, 1963.